Advance Praise For
A DEATH IN MEXICO

"Jonathan Woods has arrived. *A Death in Mexico* is a great and telling ride south of the border into madness and mayhem. I loved it. I want to read more about Inspector Hector Diaz."
—Michael Connelly, Edgar Award-winning author of *The Lincoln Lawyer* and the Harry Bosch crime novels, most recently *The Drop*

"*A Death in Mexico* is the knock you on yer arse book of 2012, the one you roar: 'This rocks!'"
—Ken Bruen, Shamus Award-winning author of *The Guards*, *Blitz*, *London Boulevard*, and the new Jack Taylor crime novel *Headstone*

"In *A Death in Mexico*, Jonathan Woods has an itchy trigger finger, flinging literary bullets at the page with precision, confidence, and playfulness. He writes twisted scenes that had me laughing in wonderfully inappropriate ways. And right when the action is going mach speeds, he somehow whispers a poignancy right in your ear."
—Joshua Mohr, street poet of San Francisco's Mission District and author of *Termite Parade* and *Damascus*

"Jonathan Woods' *A Death in Mexico* is more than a police procedural, it's a portrait of a wounded man trying to make sense of a world that increasingly makes none. Woods stands with Simenon and Derek Raymond as a master of the form."
—Scott Phillips, master of noir and author of *The Ice Harvest* and *The Adjustment*

"Reading Jonathan Woods' *A Death in Mexico* is similar to using 80 grit sandpaper on your eyes, as it takes you on a painful journey into the darkness of modern Mexico. *A Death in Mexico*

is as blood-haunted as the history from which it is spun."
—Frank Bill author of *Crimes in Southern Indiana*

"With *Bad Juju & Other Tales of Madness and Mayhem* and its deliciously twisted tales, Jonathan Woods blew into town as the new bad boy of American noir. Now, *A Death in Mexico* shows he's here to stay. This stylish, gritty, no-holds-barred novel establishes Woods as a master storyteller in the tradition of Chandler, Hammett and Mosley."
—Ben Fountain, 2007 PEN/Hemingway Award-winning author of *Brief Encounters with Che Guevara* and the forthcoming *Billy Lynn's Long Halftime Walk*

. . .

Praise for Woods' debut, *Bad Juju & Other Tales of Madness and Mayhem*

"Violence, sex, and gonzo plot twists fuel Woods' diverting collection of 19 stories, most set in sun-and-blood-drenched borderlands. [These stories] amp up the volume to 11... Throughout, a penchant for vivid imagery slaps the reader around like a boxing bag."
—*Publishers Weekly*

"*Bad Juju* delivers a dance of life and death that soars and plummets like Fred Astaire on methamphetamine."
—*Booklist*

"*Bad Juju* is hallucinatory, hilarious, imaginative noir."
—*New York Magazine*

"Tales of erotic or absurdist noir...executed with enormous skill by a writer of formidable talent."
—Jon L. Breen, *Ellery Queen Mystery Magazine*

A DEATH
IN MEXICO

ALSO FROM NEW PULP PRESS

A DEATH
IN MEXICO

JONATHAN WOODS

A NEW PULP PRESS BOOK

First Printing, May 2012

ISBN-13: 978-0-9828436-8-0

ISBN-10: 0-9828436-8-2

Printed in the United States of America

Visit us on the web at www.newpulppress.com

For Dahlia

and for Herschel, Camille and in memory of Charlotte

She laughed suddenly and sharply and went halfway through the door, then turned her head to say coolly: "You're as cold-blooded a beast as I ever met, Marlowe…"
—Raymond Chandler, *The Big Sleep*

¿LE GUSTA ESTE JARDIN
QUE ES SUYO?
¡EVITE QUE SUS HIJOS LO DESTRUYAN!
—Malcolm Lowry, *Under the Volcano*

And Darkness and Decay and the Red Death held illimitable dominion over all.
—Edgar Allan Poe, "The Masque of the Red Death"

A DEATH
IN MEXICO

Chapter 1

A winter mist like the haze that draws over the eyes of a corpse shrouded the *Jardin Principal* of San Miguel de Allende, Mexico, high in the rugged Sierra Madres. As if decapitated, the stone façade of the main cathedral *La Parroquia* disappeared abruptly into thickening fog. In the dim light of a street lamp, the black arms of a cast iron bench glistened with moisture.

A bell rang two a.m.

Two revelers, supporting each other, stumbled up the steps on the north side of the *jardin*. At the top they swayed back and forth like dancers.

A black shawl fringed with glass beads covered the woman's bare shoulders. Jet hair, cut in an expensive, modern style, hung like a drawn curtain. The rhinestones on the bodice of her strapless dress shimmered even in the half-light. The man, dapper in a dark suit, stood noticeably shorter than her. When she leaned into him, he cupped his hand over her breast. She pushed him violently away.

"Get your hands off me, you shit."

"Oh, come on, give us a feel, baby. You know I love you."

"You're drunk. And I'm dog-tired. I want to go to bed and sleep for about three days. But not with you."

She turned and set off across the plaza, her high heels click-clicking on the stonework like a set of nervous false teeth, the drizzle washing her face.

Disoriented, the man stumbled backwards to the edge of the *jardin*. An unprotected parapet offered a two-meter drop-off to the street. He tottered on the edge for a dicey moment or two.

A simple misstep and he would have pitched headfirst, his skull cracking on the pavement below. *Sayonara.*

Somehow he avoided disaster.

"Wait," he shouted at the disappearing figure of the woman. "You nearly killed me, you crazy *puta.*"

He stumbled after her.

In the hush of the fog, his steps were amplified into drumbeats, marking his lurching progress. Ahead of him the woman passed under a streetlamp. A shiver ran through her body. Was it fear? Anger? Loathing? Or just the chill of the night?

The spike heel of one sandal caught in a crack between two stone slabs. When she tried to jerk free, the sandal's strap broke. With a cry she pitched forward onto her hands and knees. The gritty surface of the stones lacerated her knees and palms. Pain spiked into her brain. She momentarily blacked out.

As the man came up to her, she shook her head from side to side to dispel the pain.

"Jesus, Consuela. Are you okay?"

"Of course I'm not okay."

The man helped her stand. A dark dribble of blood inched down the front of her leg.

"You're bleeding."

"No shit, Leo."

Consuela leaned down and removed the other sandal, then threw the pair as far as she could into the darkness. Barefoot, limping, she moved on across the plaza. Leo took her arm.

They traversed the *jardin* from the northwest quadrant to the southeast, detouring around the cupolated shelter where a brass band played on summer evenings. Dark porticos like hunched laborers loomed ahead on the eastern edge of the *zocalo*. A drizzle began to fall again.

Two feral cats hissed at the approaching couple. Reluctantly the cats withdrew beneath some bushes.

"What's that?" asked Leo.

"What?" Consuela's voice was querulous.

"Over there." He gestured at a dark shape on the ground. "What those damn cats were so interested in."

"It's a bag of garbage someone threw away. Come on, Leo. I want to get back to the hotel before daylight."

But Leo wouldn't move on. Letting go of Consuela, he took several steps along a side path toward the bag of trash.

"Leo. Please. Can't we just go?" Her words were a prayer.

"It's a person."

"Oh, for Christ's sake. It must be an Indian drunk on *pulque*. Don't get too close. You'll catch a dose of fleas. Or worse."

He bent down.

"Leo. I'm sure he has the plague."

But she came up behind him, fascinated by this little mystery in the dark and silent night. Leaning over his shoulder, looking down at the curved shape stretched on the pavement and hidden under some dark covering.

"It's a woman," said Leo.

He went down on one knee and struck a wooden match. In the flare, the edge of a black peasant dress embroidered with orange and blue flowers protruded from beneath a rough, hand-woven gray blanket. Below the hem appeared two small bare female feet.

"Is she dead?" asked Consuela. "I've never seen a dead person, except my grandmother in her coffin."

Leo reached toward the edge of the blanket. Consuela put a hand on his shoulder. Her fingers gripped the cloth, and the flesh beneath, as Leo threw back the blanket.

The body of a young woman lay exposed on the damp ground. Heaps of blond hair shimmered. A delicate gold chain around her neck led to a gold crucifix lying on the stone pavement like the carapace of an exotic insect. The front of the woman's dress had been torn asunder, the buttons violently stripped away, to expose her flesh like an obscenity.

The match guttered. Leo struck another.

Her prominent cheekbones were those of a starlet. Twin rows of small, white teeth grimaced between bruised lips. Leo and Consuela absorbed each of these particulars. But one detail overshadowed all the others. Her eyes were empty sockets rimmed with dried blood. A nightmare remembered upon waking.

Leo's face went as slack as a punctured tire. Behind him Consuela wouldn't stop screaming.

When Leo grew tired of her high-pitched ululations, he drew back his fist and struck Consuela in the nose. Stunned by the sudden pain, she swallowed her scream, choking on the blood gushing from her nostrils. Tears like glistening drops of glass clung to the corners of her eyes.

Chapter 2

Though he remembered nothing of it, the residue of the dream wouldn't let Inspector Hector Diaz return to sleep. For an undetermined time he lay in the dark, listening to the tide of his blood.

Then he turned on the light, stood and walked into the bathroom to urinate. The muscles of his arms and legs were twisted knots of rope. His gray-green eyes as limpid as raindrops on a tin gutter. From the closet rack he took down a gray wool suit – one of four identical gray wool suits hanging there – and a burgundy silk tie. From the bureau a starched white shirt.

Outside, Diaz stood in the shallow doorway of his apartment building, as a chill mist pissed down his neck. Even the beggars would be indoors tonight, he thought. Turning up the collar of his suit jacket, he dove into the night streets. Around a corner he came to a stairway leading down into impenetrable darkness. He hesitated for a moment, as though he was at risk of reentering the nightmare that had awakened him. Then he went down the steps quickly, his shoes grinding on grit. Finding a door handle by touch alone, he entered a passageway with yellow, bitter light at the far end and came into a late night haunt filled with cigarette smoke and five or six habitués.

The priest, disguised in a shapeless navy blue sweater and wool beret, sat at a table against the far wall. A shot glass of dark rum resided before him. When Diaz took the chair opposite, the priest looked up at him with blank fish eyes. The skin around his nostrils was tight and blanched to the whiteness of eggshells. Stinking drunk as usual, thought Diaz.

The priest raised his glass and drank the full measure of rum. A mote of recognition drifted into his eyes.

"About time you showed up," the priest said. "There's evil out tonight."

"What else is new, Philippe?"

"The innocent will be slaughtered."

"And your God does nothing about it."

Obfuscation knotted the skin between the priest's thick eyebrows. He ran two fingers across his razor-nicked chin.

"It's for us to overcome evil. In order to find our way to God. The Fathers taught us that, Hector. You can't have forgotten that."

The priest tapped his shot glass loudly on the table to emphasize his point. Or to call for another drink. Diaz wasn't sure which. Maybe both.

"I never believed those lessons," said Diaz. "As far as I can tell, we're losing the war. If it's not already lost entirely."

"No. No. My friend. Not with the likes of you to fight for us," smiled the priest.

"I'm dog tired," said Diaz. "And I'm afraid to go back to sleep."

"Then sit down and have a drink. Or three." The priest made a beneficent gesture. His hand still held the empty shot glass.

At that moment Tia, the proprietress of the *bodega*, arrived bearing gifts in the form of another glass of rum and one of mezcal. A pear-shaped, jovial woman in her fifties, she had been to Hell and back. For her the glass was always full.

"Inspector Diaz. A pleasure to see you this evening." Before Diaz could react, she drew him from his seat and, clasping him in an affectionate hug, propelled his nose into the deep perfumed cleavage of her lush breasts. Diaz went with the flow. The overpowering scent of her body, like nothing else in this world, made him instantly stiff. In the next moment she pushed Diaz away and turned to the priest. "And you, Philippe. No pounding on the table, no ranting speeches or any other nonsense. Or you're out on the cold street."

Tia leaned down and nibbled the priest's ear. The priest pulled her into his lap, where she squirmed coquettishly before breaking free and going off to attend to another customer. Diaz took a sip of mezcal while his eyes followed the exaggerated rhythm of Tia's departure.

"A fine warm-hearted cunt," lamented the priest. "If only my *cojones* weren't already pledged to the Holy Spirit."

"That's a perfect example of how fucked up life is in old Mexico," said Diaz, lighting a cigarette. "You're off in some bathhouse of the mind getting it on with the Holy Ghost, while the meek and downtrodden are arming themselves to the teeth to protect their drug turf. And I'm left trying to maintain law and order for the benefit of the rich and famous, who are mostly too busy doing lines of coke to notice the sky is falling. Sometimes I wish Mexico's ancient gods would come back and clean house. They may have been a bloodthirsty bunch, but they kept everyone in line."

The priest's eyes came suddenly alert.

"Careful, Hector. You have no idea what you're asking for. Ancient Mexico was ruled by pure evil."

Diaz laughed.

"No more evil than what exists out there in the night. You said so yourself when I first sat down."

Diaz finished his drink in a single gulp and stood up. The burn of the mezcal reminded him of the mentholated chest rub his mother had abused him with whenever the flu laid him low.

As Diaz leaned at the bar collecting another round of drinks, his cellphone rang. For a moment he thought about letting it roll to voicemail. A call to a cop at three in the morning meant only one thing. Someone was dead or dying.

Then he flipped the phone open and held it to his ear. "Diaz."

Chapter 3

The central substation of San Miguel's *Policia Preventiva* consisted of a single large room one flight up on the west side of the *jardin*. The high-ceilinged space was empty of human activity, its drab walls barren except for a bulletin board of official proclamations and a large institutional clock. In a darkened storage alcove at the back of the substation, Sergeant Ramon Silva lay stretched full length on a cot, snoring contentedly.

When Consuela began to scream, the alien echo down the hallways of his dreams transformed into the cries of his mother looking for her lost son. "I'm here, I'm here," he whimpered. But she couldn't find him. Her cries came closer, then receded again. A groan of anguish escaped the Sergeant's lips.

Suddenly he awoke and propped himself up on his elbows. His eyes were slits in the rough burlap of his face. Silence enveloped the room except for the slow, melancholy ticking of the clock and the patter of mice feet.

Silva sat on the edge of the cot, rubbing his neutral eyes. Had there been a scream? Some shit was always coming down, interrupting even the small pleasures of his existence. Citizens were constantly being set upon, robbed, raped and murdered. And he, Ramon Silva, was expected to get involved, come running to the rescue.

Silva hated night duty. Come to think of it, he hated his entire existence as a cop. There was no money in it; he even had to buy his own weapon and ammunition. And way too much risk. Some *Los Zetas* wannabe trying to make a name for himself was always lurking around the next corner waiting to put a bullet between your shoulder blades.

In the main room of the substation, Silva splashed cold water on his face from the sink in the corner. He looked in the mirror hanging above the sink and for a moment saw someone he didn't recognize. Greed-gnawed eyes, flaccid cheeks stained by the stubble of a heavy beard, a wide Mongolian nose, and a thick-lipped mouth tight with anger. An open shirt collar, frayed and grease stained, outlined a neck as thick as a stone obelisk. In defiance, Silva spat a gob of phlegm into the porcelain bowl and turned away.

Where the hell was Corporal Florio? Probably outside somewhere, making out with his fat *puta* of a girlfriend. Silva decided to go downstairs for some fresh air and a cigarette. And to rescue Florio from the clutches of that temptress.

Squat and massive, Silva stood beneath the colonnade, glaring into the mist-clotted darkness, a hand-rolled cigarette hooked in the corner of his mouth like a fixture. Nearby, the engine of a Volkswagen Bug started up with the high-pitched whine of a lawn mower. Didn't Florio's girlfriend drive a Bug?

"Florio, you son of a syphilitic mule," he shouted. "*Donde usted?*"

As if in response, three humanoid shapes emerged from the thick vapor obscuring the *jardin*. Silva recognized Florio's runner's build. The other two, a man and a woman, were unknown to him. The woman, in a cocktail dress, was barefoot.

Silva waited, arms crossed, feet planted fifty centimeters apart. When they reached the edge of the park and started down the two steps to the street, he spoke:

"*Que pasa?*"

Even from across the street Silva could see the grimness of Florio's expression. His color as blanched as that of a schoolboy caught masturbating by one of the Sisters.

"There's the body of a young woman in the *jardin*," said Florio. "Murdered. And horribly mutilated."

"Murdered you say?"

The woman's hands moved erratically in nervous disarray. Her tongue licked at a trickle of blood and mucus that crept from her nose. What was that about? Silva considered the expensive cut of the man's suit, the gold and pearl studs in the woman's ears. Tourists up from Mexico City for a getaway, he thought. And now here they were, involved in a murder.

When they were all standing under the colonnade, Silva took the woman's hand. He looked into her eyes, then down at her cleavage. The cigarette still clung to the corner of his mouth. She was attractive, he decided, in an undernourished, urban sort of way. A highbrow whore from Mexico D.F.

"I'm sorry you've had such a shock, *senora*. Please accept my apologies that such a terrible thing as a murder has occurred in our little town and spoiled your visit."

His words were like a cheap *dulce*. Cloyingly sweet.

"Someone was very cruel to that girl before they killed her," said the woman.

Her companion's eyes flicked back and forth between her and Silva. Silva met them with belligerence, exhaling a cloud of smoke. Turning to Florio, Silva said:

"Get back to the body and make sure nothing is disturbed. I'll take these people upstairs and call the *Judiciales*."

Florio looked perturbed, hopping nervously from one foot to the other.

"She's already dead for Christ's sake," said Silva. "There's nothing to worry about. You don't believe in the living dead, do you Corporal?"

Upstairs, out of the fog, it was warmer. The woman slumped on a bench, her face sprawling in her hands. The man leaned on the counter separating the room into office space, crowded with desks, and a waiting area for citizens, guilty or innocent.

Silva took a bottle of *Tradicional* from a cabinet and set it and three shot glasses on the counter.

"Have a drink, *senor*. It will take off the chill. I think your friend could use one too."

Silva went to his desk by the windows and made a telephone call. He talked quietly into the handset. Overhead a florescent light buzzed. The man began pacing back and forth in the waiting area.

When he was through talking on the phone, Silva came back to the counter and poured himself a drink.

"An Inspector of our local *Policia Judiciales* will be here in a few minutes. They have to wake him up. He won't be in a good mood."

He sipped the tequila.

"What's your name?" he asked the man.

"Leo. Leo Bremmer. From *Cuidad de Mexico*. I can't believe this has happened to us. If I'd just listened to her," he nodded toward Consuela, "we'd have walked on by."

"And her name?"

"Consuela Domingue, a business associate."

Of course, thought Silva. In official situations whores were always business associates. He took a long taste of his drink, looking steadily at Leo. Then he raised the bottle and topped off his glass again.

Across the counter he watched Consuela, who, having heard her name spoken, was sitting up and staring hopelessly into a tiny, compact mirror at the disaster of her makeup. With two, tongue-moistened fingers she wiped away a smear of dried blood beneath her nose.

"Perhaps, *senor* Bremmer," said Silva, "there is no need for either you or *senora* Domingue to be further involved in this terrible matter. After all, you don't look like murderers."

Bremmer looked blankly at Silva. "She was dead when we found her," he said.

"Of course. Of course. But how did you know? Did you take her pulse? Touch her in any way?"

"What do you mean?"

"To find out if she was dead. Perhaps she was still warm to the touch. An attractive young woman appearing to be in *estado borrachera*? Passed out. The perfect opportunity for a little late night fornication, *si*? Just a little help from your friend Consuela, a little fellatio to get it up. After all you were intoxicated too, weren't you, *senor*? And in all the excitement somehow she dies."

"What the hell are you talking about?"

"Just considering one of the possible theories of how a woman ends up murdered in the *jardin*."

Consuela leaped to her feet and leaned across the counter, her lips an inch from Silva's nose, which was as pockmarked as a lunar landscape. Her eyes burned like flares at a fatal accident. Her breasts, revealed by the flimsiness of her evening dress, were sexless in her rage.

"Fuck you, Sergeant! We're not playing that game. As soon as it gets light we're driving back to Mexico City. And I hope never to see either you or this town ever again."

Silva drew back as if Consuela's breath was tainted. His thick lips barely parted as he spoke.

"Game? There's no game, *senora*. If you want to leave this jurisdiction, security must be provided. At the very least, you are material witnesses. And in the worst case…"

A weariness invaded Consuela's face again. It was suddenly apparent how she would look on the day of her death. The clock on the wall said the time was three ten in the morning. The night hung with the heaviness of a bloated corpse. As if the light of day would never come.

Leo rested a hand on Consuela's bare shoulder. She shrugged it away. Then she resumed her seat on the bench in the waiting area. The skin of her forehead knitted into a zigzag of fretfulness; she stared at the opposite wall. Its only ornament was a rustic crucifix hanging from a nail.

Leo licked his lips.

"How much to get us out of here?"

Opening a packet of tobacco, Silva rolled a fresh cigarette, his pudgy fingers moving deftly back and forth. He lit it and smoked. His eyes were again on Consuela. But she gave no reaction.

"For security, so that you can return to *Cuidad de Mexico* without undue delay? I think 10,000 *pesos* should be sufficient. And, of course, a signed and notarized affidavit about finding the dead girl."

"I don't have that kind of cash with me."

"The ATMs work day and night, *senor* Bremmer."

Leo reached into his suit jacket and removed a leather wallet. A wad of banknotes filled one compartment. He ruffled through them, his lips moving silently.

"Three thousand," he said.

"Let me see that."

Silva reached out his hand to take the wallet. Like a sprung trap, another hand descended out of nowhere and gripped Silva's wrist. The wallet, already released by Leo, fell with a ka-thud to the floor.

"Did I come at a bad time, Sergeant?" asked a gravelly voice.

The questioner, dressed meticulously in a gray suit, starched white shirt and burgundy tie, was as tall and thin as a wraith. His black hair was long but carefully groomed.

Nicotine-stained fingers released Silva's wrist. Silva's other hand massaged the red chafing left behind.

"Inspector Diaz. I didn't expect you so soon."

Chapter 4

Despite its height, the room was claustrophobic. Perhaps because of its narrowness: it had once been a back hallway of an Eighteenth Century *palacio*. Or was it the brown and yellow floor tiles installed in the 1930s, whose gaudy geometric pattern overwhelmed the otherwise minimalist space? Most likely of all it was the presence of the body of the dead girl, lying utterly still on the stainless steel examination table.

Inspector Diaz's brilliantly polished shoes hooked the edge of a metal wastebasket, then pushed away. Diaz, the daredevil, tilted backwards in a wooden chair, balancing on its two rear legs. His thin face exuded the sallow asceticism of a conquistador in love with God and Aztec gold. But his eyes like deep *cenote* pools captured within their bottomless depths the ghost fires of an ancient Mayan lineage. Between puce lips the butt of a cigarette protruded.

Diaz's gaze followed the path of a brown spider high stepping its way up a whitewashed wall. With a sudden effortless motion, the flat of his hand could have smashed it to an indecipherable brown stain. But he bore the spider no ill will.

"Her neck was broken. The eyes were removed later. That's why there was so little blood. I'd guess based on the limited state of rigor she died about two hours before the body was found."

These remarks were tossed over the white-jacketed shoulders of a man standing at a stainless steel sink fastidiously lathering his hands. The gray stubble of his hair was as fine and velvety as the flock wallpaper of a whorehouse.

"So the killer was a man."

"Or a very strong woman."

Finishing his ablutions, Dr. Nicholas Moza turned toward Diaz. He wiped his hands on a fresh linen towel.

"She wasn't killed in the *jardin*," he continued. "There are lacerations on her heels from being dragged across the hard pavement before being dropped where she was found."

"If she was dragged like that, it means there was only one person."

"Probably."

"But why would they dump the body in such a public place?"

"Panic, maybe. Or some perverse exhibitionism."

With a sudden jerk forward, Diaz righted his chair and stood up. He inhaled a last lungful of tobacco smoke and stubbed out the butt in a glass ashtray on a cast metal stand. It joined six other butts of the same brand.

"Or as a threat, an unambiguous warning to someone," said the doctor.

Across the room Diaz could see the soft curves of the dead girl's body. The pale skin was tinted a deep blue in the florescent light. In two steps Diaz crossed the room and stood looking down at her. Her breasts were too abundant for the slight frame on which they hung: a thin, almost emaciated body. Tufts of gingery blond hair nestled under each arm and in the space between her legs. Her legs were unshaven. A purple bruise discolored her neck where it had been crushed and broken. Moza had draped a towel over the mutilated face.

In whose arms had she awakened the morning before her death? The thought flashed across Diaz's mind. Or had she slept alone? Had she smoked a joint with her coffee and sat in the sun stroking a favorite cat and reading the same paragraph of a novel over a dozen times? Did she visit friends in the afternoon and laugh at some trivial slur cast upon an absent acquaintance? All this ordinariness because it was impossible for anyone so young to know that death was waiting around the corner.

Diaz's attention turned back to Moza, who had taken a seat at his desk and was writing notes in a leather-bound ledger.

"Anything else you can tell me?"

"Age early twenties. Possibly anorexic. No needle marks. An

old appendectomy scar on her lower abdomen. A gecko tattoo on the back of her right shoulder, but no body piercings. And she hasn't had her teeth cleaned recently."

Diaz gave a low snort.

"And she's a *gringa*, not some *indio* nobody," he muttered.

"It's certainly not a fortuitous turn of events," agreed Moza.

"Everyone and his brother will want this case solved in two days. And with nary a word to the newspapers. *Gringa* murders aren't good for business. Makes the *touristas* jittery and they stay home. The cartels and their endless vendettas are bad enough."

Diaz stepped to Dr. Moza's desk and picked up a leather coin purse that had been found in a pocket of the dead woman's dress. It was of an old fashioned design with a metal clasp like two intertwining arms. Diaz snapped it open and dumped out the contents, which he already knew too well. A crumpled fifty *pesos* banknote. Three coins of small denominations. A St. Christopher's medallion. And a Texas driver's license.

The license bore the name Amanda Smallwood of Dallas, Texas. DOB: 1-28-89 HT: 5-3 EYES: BRN SEX: F RESTRICTIONS: DEAD.

The out-of-focus bureaucratic image on the license was unmistakably that of the young woman beginning to putrefy on the steel table across the room. But it didn't do justice to her beauty, illimitable even in death. After a moment, Diaz replaced the items in the purse and slipped it into a side pocket of his suit.

"Not much of a legacy," he said.

Dr. Moza closed his notebook.

"Ah," he said. "But remember, Inspector, that it's far easier for a camel to pass through the eye of a needle than for a rich person to enter the gates of heaven."

"Only if you believe in that voodoo."

Diaz shook free another cigarette from the crumpled packet of *Montanas* in his jacket pocket and lit it.

"You're sending the body to Guanajuato for a complete autopsy?"

"Of course."

"Let me know if anything else of interest turns up."

Diaz's heels clicked on the tile floor as he walked toward the exit. At the door he glared at Moza. "And don't say a word to any reporters or anyone else."

A wave of exhaustion broke over Diaz as he emerged from Dr. Moza's clinic onto a narrow cobbled street stinking of urine and festering drains. Two lines of stuccoed facades, painted in a gallery of colors, stretched in either direction. A passing dung-colored cur paused to lift its leg in mock salute to Diaz before loping out of sight up the street.

It was all too familiar. Except for attending the University of Monterey where he had taken a degree in criminal justice, a year of military service and five years as a junior police officer in Guanajuato, Diaz had lived his entire life in San Miguel. A small pond.

Already the fog was attenuating under the assault of the early morning sunlight. The bells calling the faithful to early mass sounded over the town.

A café at the corner had just opened. Diaz went in and ordered a coffee and a plate of *churros*. As the first customer of the day, the owner's wife behind the cash register gave him a warm smile. He was a familiar face. When he finished the *churros*, he brushed away the sugar granules that had fallen on his trousers and lit a cigarette.

Murders were few and far between in San Miguel. And the murder of a *gringo* was a true *rara avis*. The expat community was a world apart. Five years ago a woman from Philadelphia had shot and killed her husband. He traveled frequently on business. She claimed she thought he was an intruder. In the end it became clear that there was a mistress and a large life insurance policy. The mistress bedded both the husband and the woman from Philadelphia.

Claro, thought Diaz, the dead girl had been living a bohemian existence at the edge of San Miguel's expat community. Who else would wear *indio* peasant garb and not shave her legs or under her arms but some new age hippie running away from the world?

No doubt she heard that in San Miguel the shrooms were plentiful and the living cheap.

He considered it a strong likelihood that someone from that same insular community had strangled and mutilated the girl. Some virulent mutation of *gringo* culture. He just needed to find the road in.

But the beginning of that search could wait for a few hours.

As Diaz crossed the *Jardin Principal*, the beggars were already claiming their turf. The newspaper sellers sat half asleep on the low stone wall along the cathedral side of the plaza awaiting their first customers. Two uniformed patrolmen of the *Policia Preventiva* stood on either side of the roped off area where the girl's body was found. Diaz trudged up hill, stepping carefully to avoid a dog turd. Stopping before a nondescript wooden door inset in an ancient stone facade, he rang one of several bells. Nothing happened. He kept pressing the button. At last a sleepy female voice responded:

"Who is it?"

"It's me. Hector."

A long silence devoured his words.

"Have you fallen back asleep?" asked Diaz. "Is that how much I mean to you?"

"It's too early. And besides why should I let you in at all? You haven't bothered to come by for weeks. Maybe I have a friend staying over."

"There's been a lot of crime. I've been busy."

"Liar."

But he heard the rasping sound of a metal bolt being drawn back, then the click of the latch opening. The door swung inward and Diaz ducked through. A woman stood back from the doorway, tightening a robe about her body. Together they stepped into a small courtyard but neither touched the other.

In the early light seeping from above, the woman's face became visible. The lines of the jaw and cheekbones were angular and self-willed. Full lips set in a slight pout added a sexual hunger. There was still something innocent about her amber eyes, though they tried to deny it by their constant flickering movement. When Diaz looked at her, she touched her cropped black hair.

"You look good, Martina."

"That's a laugh. As of last Wednesday I'm forty-two years old and I just woke up. Is this the new warm and sensitive Hector Diaz? But only when it's convenient or he wants to get laid."

"Don't be hard on me. It's been a long night."

Her mouth twisted.

"Alright. Come on. It's as easy to make two cups of coffee as one."

Diaz followed her up a flight of stone steps and along a passageway that led to a small apartment. A too comfortable couch slouched next to a coffee table made from an antique door. He removed his suit jacket and laid it carefully on the couch. His tie, folded, went into a pocket. Light entered the room from a balcony. In front of this opening a small table was strewn with the smeared plates and fingerprinted glasses of the previous evening's meal. A meal for two.

Martina cleared the table, carrying the dirty dishes into a kitchen alcove. Diaz sat gazing out over the terra cotta tiled rooftops of the town. Innocent as a postcard. In his mind he turned the postcard over.

Dear Mom and Dad. Having a wonderful time in San Miguel. The weather's cool but sunny. Fabulous sunsets every day. I've made several friends from the States. My Spanish is getting better. Hope everything is OK in Dallas. Love, Amanda.

Later he would have to try to call Amanda's parents. He assumed they lived in Dallas. He would tell them that their little girl was dead but avoid giving any details over the phone. He wondered if they would have the body returned to the States. Or just bury her here, where no one would ever come by to leave a bouquet of flowers or say a prayer.

Martina set a tray on the table. On it were two tiny porcelain cups and saucers and a steaming espresso pot. She poured the coffee. When Diaz took a sip, the bitter, spicy taste instantly banished the horror of the night. But only for a moment.

"You wouldn't have any brandy?"

"Hector, you're never happy with what you're given. I don't know why I put up with you."

With a dismissive shrug Martina got up again and fetched a bottle of *El Presidente*. Diaz poured some of it into his half empty cup. Then drank the mixture without expression. Twice he refilled the espresso cup, each time tossing it back like a shot glass. Each time there was only brandy.

"That bad?"

"A twenty-two year old woman was killed last night. Disfigured and dumped in the *jardin*."

Martina's face winced.

"How was she disfigured?"

"You don't need to know."

"I'm sorry."

"And besides that, she was a *gringa*. They'll be busting my *cojones* to find the killer."

Martina got up and came around the table, wrapping her arms around Diaz's shoulders from behind. As she leaned down her robe opened. Diaz stood and turned into her. The robe hung wide. His hand touched the warmth of her stomach, then moved upward to grope her copious breasts, the nipples as hard as small glass tesserae.

Quickly she undid the buttons of his shirt, running her hands over the flesh of his chest. A ray of sunlight caught the fluid surfaces of a small, golden creature that hung by a leather cord round Diaz's neck. Part bird of prey, part deity. *Ehecatl* the wind god, borrowed long ago by Diaz and his grandfather from a forgotten Aztec tomb in the mountains, spun a draft of feverish air across Martina's breasts and downward to kiss her open thighs.

A groan of impatience seeped from her lips.

She wrenched down his zipper and, reaching her hand into his fly, found Diaz's cock steel hard. She pulled him toward the open door of her bedroom, his cock a convenient handle.

At the door Diaz noticed the bed was unmade. And another relevant fact: most recently two people had slept there.

He shrugged inwardly. What was he supposed to do? He wasn't a very consistent lover, and women had their needs.

And indeed, upon the bed Martina, buck-naked on her back, opened her airborne legs in a yawning V for victory. A smile halfway between the Mona Lisa's and that of a priestess of the golden calf looking to make the rent money crenulated her lips.

Go for the gold, thought Diaz. Discarding shoes, pants and boxers decorated with images of heart-shaped candies in various pastel colors, he dove for her nakedness. There was some jockeying for position. She stuck a pillow under her ass, and lay there heavy-eyed as he sucked her off with gusto. When she began to writhe, he stopped and lurched forward, his cock poking around in her vulva.

Whispering something obscene, she reached down and guided him in. He got on with it, the pressure building behind his nads like a steam engine about to blow. Beneath him Martina gasped and pleaded. She would die if she didn't cum soon. Why was he holding back? Why the fuck didn't he get his groove on? "Come on, baby!"

Diaz was lost in the rhythm of the thing, the tip of his dick sensually calibrated like the finest seismological sensor. When he began to yelp with anticipation, suddenly Martina was fighting him, her arms pushing vehemently against his chest. He flopped out, his overcharged brain chugging between vague disillusionment and too-far-gone-to-care.

"You're not using a condom," she complained. "Finish outside."

At that exact moment he came, white tracery arcing across her thigh and onto the hand-stitched duvet.

She pushed him sideways. "Shit. That'll leave a stain." Even as she got up to fetch a wet rag, Diaz rolled over onto his back and fell into a dead sleep.

Chapter 5

At 10 a.m. on Friday, when Diaz walked past the machinegun-armed sentry and entered the *Judiciales* station, Sergeant Roberto Ortiz's eyes sought him out. Ortiz was on the telephone. He held the handset in one hand, the other cupped over the mouthpiece. His eyebrows rose like exploding flares. Soundlessly his lips moved:

"The mayor."

Diaz patted the pockets of his suit jacket, locating his cigarettes. He extracted one, lit it and walked into his office. Standing over his desk, he picked up the phone.

"Diaz here."

"Inspector Diaz." The voice was clipped and formal. "I was wondering when you might arrive."

"How can I help you, *Don* Cedillo?"

"The murder of *la mujer norteamericana* is in every newspaper, on every radio station."

Fuck! lamented Diaz. He knew the dead girl's nationality would become a public relations nightmare sooner or later. But he had hoped for much later.

"As I'm sure you can appreciate, Inspector, this is a fucking disaster beyond calculation. I want to know everything that's being done. Everything to bring justice and closure to this loathsome affair."

"We're on it."

In his mind Diaz envisioned at the other end of the line the narrow, pointed face of a gigantic rat dressed in a pinstripe suit. The rodent leaned back in a deep leather chair, telephone pressed to his ear. His hairy, claw-tipped feet, protruding below his trouser legs, rested one on top of the other on the surface of the desk in front of him. Ignoring Diaz's terse response, the rat continued:

"Now that the newspapers have the scent, they'll be as relentless as a hooker after the rent money. Already I've been asked inestimable times to make a statement regarding this atrocity."

There aren't that many newspapers, radio and TV stations in the entire state of Guanajuato, thought Diaz.

"I'm sure you'll find the right words to restore public calm."

"Of course I will. And you, Inspector. Just bring me the killer's head by Monday morning."

"We'll do what we can, *Don* Cedillo." Dropping the phone into its cradle without waiting for a response, Diaz viciously stubbed out his cigarette, sending tobacco embers scattering across his desk. Asshole.

A fierce and inexplicable rivalry had existed between Cedillo and Diaz since the days when the nuns kept them at opposite sides of the classroom. Cedillo's election as San Miguel's mayor lit a new fire under this ancient competition. Relentlessly, he sought out every occasion to tweak Diaz about his job performance, his screwed-up existence. For his part, Diaz circulated rumors about Cedillo's raging insanity and bizarre sexual appetites. Privately Diaz didn't give a shit, though he found pleasure in baiting his rival. Soon enough some businessman would have Cedillo snuffed for demanding an unreasonable share of the take in some black-hearted scheme or other. In the meantime State Prosecutor Ortega, Diaz's roommate at university, blunted any ill effects from Cedillo's chicanery.

At the moment Diaz was interested in only one thing. Finding out who strangled and mutilated a too young Amanda Smallwood.

Standing in his office doorway, he scanned the mundane activities in the outer office. Ortiz was back on the phone, gesticulating wildly as he talked. His gray shirt, narrow knit tie and black double-breasted Italian sports jacket were the wardrobe of a TV detective. Sergeant Armando Ruiz, pink cheeked, well scrubbed and well fed, was chatting up the intern, Corporal Felicia Goya. She laughed at some remark, her retro ponytail shaking from side to side like an antique African fly brush. Garcia Sanchez, the newest Sergeant, stared morosely into outer space. What a bunch of losers, thought Diaz.

The palm of Diaz's hand slammed against the doorframe with a thunder crack that sent Armando flailing backwards, almost tipping his chair. Ortiz ended his phone call in mid-sentence. Felicia gnawed a fingernail. All eyes turned toward Diaz, who surreptitiously massaged his injured hand.

Only Garcia remained unperturbed, remote. Diaz wondered if he had a drug problem or suffered from the reverse of attention deficit disorder.

"Listen up, *cabrons*. You all know a *gringa* was murdered last night in the *jardin*."

They nodded.

"How the newspapers got the story so quickly we'll address later. For now we have only one job – to find the killer. I want to know everything there is to know about the deceased. Where she lived, who her friends were, how often she took a piss, her favorite color and whom she was sleeping with, or why she wasn't."

Ortiz interrupted eagerly:

"A woman called half an hour ago. Very upset, crying. Said she lived with the dead woman."

"Okay, Roberto. You and I will go and talk to this roommate. Armando, I want you to interview the couple that found the body. They're at the Hotel San Sebastian. Felicia, you get on the phone and find out whatever you can about the dead woman, including the address and phone number of her family."

Felicia sighed.

"Garcia will handle anything else that comes up."

Diaz glowered.

"And if that rat's ass of a mayor telephones again, play dumb."

The *Hotel De Los Tres Santos* was a tumbling down affair in the lower town, a few blocks west of the *mercado publico*. Two floors of crumbling adobe-walled rooms facing three sides of a dirt-floored courtyard. A single, scrofulous palm tree clung to life amidst the desolation.

Two men, early twenties, sat in the shade of the palm playing chess and smoking. Their attire was *gringo* slacker: T-shirts, khaki cargo shorts, flip-flops. Dirty blond hair hung long and unwashed. The only way to tell them apart was by the different beer logos imprinted on their T-shirts.

The sudden appearance of Diaz and Ortiz in business attire created no current of interest. The chess players continued their game in stoned contemplation.

With a nod Diaz walked past them to an open door marked *Oficina*. He rapped on the doorframe but no one appeared or called out.

"She's out," said one of the young men. "But anyway you don't look like you're interested in renting a room."

The other man guffawed, which turned into a strangled cough. Diaz wrinkled his forehead in annoyance.

"We're looking for *senorita* Gates."

"Little Sylvia? She's a wreck. Her friend Amanda was raped and murdered last night." The man speaking spat a bullet of saliva between his front teeth into the dirt. "You must be the cops."

"And you are?" asked Diaz.

The man looked back to the chessboard, the question ignored. Time hung suspended like a torn fingernail. The standoff ended badly when Diaz stepped forward, grabbed the man's arm and wrenched it behind his back, pulling him from his seat. Chess pieces scattered in the dirt. The other man stood up, arms outstretched, palms upturned in supplication. "Whoa," he said, backing away.

Diaz twisted harder, back and upward, simultaneously pressing him forward until the man's face touched the tabletop.

"Shit, man. You're hurting me."

"I think you forgot to answer my question," said Diaz.

"It's Bobby. Bobby McVey."

Diaz released his hold without warning and Bobby collapsed to the ground in a ganglion of arms and legs. He lay in the fine dust, massaging his arm.

"You live here, Bobby?"

McVey remained sullen and unresponsive.

"If you don't want me to break your arm, answer my fucking questions," spat Diaz. McVey's eyes darted hither and yon, a pair of panicked roaches caught in a burst of light.

"Yes, I live here."

"How long?"

"Couple of weeks."

"So you knew Amanda Smallwood?"

"She was already living in this dump when we got here."

"What was she doing in San Miguel?"

"I don't know. Hanging out. Getting high. What're you supposed to do in Mexico?"

McVey edged backwards, trying to get as far away from Diaz as possible. His companion, standing at some distance, lit a cigarette and smoked nervously.

"Were you friends?"

"She lived with Sylvia in 14 upstairs. Sometimes she'd read my tarot or we'd make dinner together. But Amanda hung with the arty crowd. We weren't hip enough for her."

"So you weren't sleeping with her?"

"Shit no, man."

Diaz squatted down so that McVey could see the Glock in the shoulder holster beneath his jacket. He reached across and tapped a finger on Bobby's forehead. "Don't screw with me, *hombre*."

"Okay, okay. She was a hot little number. Sometimes we hung out, drank some beers, smoked some pot. But we never hooked up. She had Sylvia and all her artist friends for that."

"How about your chess buddy here?"

The other man started in surprise at being brought into the conversation. He fumbled his cigarette, which fell in the dust.

"Hey, not me, man. I hardly knew her."

"Do either of you know if she had any enemies, any relationships that might have gone south."

"She had her own life, man. Neither of us was involved."

"I hope not."

For a moment Diaz considered kicking McVey in the nuts. Instead he strode across the bleak courtyard and climbed the cracked cement stairway to the second floor of apartments. Ortiz followed. Walking along a common balcony, Diaz stopped outside the open doorway of number 14. The ill-lit interior was a patchwork of intersecting shadows. As his eyes adjusted, Diaz made out a female form hunched over on an old mattress thrown across the floor. She rocked back and forth to some unheard rhythm. A candle glittered like the first evening star.

"Sylvia?" called out Diaz.

The woman looked up. Her eyes glistened with moisture in the candlelight. Another lost hippie girl in a flowered dress, thought Diaz. Amanda's doppelganger. Except her eyes weren't missing, she breathed air in and out, and she still had a soul connected to her body.

"I'm Inspector Diaz with the *Policia Judiciales*. You called us earlier."

A cry, some primal lament, broke from the girl's throat. Her rocking motion increased in intensity. Lines of tears deluged her cheeks.

"We're trying to find the person who hurt Amanda. I was hoping you could help us."

"She's dead, she's dead, she's dead."

Words chanted like a mantra from Hell. Entering the room, Diaz crouched down and took Sylvia in his arms. Her body quaked, as if in a palsy. The flesh of her arms was as soft as cream. Her tears cooled his cheek. After a while she stopped shaking. Diaz helped her to her feet and guided her outside onto the balcony. In the sunlight he discovered one strand of her hair was dyed vermilion.

They sat on a bench in the warm sun. Diaz motioned Ortiz back downstairs.

"I'm sorry about your friend," said Diaz.

"I'm all right."

"Tell me about Amanda."

As he said these words, Diaz looked up at the perfect blue sky. High, high above an eagle climbed an updraft. Or was it *Mictlantecihuatl*, goddess of the underworld, carrying the soul of Amanda Smallwood to paradise.

Sylvia's eyes were earthbound, resting on the tattered fronds of the palm tree that had somehow managed to survive in the desolation of the courtyard. Along a browned-off frond, a lizard rippled like a tiny, green wave. When Sylvia began to speak, her voice was as cold as the heart of the dead.

"We met two months ago in San Miguel's main plaza. I think we were both a little homesick. We started talking about where we were from in the States. She'd already been living here for a year. I was just off the bus from Cuernavaca. I'd been traveling around Mexico. You know, seeing the sights. We went to lunch and she asked if I had a place to stay. When I said no, she asked if I wanted to move in with her. Since I didn't have much money, it seemed like a good idea."

"You've been living together then for the past two months?"

"She was like my older sister. And a long lost friend. She knew her way around San Miguel, which made it easy for me. We were both vegetarians. And she was learning to read the tarot, which I'd studied for a while when I was at college in Albuquerque. She got me a job working part time in a bookstore."

"Then you know her friends here?"

"Amanda knew lots of people in San Miguel. Mostly artists and musicians."

"Was there anyone in particular besides you that she was close to?"

"She got along with everyone. But she didn't have a boyfriend, if that's what you mean. To her guys were a waste of time."

"Tell me about yesterday."

At these words Diaz saw the ritual sadness slip back into Sylvia's eyes, clouding her mind like the spume of a waterfall. It had been absent while she talked about her and Amanda's life in San Miguel, remembering its mundane repetitions, its trivial details. But all that had ended sometime last night. Replaced by the inexplicable arrival of death.

"Yesterday morning Amanda flew back from Dallas. She went up there once a month. I think her father is seriously ill, though she never talked much about it. I was waiting for her when she got off the bus from the Guanajuato airport and we went shopping for supper. But she seemed distracted. Hyper one moment, self-absorbed the next. I figured maybe her father wasn't doing well."

"Did you ask her?"

"No. I didn't want her to snap at me. Amanda had a temper, especially when it came to personal stuff. When we got back to the apartment, she said she needed to go by the *Instituto de Bellas Artes*. To see the work schedule. She modeled there. I guess maybe you know about that. They paid well. And she was in love with her body."

After a pause, perhaps to resurrect a memory of Amanda's anatomy, Sylvia continued.

"We planned to meet here for supper but she never showed up. I figured she went to a party. Amanda loved parties. I hate them."

Diaz nodded in sympathy. He also hated parties.

"When I got bored waiting for Amanda, I went downstairs and drank a few beers with Bobby and Jim. Then I went to sleep. I had a nightmare and woke up with a feeling of dread."

Sylvia licked her dry lips.

"It was pitch black out. A cold fog was coming into the room because I left the door open for Amanda. But she never came home. I closed the door and lit a candle because I was afraid. Then I must have fallen asleep again."

"But this morning you called the police. You knew she was dead."

"When I awoke the fog was gone. The sun was bright and ordinary, like it always is here. Amanda's side of the bed hadn't been slept in. It wasn't the first time."

She stopped talking, thinking about something. Then she continued to the end.

"I felt like I had a hangover, so I drank four glasses of water and sat in the sun, reading a book. That's when Jimmy came upstairs with a copy of *Atencion*. That's how I found out she was dead. A cheap headline. I called the *policia* from a payphone down the street."

"Do you have any idea who might have wanted to hurt Amanda?"

Sylvia shook her head. Tears were again coursing down her cheeks.

Diaz removed a cotton handkerchief from his jacket pocket, noted that it was clean and handed it to her.

"Thank you for your time, *senorita*. I'm terribly sorry. Please call me if you think of anything else."

"I loved her," came a whispered response.

At the bottom of the stairs Diaz blew out a loud gust of air. Bobby and Jim had disappeared. Ortiz leaned against the adobe wall, using a small metal file to meticulously remove the dirt from beneath each fingernail and smooth and round the edges.

Diaz walked past him and out into the street. Ortiz slipped the nail file into his pocket and hurriedly followed. When they were walking side by side, Diaz turned his head and spoke:

"You know, Roberto, if you don't make it as a cop, you can always get a job as a manicurist."

Chapter 6

Diaz's cellphone rang while he and Ortiz were eating a late lunch. It was Sergeant Armando Ruiz calling to say that the couple Diaz sent him to interview were not at the hotel. But, he assured Diaz, they hadn't checked out.

Diaz looked at his stainless steel Rolex, an anniversary present from his former spouse. Two weeks after she gave it to him, she filed for divorce on the grounds of mental cruelty. Seven years later it was still a good watch, a classic design. Its self-winding spring alleviated Diaz's lurking fear of battery failure at some critical moment. Of course he always found something else to fret about.

When Reyna gave him the watch, wrapped in gaudy silver paper, it was common knowledge their marriage was in the toilet. Few marriages survive the death of a child at age twelve from a random bullet fired on New Year's Eve. Estella would have been nineteen last week.

Diaz always wondered why his wife gave him such an expensive gift at that moment in time. Maybe she'd gotten a deal from her uncle who owned a pawn shop in Leon. Or maybe it was from a sense of guilt because she was already sleeping with his replacement.

"Armando, it's been over three hours since we left the office. How come you're only calling me now about this problem?"

"Just after you left, Carmen called me in a panic. She thought she was having another miscarriage. I had to rush home and take her to the doctor. He said it was just indigestion. Thank God. She's back home now. But when I finally arrived at the hotel, *senor* Bremmer and *senora* Domingue had left to meet someone for lunch."

Yes, thank God, thought Diaz. Armando's wife had lost two pregnancies. A third miscarriage in less than two years would surely doom their marriage. The entire *Judiciales* unit was rooting for them.

"Did they tell the hotel receptionist when they'd be back?" Diaz asked.

"No."

"Then wait in the lobby until they show up."

"Yes, sir."

Armando was a conscientious cop, thought Diaz. He just had screwed up priorities. Or maybe not. If Diaz hadn't buried himself in his investigations, would he still be married? But did he still want to be married to Reyna? And what about Martina? These conundrums opened a vista of twisting emotional byways and cul-de-sacs.

Diaz stuffed another chunk of grilled *cabrito* into his mouth, followed by a slice of pickled *jalapeno*. The latter sent a piquant tingle of sexuality across Diaz's palate.

"Call me when they show up." He punched off the connection.

"Armando screw up again?" asked Ortiz.

"I don't want to get into it."

Ortiz gazed out through the open door of the restaurant. A secretary, dressed to the nines and with extra long legs emerging from beneath an extra short skirt, sauntered by. Her high heels wobbled on the uneven stones of the sidewalk.

"Well," said Ortiz. "How would you like to get into that instead?"

Perhaps sensing twin pairs of male eyes undressing her, the woman straightened her shoulders and increased her pace.

Diaz nodded sagely but said nothing, his eyes following the pleasing convexity of the woman's buttocks as they disappeared from view down the street. It would not, he thought, be seemly for the head homicide detective of the *Policia Judiciales* in San Miguel to engage in ribald commentary regarding the passing fauna. After all, this was the new millennium. The sexes had reached a new

JONATHAN WOODS • 33

equality, if not fraternity. And he had to consider the position of Felicia, the new intern. Attractive though she might be in a tomboyish sort of way, in another three months she would be the junior investigating officer in the unit, armed like the rest of them with a Glock 9mm.

Diaz wiped his mouth with a paper *serviette* the size of a postage stamp, crumpled and tossed it amid the leavings on his plate and lit a cigarette. What did they have? A dead American hippy girl with her eyes ripped out. A girl who earned money as an artists' model and who slept with at least one woman and perhaps others, male and/or female. *Claro* she was someone, as Sylvia Gates put it, who knew her way around San Miguel. Until she got in too deep.

There was a whiff of sexual perversion in the air. The possibility of some deep and abiding obsession that had worked its way to the surface in the form of murder and mutilation. It was time to visit *El Instituto de Bellas Artes*.

"Then go fuck yourself!"

The slim, young woman expressing this anatomically difficult wish, turned and stormed past Diaz. She held her body as stiff and unyielding as a starched shirt.

The recipient of her fury was a man with thinning hair, goatee and dishonest eyes seated behind a paper-strewn desk. If asked, Diaz would have guessed early 50s. His face accepted the slur without emotion, while his lips murmured some counter-insult come to mind too late to be articulated. One finger tapped out an irregular rhythm of irritation on the desktop.

Diaz, previously lurking in the miniscule reception area, entered the office. Their eyes collided, then spun away. A defensive grimace curled the man's lips as he spoke.

"Everyone thinks they're a genius. The next Freda Kahlo. But no one wants to work their butts off to get there. Think it'll just happen while they're sitting around in cafes drinking beer and chain smoking."

"A disgruntled student?" asked Diaz.

The man blew out a puff of air in dismissal.

"She'll get over it. Then she'll either buckle down and do the work or drop out of the program. It's usually the good-looking ones that complain the loudest and want to do the least. Once they figure out every male in the room and half the females want to get into their pants, they think everything should be handed to them on a silver salver."

The man's thumb and index finger nervously massaged the tip of his earlobe, which was pierced by a tiny gold ring.

Suddenly aware he was rambling on to a total stranger, the balding administrator stood up. His fingertips touched the desktop for ballast.

"Eduardo Flores, *Director*. How may I help you, *senor*?"

Diaz handed him his *Judiciales* photo ID. At the same moment Ortiz edged into the remaining unfilled portion of the tiny room and sat down.

"Inspector Hector Diaz. This is Sergeant Ortiz."

Flores considered Diaz's ID as if it might contain some cabalistic message – or a coupon for a half-price dinner special. On the wall behind Flores, amid framed diplomas and other credentials of *El Director*, resided a black and white photograph of a group of students surrounding a dower Garcia Bustos, protégé of Diego Rivera. Among the students, Diaz recognized the face of a very young Flores.

"*Ciertamente*, Inspector Diaz, it's a great pleasure to meet you. Your name is synonymous with crime busting in San Miguel. Please, have a seat." He gestured to twin chairs in front of his desk, one of which Ortiz already occupied. "How may I help you? Would you care for something to drink?"

"We're investigating the murder of Amanda Smallwood. She was a model here at the *Instituto*."

Flores collapsed into his chair, shaking his head wearily from side to side.

"Terrible," he groaned. "When I read about her murder in the newspapers today, it was an enormous shock. Such a sensual young woman, her life snuffed out like a candle." Lines of worry creased his forehead. "This is very bad for business, you know. Many of our students come here on exchange programs from universities in *Los Estados Unidos* and Canada. Their parents may now think twice about allowing their sons and daughters to travel to such a primitive and dangerous place as San Miguel."

"*Director* Flores, what can you tell us about *senorita* Smallwood?"

"Came here about a year ago. In response to an ad we ran for studio models. She had no experience modeling but she was very attractive and possessed an excellent anatomical form. If I may be entirely frank, her breasts were beyond voluptuous. As a trial I took her into a sketching class. She disrobed and sat on the podium without embarrassment. From that time forward she has modeled regularly for us. Usually three or four times a week. And now…" He spread his hands.

"She got along with the students and professors?" asked Ortiz.

"She was very reserved while doing her work at the *Instituto*. Some of the students, women I mean, were jealous of her beauty. But she was very professional, never flirted with students or faculty. There were always those men and women who fell in love with her from time to time. She always managed to disengage herself from them without making anyone angry."

"So you're saying she didn't have any enemies?" interrupted Diaz. "Not even one or two of those thwarted lovers?"

"Of course some people spoke badly of her. Among the faculty Dr. Duncan constantly complained she never held her poses long enough and was too thin to be a proper artists' model. But Duncan is never happy about anything. And, of course, there were the usual rumors about her life outside the school."

Diaz stifled a yawn. Administrators were universally long-winded. He knew he shouldn't have eaten such a heavy lunch after getting little sleep the night before. Finding his cigarettes, he placed one between his lips.

"*Dispenseme*," said Flores. "I would appreciate it if you didn't smoke in here. Such a small space." He indicated his closet sized office. "And I suffer from asthma."

In violent irritation Diaz snapped the cigarette in two and dropped it on the floor. He sat forward, the hard edge of the chair a throbbing discomfort.

"What sort of rumors?"

"Gossip isn't really my specialty, Inspector."

Diaz rested one arm on the edge of the desk and leaned menacingly across.

"I don't give a rat's ass about your sensibilities, *Director*. I'm trying to find the killer of a young woman who, by her age, could easily have been your daughter. He's sitting out there right now sipping a beer and lighting up a cigarette and watching the passing scene. Considering his next victim. We need to know everything and anything about Amanda Smallwood to help us find him."

Even as he snarled at *el Director*, Diaz's complexion paled. A twinge of indigestion burrowing through his interior maze like a parasite dressed in a ninja outfit. Or maybe like Armando's spouse he too was having a miscarriage – but of the soul. He smirked inwardly at his sardonic wit. Then he thought: what a pompous ass you are.

A thin glaze of sweat glistened on Flores's forehead. He fumbled in his pocket for a none-to-clean handkerchief and used it to wipe his face.

"These details are of the most tenuous quality."

"Of course. Continue."

"As you may know, she lived with another American girl, somewhere in the lower town. Her name is Sylvia Gates?"

Diaz nodded.

"Also a very nice young woman with exquisite alabaster skin. I met her one time when she came with Amanda to an event here at the *Instituto*." Florio shrugged. "Anyway, it was said that Sylvia and Amanda were intimate."

"You had a thing for Sylvia and Amanda?" interjected Ortiz.

Flores's body tightened. He sat up, his cheeks flushed.

"You must be joking."

"You were perhaps dreaming of something out of the ordinary? A *ménage a trois*?"

Flores's hands balled into fists.

"I demand that you revoke your slanders immediately."

"Don't mind Ortiz," said Diaz. "He likes to play the wild card. We're already aware of Smallwood's predilection for Sylvia

Gates. Can't you tell us something more interesting than that, *Director*?"

Flores's body language threatened his imminent collapse into a pout.

"Just the usual. She was sleeping with this or that artist in San Miguel. But no one associated with the *Instituto*."

"Names, Dr. Flores," growled Ortiz. "Of everyone she was rumored to have hooked up with or was considering. Male or female. Flora or fauna."

Silence hung like a drop of water on the lip of a faucet. From the outer office/reception area, a space even smaller than Flores's domain, came the tap-taping of plastic fingernail extensions on a plastic keyboard. When Diaz and Ortiz first arrived, the secretary's station, with its computer terminal and telephone, was unoccupied. The door to Flores's office had remained open during the interview.

Then the drop fell.

"I really don't think I can help you with names, Inspector."

"Fine sentiments, I'm sure, *Director*. I just hope that when names are mentioned, yours isn't on the list." Diaz stood. His intestines palpitated with unease. "Now we'd like a tour. See where Amanda Smallwood worked." The words "plied her trade" had come to mind, but Diaz rejected using them.

Flores slipped into a corduroy jacket with suede elbow patches and led the way out of his office. A fortyish woman, with heavily lidded eyes outlined in purple and raven hair pulled back and secured with a red velvet ribbon, sat behind the secretary's desk. As the three of them filed past, she glanced up momentarily from her typing.

"I'm showing Inspector Diaz and his associate around the *Instituto*, *senora* Pinto," said Flores.

Flores led Diaz and Ortiz down an ill-lit corridor with ochre painted walls and a red tile floor. Each time Diaz's nether regions gurgled, he felt a strange kinship with the color of the walls. Flores droned on:

"The *Instituto* was originally conceived as a *palacio*, built at the turn of the century. Not very old compared to most buildings in the heart of San Miguel. But the patron had grandiose ideas.

When he died suddenly, the heirs abandoned the project, though it was close to completion. Since that time, it's been a school. First a private military academy. Then, after World War II, a haven for artists."

Flores turned down a narrow side-corridor.

"This is our main painting and drawing studio. A class is in session."

From chiaroscuro they entered a room flooded with light. It poured in through tiers of small-paned windows filling most of one wall. Beyond, the sky was an invincible blue.

Fifteen or so men and women sat at tables or scrunched on metal stools, drawing pads open, charcoal scuttling like many-legged insects across the coarse surfaces of paper. In a corner of the room, on a raised platform, a woman, naked, rested her buttocks on a wooden chair. The rest of her body was twisted over one arm of the chair in a contortionist's dream, one hand grazing the floor, the other raised like a swimmer's in mid-stroke. An elaborate scheme of garish tattoos intertwined down her arms and across the tops of her breasts. Each nipple, the size and color of a rare and weathered Roman coin, was pierced by a gold ring.

Diaz frowned, as his mind considered the pain involved in acquiring such body ornaments.

"I see you found a replacement for the deceased quickly enough."

"We have six figure drawing classes a week as well as a painting seminar involving the human figure," said Flores. "Amanda was only one of the models we use."

Several students looked up at the sound of voices.

A hollow-cheeked woman stepped urgently toward them. Her long hair, streaked with gray, was thrown back carelessly over her shoulders. She held her index finger to her lips. Her sparrow eyes held a wild look as though suddenly aware of a descending predator.

"May I help you, *Director*?" she whistled between buckteeth.

Flores's knee-jerk smile unsuccessfully masked his fear of this quixotic creature.

"I'm showing these gentlemen around our campus. A quick

JONATHAN WOODS • 39

look at your class in action, *Profesor* Stein, and we'll be gone."
Flores looked hopefully at Diaz.

One of Diaz's eyes winked at Stein. Or perhaps it was a muscle
spasm brought on by his tiredness. She squinted at him with hos-
tility.

"You knew Amanda Smallwood, *Profesor* Stein?" he asked.

"So that's what this is about." Her gaze shifted from Diaz to
Flores and back. "You're with the *policia*?"

Instead of answering her, Diaz abruptly swung about and exited
the room. He couldn't deal with aggressive women when his intestines were in turmoil. Single file, Flores and Ortiz followed.

Back in the main hallway, Diaz looked left and right, wondering
where the nearest lavatory might be located. Ortiz spoke:

"The nipple rings are fake, right?"

"I don't think so," said Diaz. "I imagine women like that are
very provocative in bed. But be forewarned. She probably collects
dicks as souvenirs. Like shrunken heads."

Ortiz winced. Several students walked by laughing. The pulsa-
tions in Diaz's nether regions eased. He turned to Flores, who was
nervously rubbing his hands together.

"Amanda Smallwood modeled for Profesor Stein's class?"

"Of course."

"Then Sergeant Ortiz will need to interview *Profesor* Stein
and her students." Diaz caught a shadow of disappointment creep
behind Ortiz's eyes. "And the tatted model too."

"Of course. But can he wait until the class ends? I hate to
disrupt the curriculum."

Diaz shrugged. "I understand your desire not to provoke *Profesor* Stein. I'm sure she can be a royal pain in the ass."

Flores clicked his heels together in appreciation.

"The drawing class ends in half an hour. I'll have *senora* Pinto
arrange for each student to meet with Sergeant Ortiz individually.
Our board room will be suitably private."

"Don't forget the model and *Profesor* Stein."

"Anything else I can do for you, Inspector?"

"Not for the moment."

"Good. Then I must fly to an appointment."

"We don't want to hold you up, *Director*."

Diaz and Ortiz watched Flores hurry down the hallway.

"There's something dishonest about that man," said Ortiz.

"He's an administrator. He prevaricates to protect the integrity of the institution against the plots and counterplots of everyone - students, teachers, staff, outsiders. But the conspiracies are all in his head. Stalin was the extreme example. He had everyone killed, then lied to himself that it was for the common good."

Diaz lit a cigarette and sucked in a deep draught of smoke. Ortiz slouched forlornly against the wall, hands in the pockets of his blazer.

"Hey, Roberto, don't show so much enthusiasm about your afternoon and evening assignment. Maybe the interviews will turn up something useful. Though I doubt it. See you back at the station."

Cigarette between his lips, Diaz adjusted the knot of his tie, his long, narrow fingers judging its precise verticality. "And don't ask that model out. She's sure to be hazardous to your health."

As Diaz walked past Flores's office near the school entrance, *senora* Pinto sprang towards him, one arm raised above her head. For an instant he thought she was going to assault him, a variation of the shower scene in Psycho. Then he realized she was holding a piece of paper in her hand, not a knife.

"Inspector Diaz. A call came for you."

"Thank you, *senora* Pinto." He recognized Armando's cell-phone number.

"Inspector Diaz...."

"*Si?*"

"About *senorita* Smallwood. I'm sorry for her and her family."

Senora Pinto gnawed seductively on her lower lip. Then burst out:

"I heard you ask *Director* Flores about her lovers. There was an artist. He used to come by the *Instituto* to pick her up. She confided in me about him. He was from L.A., not some provincial Mexican backwater. Amanda was crazy for him. But it was difficult. He lived with another woman. And she had to consider Sylvia. She didn't want to hurt Sylvia."

"And the name of this lady killer?"

"Gregory Gregorovich. He has an opening tonight at the Galeria Rana."

"Not a very *norteamericano* sounding name."

A squint of puzzlement narrowed her eyes.

"Never mind. Thank you for giving me this information." Pain seared through his gut like the razor teeth of a hungry piranha. He hurried out to the street.

It was a ten-minute walk back to the *Judiciales* station. The ageless taco seller was in her usual spot by the arch under the old viaduct. Her father, his face crazed like the surface of a time-corroded tile, sat motionless beside her cart, his head crowned by a straw hat of an ancient Indian style. For a moment, as Diaz passed, the old man morphed into an Aztec shaman draped in the rare pelt of a jaguar, around his neck a gold pendant of the cox-cox bird. I must have a fever, thought Diaz.

Above the ornate, mosaic dome of *El Templo de la Concepcion,* a fringe of tattered clouds were tinted gold and rose by the declining sun. The narrow side streets were already darkened with long knives of shadows.

It was almost five o'clock when Diaz entered the station. As he stood in the vestibule considering his options, Corporal Goya approached wearing a smile of accomplishment. She handed Diaz a slip of paper bearing the telephone number of Amanda Small-wood's father in Dallas, Texas.

Diaz took the message slip, muttered an incomprehensible word or two of encouragement and fled down the corridor to the unisex bathroom. For a long time he sat hunched in the dank stall, a look of general unhappiness on his face. At eye level someone had scratched the word "dickhead" on the tiled wall.

Chapter 7

Gregory Gregorovich, *artiste de erotica* and L.A. exile, eyed the tall blonde in the straw hat sauntering through the *Jardin Principal*. She reminded him of a very long, slow, opium dream. Though in fact she was quite a bit older than he usually went for.

The morning sunlight glinting off the sheen of her red lipstick was blinding. Her body fit nicely into tight black pants and a lacy red blouse. Gregorovich threw a ten-peso coin at the newspaper hawker, grabbed a copy of *Atencion* and hurried across the *jardin* to catch up with her.

The vendor called after him. He'd forgotten to take his change. Gregorovich kept going.

The blonde exited the *jardin*. Across the street she dawdled in the shadows of the arcade, looking in the shop windows. Slowing his pace, Gregorovich pretended to be preoccupied with the view of the cathedral against the crystal blue sky. In front of the cathedral a group of peasanty-looking men and women were constructing a floral arch in preparation for some religious festival. Out of the corner of his eye Gregorovich saw the blonde minx slip into one of the stores.

He leaned against a sun-stroked wall of the arcade and opened his copy of *Atencion*. The main headline read: Woman Murdered in *Jardin*. But he had no time to even scan the article. His obsession of the moment suddenly exited the shop, walked at a breathless pace along the arcade and turned the corner onto *Calle San Francisco*. Stuffing the paper into the pocket of his crumpled linen blazer, he hastily followed her.

I'm a fool, he thought, not to go back to Fran Kovacs this

minute. Beg her forgiveness. After all she'd saved him from the street. Given him a place to paint, rent-free. They'd even spent the occasional sweat-drenched night in each other's arms, when she was in the mood.

Last night she'd insisted they go to Brian's birthday party. Gregorovich drank tequila. Fran danced to the live band. After the cake routine, Gregorovich wandered upstairs with some people to smoke pot on the roof. Someone was passing out tabs of Vicodin. Later still, when Fran came looking for him to leave, he threw up all over her. This while sitting in his boxers next to a little *chica* who'd lost all her clothes.

By the time Gregorovich got dressed and ran after Fran, she was down the hill and out of sight in the mist. He found her house bolted tight against him and the lights out.

For a while Gregorovich wandered the fog-bound streets. The trees in the *Jardin Principal* were trolls hunched against the night. At last the damp cold and his own exhaustion drove him into one of San Miguel's multitudinous churches. Candles flickered before a statue of the Virgin. The vast, gloomy space smelled of damp plaster and mold. He fell asleep in one of the pews, with his linen jacket pulled over his head, hands clamped between legs for warmth. Now, in the thin sunlight of a new day, instead of going home to Fran, he was drawn inexorably after the blonde.

Up ahead the blond bombshell suddenly darted like a skittish reef fish into a famous café. When he walked past its open windows, she was sitting alone at a corner table. The place was jammed. A cramp in his stomach reminded Gregorovich he hadn't eaten since the previous lunchtime.

Half a block beyond the café he stopped and examined his reflection in a shop window. Black T-shirt, jeans, still mostly white linen jacket. Hair slicked back at a public fountain. More or less acceptable, he thought. He sniffed under one arm. Though tending toward the ripe.

He turned back around and entered the restaurant. Ignoring the pudgy *primero camarero* trying to head him off at the pass, Gregorovich veered to the blonde's table. There were two empty chairs.

"Is this seat taken?" he asked in English.

She glanced up quizzically.

"Gregory Gregorovich at your service," he said. A century earlier dressed in the uniform of the Czar's lancers, he would have clicked his heels together and bowed. Instead, without waiting for a response, Gregorovich pulled out one of the chairs and sat down.

"Do I know you?"

"There are no tables and I'm starving," he said.

She looked at him, then turned her eyes away. "I'm expecting some friends."

"I hope they're amusing."

A smile crept like a dangerous insect across her lips, then turned to pique.

"At the least you're presumptuous, Mr. Gregorovich. More likely you're an ass."

Up close, tiny creases were visible along the tops of her cheekbones. Wine dark shadows stained the skin beneath her eyes. He guessed she was in her late 30s and didn't sleep well. Her breasts beneath the supple fabric of her blouse were wide and flat, the shadow of the nipples visible in bas-relief. Despite the heavy rings under her eyes, she was astonishingly beautiful.

"Gregory," he said, offering his best schoolboy-ish grin. "Since I'm from L.A., I'm pushy by nature. A matter of survival. Are you English?"

She drank from the glass of wine in front of her.

"Canadian, actually. But I live in Mexico."

He noticed a wedding band and a modest diamond.

"You're alone in San Miguel?"

"I don't think that's any of your business."

He looked contrite.

"Sorry."

"My husband's with the Canadian embassy. At the moment he's back in Ottawa. For meetings. And freezing his ass off."

A waiter appeared.

"I'm waiting for some friends to join me," she said to him in fluent Spanish. "But this gentleman wants to order now."

Gregorovich glanced at a menu. "*Enchiladas de pollo con salsa verde. Agua mineral.*"

"Your accent's lousy," she said.

Gregorovich shrugged. He glanced past her at the end wall of the room, crowded with photographs and caricatures of the comely female TV personality from Mexico City who owned the café.

"Why did you choose to sit at my table? There are other empty seats."

"Actually, I saw you walking in the *jardin*. I followed you. When you came in here I realized I was starving. Since I'm broke, I thought you might take pity on me and buy me lunch."

"I'm flattered you took me for such an easy mark."

"I thought you looked stunning. I couldn't help following you."

A sudden storm of apprehension darkened her eyes. Had he gone too far? Projecting too much of a Jack the Ripper persona? For a moment Gregorovich was afraid she would summon the headwaiter and have him thrown into the street. Luckily the enchiladas arrived. He grabbed his knife and fork and began to eat with zest.

Sipping her wine, she watched him eat. He glanced up at her occasionally as he stuffed his face. Slowly her forehead unwrinkled. When his plate was empty, he leaned back and looked steadily at her.

"I'm sorry if I…"

"Don't," she said. "You were starving."

"You wouldn't have a cigarette?"

She laughed.

"I think it's time for you to go."

"If you're not doing anything more exciting, you're invited to an opening this evening at the *Galeria Rana*. On *Calle 16 de Abril*. From 8 to 11. I'm showing some new paintings, along with several other artists."

Her eyes looking beyond him, she raised one arm and waved. Gregorovich turned sideways to observe a man in a dark business suit and a tall woman in a miniskirt coming toward the table.

"You can bring your friends."

Gregorovich's blond meal ticket stood and embraced the woman, then the man, kissing him on both cheeks. The woman cocked her gaze quizzically at Gregorovich.

"Jane," she said. "Aren't you going to introduce your friend?"
Jane looked startled.

"Oh, sorry. This is *senor* Gregorovich. We just met in the plaza.
A starving artist. He was just leaving."

"Yes," Gregorovich said. "I'm off."

The waiter was hovering with the ticket for Gregorovich's
enchiladas. Jane told him to put it on her bill and he went away.
Gregorovich smiled again at Consuela, gave Leo a nod. As he
turned to Jane, their hands grazed. She jerked back, as if stung.

"Maybe I'll see you tonight."

She appeared bemused.

"At the opening."

"Oh, yes. Maybe."

Having no further reason to remain, Gregorovich walked
quickly to the door and outside, without looking back.

As he strolled back toward the *jardin*, working a toothpick
leisurely between his ivories, he couldn't jettison the image of
Jane's face from his mind. Finally, after wandering the streets for
an hour, Gregorovich went into *La Parroquia* cathedral and offered
a prayer that all would be right with the world – and another that
Jane would decide to show up at the gallery opening.

Back in the sunlight, blinking like a mole, he wondered if he
should go back and patch things up with Fran. But the promise of
Jane proffered something entirely new and dazzling. You stupid,
crazy bastard, he thought.

Minutes later he stood at the bar of the *Cantina Gato Negro*
sipping a shot of tequila. A known quantity at the *Gato Negro*, they
always extended him a small line of credit. He opened the copy
of *Atencion* and began to read the story about the woman found
murdered in the *jardin*. The dead woman's name was Amanda
Smallwood.

That sounded familiar. Was she someone he'd slept with in
another life?

Then it struck him like a wild pitch. Holy shit! Amanda Smallwood was the shameless vixen who had posed for his most recent
paintings. Gregorovich motioned urgently to the bartender for a
refill.

so far they haven't harmed me.

but they're out there, whispering together in the dark corners, their voices just on the cusp of hearing.

sometimes they hide inside the mirrors, just below the edge of the frame where you can't see them unless you're standing right in front looking down over the edge. sometimes i catch their movements in the periphery of my vision. a flash of silver or black. or a splash of red.

red is the worst because i know then that they've been on a successful hunt and are devouring their kill. their lips and chins smeared with blood.

sometimes i only hear them snuffling behind the sofa, their hands held over their mouths and noses. or whispering as they tiptoe across the roof of the studio. later, when i look behind the couch i find where they've urinated, leaving little yellow puddles. when they've been on the roof playing among the clay pots of bougainvillea and geraniums, there's always telltale debris. broken stems. fallen and crushed blossoms. sometimes i leave them a plate of leftovers or a dead cat. that seems to satisfy them for a while.

they were the worst during the last year i lived in la. that's when i had the trouble with the girl. they kept urging me to fuck her. afterwards, her mother said she was too young and threatened to get a lawyer or go to the police.

it was they who encouraged me, demanded that i do it. a rite of passage.

when i demurred, they smeared threats in red lipstick on my bathroom mirror. i feared they were not idle.

afterwards, when the girl's mother demanded money, i left la and came here. for months they didn't know where i was. but soon enough they sniffed out my spoor.

they're here now in ever increasing numbers and i'm getting spooked again.

Chapter 8

"Armando?"

Static crackled over the ether; then a vast, cosmic emptiness descended, as if Diaz's mind had been teleported into deep space.

"Hello. Hello. Armando, are you there?" The small, silver rectangle with its minute keypad and screen illuminated by phosphorescent-blue backlighting remained mutely non-responsive. Diaz wanted to slam the cellphone onto the tile floor of the bathroom and watch it shatter into a dozen jagged fragments of useless componentry.

Instead he set it on the edge of the sink and looked glumly at himself in the mirror. His color was as anemic as a flour tortilla. Maybe I should go home and get some sleep, he thought. Amanda Smallwood was as cold as the surface of the moon. Only madmen and magicians believed you could revive the dead. So what was the big hurry with this investigation?

The answer to that question flashed in his head in an explosion of neon light: BECAUSE THERE'S A FUCKING MANIAC OUT THERE AND IT'S YOUR JOB TO FIND HIM.

He splashed cold water on his face. That was an improvement, though a headache dripped slowly into his frontal lobe like a toxic chemical leaking from a rusted barrel.

The cellphone trilled.

"Hector? It's Armando."

"Where are you?"

"I'm at home."

Diaz glanced at his watch. It was ten minutes to six.

"How did the interview go with the couple who found the body?"

"That's what I wanted to explain to you. They came back to the hotel and then they left again."

"But you talked to them, right?"

"I don't know what happened, Hector. I guess I'm not sleeping too well, worrying about Carmen's pregnancy. I waited in the lobby area like you said. But I must have nodded off. The new receptionist who came on at five woke me up, but the couple had come and gone. I missed them by minutes."

"Why didn't you go after them?"

"The note they left with the concierge said their plans were indefinite until eight, when they would be attending a gallery opening. So I came home to check on Carmen. She's feeling much better. And I missed lunch, so I'm having a *comida*."

Diaz rolled his eyes. Simultaneously he felt a twinge of jealousy for Armando's obsessive attachment to his pregnant wife.

"Stay home, Armando. I'll go to the gallery opening. You take care of Carmen tonight. I'll see you in the morning."

"Are you sure?"

"Positive."

"Don't you want to know the name of the gallery?"

"Let me guess. It's the *Galeria Rana*."

There was a long silence at the other end of the connection.

"How did you know that, Hector?"

"Goodnight, Armando."

Sergeant Jorge Quevedo leaned on one elbow, phone propped against his ear, one leg leisurely thrown over the arm of his chair. He had night duty. Otherwise the station was empty when Diaz returned from his intestinal trials. Quevedo nodded to him but continued talking on the telephone in a hushed voice. Diaz wondered whether Quevedo was working a case or just hustling his girlfriend.

Lightheaded, Diaz stumbled into his office and pushed the door shut behind him. Pitch darkness instantly disoriented him. He groped wildly for the light switch and the overhead light blinked on.

He slumped into his chair. It was always reassuring, he thought, when the lights came on. The way the world was going, he wondered how much longer you could rely on such basic amenities. Soon enough the terrorists would begin blowing up the hydro-electric dams and the nuclear-powered generators. And the lights around the world would shut down. What garbage.

Diaz's forehead was beaded in sweat. The residue of whatever bug had played havoc with his plumbing. He took a fresh cotton handkerchief from a pile in his bottom drawer. From the same drawer he removed a dispenser of lavender eau de cologne and sprinkled some on the handkerchief. Holding the handkerchief to his forehead, he closed his eyes, leaned back in his chair and began to breath in and out in a deep, slow rhythm.

After a while he opened his eyes again, leaned forward and picked up the telephone handset. There was dial tone. Another miracle. He punched in the number that Felicia had given him.

After the eighth ring he was about to abandon the call. Then the line was picked up and a deep, booming American voice said:

"Hello. Who's that?"

"I'm calling for Mr. Smallwood."

"Who wants him?" challenged the voice.

"This is Inspector Diaz of the Judicial Police in San Miguel de Allende, Mexico."

"Mexico? Police? Is this a joke? Who the hell is this?"

"Am I speaking to Mr. Smallwood?"

"Of course I'm Smallwood. Bass Smallwood. Who the hell did you think I was?"

Diaz imagined a rough hewn, barrel-chested figure with scuffed cowboy boots and rugged blue jeans standing at the other end of the line, the telephone like a toy in his massive hand. Bass Smallwood didn't sound like someone suffering from a debilitating illness.

There were no good words to say what had to be said to this man.

"You have a daughter named Amanda?"

"Yes." Sudden raw fear vibrated in the voice. "What about her?"

"I'm afraid I have to inform you, Mr. Smallwood, that she's deceased."

A stillness descended, like the moment just before a piano falls out of the sky and crushes an innocent bystander.

"It's a sick joke you're playing, sir. You won't get away with it."

"I'm with the police in San Miguel de Allende, Mexico. Your daughter Amanda was living here. Last night she was murdered."

A loud, crashing sound echoed over the line, as if the handset had been dropped or thrown to the ground. Diaz heard a muted groan. He waited, his mind in stasis.

There was a scraping sound, then the voice of Bass Smallwood again, subdued, hollow:

"You say your name is Diaz?"

"Inspector Diaz of the *Policia Judiciales* in San Miguel de Allende."

"And you're sure about the deceased person – that it's Amanda."

"There was a Texas drivers license with her picture. I'm sorry."

"I'll be on the first flight to Guanajuato in the morning."

"Are you sure you're able to travel, sir?"

"Of course I'm able. It's my daughter."

Bass Smallwood's voice broke into fragments, as a cry of human devastation erupted across the connection. Then the line went dead.

Diaz wanted a drink but knew his bowels would rebel with a vengeance. He lit a cigarette instead. Standing in the door of his office, he watched Quevedo diligently tapping at the keyboard of his computer terminal, entering a crime scene report. Or sending an e-mail to his girlfriend.

"How's the hotel burglary case going?" asked Diaz.

Quevedo stopped typing and swiveled in his seat. He ran a hand through his longish thinning hair.

"Who the hell knows? I'm looking for a guy with a mustache, bad skin and a gold front tooth. A man of that description was seen hanging around near the times when several of the break-ins occurred in which jewelry was stolen. It probably fits half the bottom feeders in all of Mexico."

"Good luck with that."

Quevedo rubbed the fingers of one hand contemplatively back and forth on his chin. One arm rested across his stomach, which was taut from constant weight lifting and floor exercises.

"*Claro*, it has to be an inside job," he said. "Most tourists don't bring a lot of jewelry to Mexico. The thief has to know in which rooms there's a spouse or girlfriend insisting upon flaunting her expensive baubles in the restaurants and clubs. To know that, you'd have to work at the hotel."

"Keep after it. Something will break. They'll have to sell the jewelry somewhere."

"The problem is there are three high end hotels involved so far and too many employees and contractors for one person to interview."

"Maybe tomorrow I can let Armando give you a hand, if that would help."

"I'll take what I can get."

Diaz went back into his office and looked at his phone messages. The mayor had called again and someone named Morales from the Federal Police in Guanajuato. Diaz knew *Don* Cedillo, the rat mayor, only wanted to chew on his ass for not making an arrest yet. He had no idea who Morales was or why he might have called. In any case he didn't feel like talking to either of them. And since it was after seven o'clock on Friday, it was unlikely that either of them would still be in their offices.

There was no record of a call from Dr. Moza about the autopsy. Diaz frowned. He dialed Moza's office but got the answering machine.

"Nicholas. Diaz here. I hope you're not spending all your time taking care of the living. I need the autopsy results on the dead girl. What's the hold up? Call me before midnight."

There was a fifty percent chance Moza would check his messages, thought Diaz. After all, someone might be dying and in need of a doctor, even on a Friday night. He looked at the clock on his desk – a memento of twenty years of service. Four pseudo-Greek columns, two on each side, like a miniature gazebo. Its fake roof engraved with his name and the dates of his police service. The clock face was suspended in a circle of beveled glass. The clock's brass plating was tarnished and, on one of the columns, had started to peel away from the base metal underneath.

After fixating on the clock face for several seconds, Diaz realized what was wrong. The clock had stopped. It was either five minutes to noon or five minutes to midnight. Overcome by a sudden wave of exhaustion, he closed his eyes, squeezing the inside corners between thumb and index finger. He knew how the clock felt. An endless circle of days going nowhere.

Then Diaz saw the white envelope lying in front of the clock. He picked it up. The front was blank. Without addressor or addressee. But his fingertips quickly identified on the back flap the embossed seal of the State Prosecutor's Office. Slitting the envelope open, Diaz removed a deckle-edged card with the same seal at the top. Beneath the seal was the familiar antique scrawl of Prosecutor Ortega:

This one is not what it seems. Watch your back.

There was no date or signature.

Diaz tore the card into small squares and burned them in his ashtray. It took a while because the card stock was thick. As the miniature blaze took hold, he suddenly became worried that the heat and smoke might set off the recently installed sprinkler system. Luckily, it didn't.

For a moment Diaz wondered whether the sprinkler system even worked. Or had a corrupt contractor installed a sham sprinkler system? Ah fuck it.

When the last deckle edge morphed into black ash, Diaz's self-winding Rolex told him he still had almost half an hour to kill before the festivities began at the Frog Gallery. He decided to have a drink after all.

Chapter 9

Jane Ryder squinted at the dry cuticle of her left index finger. Then jammed the orange stick between nail and skin and reamed it back and forth several times. Taking a pair of razor sharp cuticle scissors, she snipped away a crescent of dead flesh.

In between working each finger she sipped a tall, murky *mojito*.

What was I thinking? she asked herself.

A mere six hours before she'd been sitting in a trendy San Miguel café drinking white wine and flirting with a cocky pickup artist. He reeked of boorish self-confidence and cheap B.O. A pale, hollow eyed portrait, cheeks and cleft chin peppered with stubble, hair long and finger combed. He exuded the appearance of the bankrupt progeny of some Russian viscount killed by a Red firing squad in 1917.

Why wasn't she surprised when he turned out to be both Russian and a penniless painter?

When Gregory Gregorovich sat down at her table, she should have had him thrown into the street. Instead she had bought him lunch.

His white linen jacket looked seriously slept it. Undernourished, he needed a shave, a shower, a haircut and a fumigation. His eyes told of little sleep the night before. When he said he was hungry, she knew he was telling the truth. He needed a helping hand, someone to take him on as a project. Before he crashed and burned.

Of course she'd always been a pushover for stray cats and orphaned baby rattlesnakes.

And now she was going to meet him again in less than two hours.

For an instant she wondered what her husband Niles was up to during his free time in Ottawa when he wasn't promoting his latest Mexican development project up the bureaucratic escalator. She had declined to go with him. There were only one or two people she might have cared to see in Ottawa. And none of them during the month of February when the snow creaked under your boots and the mucus in your nose froze the moment you stepped outside. Anyway, having Niles at home or away was pretty much the same.

Instead she'd gone to San Miguel for the weekend with her friends Leo and Consuela.

And now everything was totally in the deep end. When Gregory Gregorovich stood up to leave, upon the arrival at the café of Consuela and Leo, his hand ever so slightly brushed against hers. That was when she fell off a cliff with desire.

How juvenile was that?

She knew she was tumbling helter-skelter out of control. But she didn't care. People she had known who were younger than her were already dead.

This could be my last chance, she thought. My last good fuck.

With one hand she picked up her book, a James Crumley crime novel, and started to read. Then set it down again as she drifted back in time.

"Maybe I'll see you tonight," he had said. She must have looked dumbstruck because he added: "At the opening."

"Maybe," she had said in her most noncommittal tone. While inside her head she was screaming: Yes, yes, yes, like some Irish strumpet.

After Gregorovich departed with a nod and a wink, Consuela, over Cobb salads for herself and Jane and *enchiladas suiza* for Leo, had told a wild story about finding a young woman's dead body in the *jardin* while stumbling back to the hotel last night. A beautiful blond white girl lying in the dark, strangled, her eyes ripped out.

A knock at Jane's hotel room door interrupted these recollections.

"Just a minute."

Jane set her manicure implements on the night table, took a final swig of the *mojito* and pulled her robe closed around her voluptuousness. When she unlatched the door, Consuela bustled into the room.

"So who is this guy Gregory Gregorovich you're seeing at the opening?"

"An artist I met in the *zocalo*."

"Of course. An artist. I hope he's good in bed."

"Well, I'll have to find out, won't I?"

"What if Niles…"

"What if Niles…" repeated Jane in a high, airless, Truman Capote-ish voice.

"It's your funeral."

"No, it's not. At best life is short and fickle. At worst you're screwed the day you're born. Cancer, AIDS, a drive by shooting. The dead girl you found wandered into harm's way and chance turned his back. There are no safe bets."

"But what if this guy is the murderer? He looked like a street person to me, a drifter. Someone told Leo the *policia* think the killer is a drifter."

"Please. He's not a murderer. I'd know."

Jane looked at Consuela with exasperation.

"Now get out of here so I can take a bath."

After the door clicked shut on Consuela and the corridor, Jane ordered another *mojito*, armed with which she spent an hour soaking the world away. When she emerged, she gazed down at her electric-pink body and winced.

Why would some swaggering bohemian painter bother with me? she asked herself.

But watching him across the table as he wolfed his enchiladas, he looked like a man at the end of his tether, a tomcat who had used up too many lives. She was counting on the fact that Gregory Gregorovich was running on empty.

With mounting desperation she slathered on a variety of unguents and restorative creams. She bagged the idea of makeup except for a swath of tomato red lipstick across pursed lips and a daub of eye shadow.

Maybe I'll get lucky and he won't notice the fine print, she thought.

She tried all three of the cocktail dresses stashed in her suitcase, finally opting for a silvery bit of petrochemical artifice that hung off one shoulder.

At 8:30 p.m. Jane, Leo and Consuela tumbled into a green & white cab. Wedged between the two of them, bare thighs glued to the vinyl seat, Jane felt like a third class tramp trapped in a tawdry nightmare. A Jean Rhys heroine.

When Leo lit a cigar, a raging headache exploded in Jane's forehead. Her stomach churned. Desperately rolling down the passenger window she leaned across Consuela and spewed *mojitos* and bile into the street. They stopped at a pharmacy so she could buy a small bottle of mouthwash.

A few minutes later they exited the cab in front of a glass façade of pulsing lights that was the *Galeria Rana*. Entering the gallery, Jane glimpsed, across a room thronged with San Miguel's glitterati, the Russian artist. Surprisingly he'd actually shaved and put on a fresh shirt. He was talking to a man with the low budget glossiness of a salesman who'd stumbled on the secret of a high six-figure income. Puke!

Then again, she thought, maybe he's some wealthy collector. A person of serious taste, despite himself. And for all I know, Gregory Gregorovich is just a talentless hack.

Suddenly another wave of nerves raged like a squall though her stomach.

Or a murderer.

Chapter 10

Leaving behind the *Gato Negro's* stench of sweat, booze and loneliness, Gregory Gregorovich stumbled through San Miguel's ancient streets, pondering the grave Indian faces, trying to comprehend the idea of Amanda Smallwood's murder. But instead of Amanda's impish leer, a vision of the blonde named Jane kept materializing in his head. Would she make an appearance tonight at the *Galeria Rana*? Or had their encounter been just another random intersection of molecules in a cold universe?

Chance, or a lack of other options, at last brought Gregorovich to the front door of the gallery. Surely, he thought, Brian Dillinger owner of the *Galeria Rana* would have the inside scoop on Amanda's shocking demise. But upon entering the gallery, he found no one around. Only Gilberto something-or-other, the assistant manager, unpacking a case of white wine and putting the bottles into the wine cooler.

"*Hola.*"

Gilberto gave a snotty little nod in reply.

Gregorovich blew him a kiss and descended to the gallery's basement. A nether region consisting of spider-inhabited storage space and a slick conference room for closing sales. After a quick wash-up in the bathroom next to the conference room, he shaved painfully with a dull razor he found in a cabinet next to the sink. A closet disclosed three laundered and pressed blue shirts, no doubt belonging to Dillinger. Gregorovich tried one on. It fit okay *mas o menos*, if a little long in the sleeve and a little tight in the gut. Suddenly exhaustion weighted on him like a heavy rain. Crawling under the conference table, he instantly fell into a fairyland and dreamed of a stark naked Jane Ryder streaking across a Dali-esque landscape.

The next sound Gregorovich heard was a woman's throwaway laugh.

"Wrong door, sweetie," tittered another female voice.

As he sat rubbing the obfuscations of sleep from his eyes, he heard their inebriated banter through the paper-thin wall as they catalogued the defects of their male companions. Then the flush of a toilet.

Gregory's Japanese digital watch showed 20:32. The opening would be in full swing.

At the top of the stairs, Gregorovich gazed upon the motley throng that drifted about the gallery like confetti burst from a party favor. Most of the women were beautiful. Some strikingly eccentric. A few utterly grotesque. The men either rich business-men or impoverished artists and drug addicts. It was a perfect crowd to reenact Prince Prospero's masked ball. But who would play the Red Death?

Making his way through the crush, Gregorovich found Brian Dillinger wedged in an oblique corner of the room, button-holed by an ancient dowager with enough diamonds around her wattled neck to choke a horse. With unctuous formality Brian drew a withered, toad-skin-covered hand to his lips. Her other claw rested on the arm of an impecunious relative who accompanied her everywhere like a shadow. Wearing round tortoiseshell sunglasses, the caretaker's face was as impassive as that of a hired assassin.

"*Senora* Limon," said Brian. "The two paintings will be deliv-ered to your *estancia* tomorrow. Then you can choose the one that fits most perfectly in your salon. It gives me the greatest honor to serve you, *senora*. As always, your taste is impeccable."

Obsequiousness is next to godliness, thought Gregorovich. At least in old, moneyed Mexico.

Julia, a pretty young woman with melancholy breasts who worked in the gallery, stood to one side, waiting patiently. Brian looked beyond the stooped figure of wealth and privilege and found Gregorovich standing at the edge of this quaintly Latin tableau.

"Now if you'll excuse me, *senora*. Julia will talk with you about logistical details."

Brian dove past the sexless creature and grasped Gregorovich in a wrestler's grip. They stumbled backward through the crowd, their heads tucked close together like an investment banker imparting insider information to his acolyte.

"You've heard the news? Someone's iced Amanda. Rumor is she was a bloody horror show. It'll be a closed coffin funeral. You didn't do it did you, Gregory?" A cough of laughter escaped Dillinger's lips.

"What the hell is wrong with you?" demanded Gregorovich, breaking free of Dillinger's hold. "Of course I didn't do it!"

A narrow smile sliced Brian's tanned face.

"The buzz is she was murdered by a crazed drifter down from the States." He shrugged his shoulders, hands raised in the mock-histrionics of a sitcom star. "I thought of you immediately, Gregorovich. Your penchant for ravishing underage chicklets in far away L.A. makes you the perfect candidate."

"Screw you." But even as Gregorovich spun away in anger, Dillinger's arm was around his shoulder again. "Poor Gregorovich. Don't be pissed. Come on. I'll buy you a glass of wine or introduce you to a beautiful woman."

Gregorovich knew there was no way he could kiss off Dillinger. Rich and powerful, the man owned one of the three galleries in San Miguel that mattered. The very one through which Gregorovich hoped to make his comeback.

"I think you owe me both."

They went over to the bar where Gilberto was doling out the glasses of *tinto o blanco*. Dillinger told him to open a special reserve bottle. When Dillinger's back was turned, Gilberto made a face at Gregorovich.

Like old prep school chums, Gregorovich and Dillinger stood tasting the fine vintage and surveying the scene.

"A good crowd tonight," said Dillinger. "They seem to be in a buying mood. Three of your paintings have already sold. I'm sure it's because of Amanda's murder. There won't be any more paintings of her. At least from the flesh."

Dillinger emptied his glass in two quick gulps.

"Maybe before every opening we should have the reigning female model killed. A sort of postmodern Aztec ritual to gain the favor of the gods. It could be shown on late night cable right after the news from the Middle East."

Through a break in the crowd, Gregorovich suddenly saw the waspy profile of Jane Ryder caught in the flashing neon above the gallery entrance. The garish light ricocheted off her hair in tendrils of fools gold. A wave of unfamiliar nervousness quickened Gregorovich's pulse, set his blood racing. He touched Brian's arm and pointed across the room.

"Her," he said. "Introduce me to her."

Dillinger squinted, rucking the skin at the top of his cheeks.

"Which one?"

"The tall blonde."

"But I have no idea who she is. Though from here she looks quite ravishing for a cougar slut. Give me one good reason why I should give her to you?"

"Because you promised."

"That and five thousand *pesos* will get you knifed and thrown into a dumpster behind the Palace of Justice in *Ciudad de Mexico*."

In the meantime, Jane, having espied Gregorovich, jostled her way toward them through the ebullient mob. Her dress was silvery and minimalist. The same iridescent red that had shimmered in the morning sun of the *jardin* was scrawled across her lips, which twisted into a wry smile as she approached.

Gregorovich was mesmerized.

In the next instant Dillinger stepped into her path.

"I'm so glad you were able to come tonight," he said, leaning in and kissing the air beside each of Jane's cheeks, his hands on her cool shoulders. "You look lovely."

He grasped her hand. "Before you say anything, there's someone I want you to meet." He swung her in an arc toward Gregorovich.

"Gregory Gregorovich is one of the artists exhibiting tonight.

He has the unique talent of turning beauty into pornography. Or is it the other way around?"

"Actually Gregory and I are old friends," she said blithely. Her scent, a mélange of soap, perfume, sweat and musk, burned up Gregorovich's nostrils like a brush fire. She turned and looked at Dillinger. "I'm afraid you have me confused with someone else in your past. We've never met before this moment."

Dillinger made a deprecating twitch of his mouth. "A pity."

"This is Jane," Gregorovich interrupted before Dillinger could make some further cutting remark.

She held out her hand. "Jane Ryder."

"Brian Dillinger. I own the gallery."

"How nice for you."

At that moment Jane's entourage consisting of Consuela Domingue and Leo Bremmer arrived, precipitating a further round of introductions. Brian told an amusing story at the expense of someone famous who kept a home in San Miguel, then excused himself. Leo made a beeline for the bar with Consuela in desperate pursuit.

Left alone with Jane, Gregorovich felt school boyishly inept, at a sudden loss for words. Jane hooked her arm in his.

"Well, come on, *senor* Gregorovich," she said. "Don't stand there like a petrified turd. Show me your paintings. I'd like to judge for myself whether Mr. Dillinger's critique is accurate."

At that moment Gregorovich realized he was madly taken with this woman who called herself Jane Ryder. She was ravishing and ravishable. He was breathless with anticipation.

They crossed the gallery together and stood in front of one of his paintings. In it a nude Amanda Smallwood jutted her buttocks skyward, awaiting the favors of a rampant satyr. Concealed behind a crumbling Greek column to one side, a doltish shepherd gawked, his face consumed by lewd expectations.

"A friend of yours?"

"The satyr?"

"No, stupid. The shameless *puta*."

"Just a model."

"If she lives in San Miguel, I'm in trouble."

"Actually she was murdered last night."

"Don't joke with me."

"It's true."

Jane's fingernails dug into his arm like the teeth of an agitated ferret. Beneath her perfume, Gregorovich smelled the rank spoors of fear, violent death looming in her imagination like some fecund and poisonous fungus.

He took her hand. It vibrated as if injected with an electric pulse.

"I've been thinking about you all day," she said in a whisper. A mumbled confession to drive away the horror of Amanda's bloody denouement.

Gregorovich looked at her. Her eyes were filled with hope and lust.

"Let's get out of here."

As they hurried from the gallery, Gregorovich glanced back across the room. Through the haze of cigar and cigarette smoke, Dillinger stood halfway up the stairway to the loft exhibit space. Oddly enough Gregorovich was sure Dillinger was watching them.

Ten minutes later a taxi, bearing Jane and Gregorovich locked in a squirming, panting embrace in the back seat, crept to a halt at the top of the gravel-paved entrance to two stories of crumbling red bricks and mortar known as The Pines Hotel.

In the whitewashed office a drowsy Mexican in a frayed argyle sweater vest and grease-spotted tie, motioned for Gregorovich to fill out a registration card.

"Is the bridal suite available?" Gregorovich asked.

"Only one suite, *senor*. It iss available for you. But the shower iss no workin. You usse another whone jist dowhn the 'all."

"*No problemo.*"

Somehow Jane managed to count out the cash for three nights in advance, while Gregorovich's hands roved distractingly across her derriere. Then they were outside again, hurrying cattycorner down a cement walkway through the ragged garden toward a far wing of the hotel. A low wattage bulb burned vaguely above a metal door. The night air was cool; stars glistened like cheap glass beads. A lone bat torpedoed back and forth in the space between two palm trees.

For an instant Jane wondered whether Gregory had ever stayed at The Pines before. Under similar circumstances. It was not a question she wanted the answer to.

He held open the metal door to the far wing. A sensor switched on the lights in the stairwell. They bounded upward two steps at a time, Gregory in the lead.

"Why did you ask for the bridal suite?"

"I thought I might do some painting in the other room...you know, in between...."

"Bastard." But her hands were already inside his pants groping his cock and balls as he fumbled with the door key.

Once inside but unable to find the light switch, they stumbled over sharp-edged rattan furniture, then slid to the floor where they kissed and groped and discarded all items of clothing in a rough and tumble reminiscent of a high school wrestling match. As Gregory nuzzled and nibbled her carefree breasts, Jane grasped for his dick. It was a doozy: long, hardwood hard and curved like a boomerang. She wanted it inside her *pronto*. Even as this thought materialized, his cock began to twitch and bob like a dousing wand and in the next instant an explosion of hot sperm splattered across her stomach.

Jesus, not fucking PE! Jane cursed silently. Niles, when they were first married, had suffered from that affliction. It had taken years of therapy to ferret out the cause and kill it.

The edgy artist's dick was now a limp shadow of its former self.

"Sorry," said Gregory. "Got a little overexcited."

With a sigh Jane licked her lips, then leaned forward and began the tedious task of reigniting his ardor.

Chapter 11

The *Galeria Rana* was a gigantic white sugar cube dropped amid a row of trendy shops and bars in a newly developing part of the lower town. To get there took a good twenty-minute walk from San Miguel's old, colonial center, a breeze by cab. At nine fifteen p.m., a green and white cab with badly worn brake pads squealed to a stop in front of the gallery. Moments later, Inspector Hector Diaz's slender figure, in a wavering state of inebriation, emerged awkwardly from the wrong rear door of the cab. He was more than an hour late. Better late than never, he thought.

Before he could turn to close the door, the taxi sped away, sending up a cloud of dust from the partially paved street. Diaz stood looking up at the gallery, a fresh handkerchief held over nose and mouth. Like some neurotic mantra, green, pink and periwinkle neon flashed on and off from the translucent depths of the glass brick facade. From a niche above the entrance, a fat, copper-green frog stared back at him.

Diaz's progress from street to sidewalk was erratic, as the pulsing neon beckoned and then repelled him. A rumbling aftershock of whatever bug he had acquired at lunch plummeted through his entrails. Three mezcals on an empty stomach in the bar at *El Iris* had been a mistake. If he was lucky, a generous assortment of finger foods to counteract the alcohol's effect awaited him inside the gallery. Or at least the palliative calm of a locked bathroom.

From the edge of his vision, he caught movement. A stray dog as thin as a fading memory loped down the center of the street. When it turned its head, the face of the devil leered at Diaz with bone-chilling enmity. Diaz faltered, his hand grasping instinctively for the silver cross that he had stopped wearing around his neck since his fourteenth birthday. His hand found instead the golden image of *Ehecatl*. Could this ancient god of storms protect him against the Christian devil? Neither he nor the other ancient deities had served *Montezuma* well against the blood-drenched onslaught of Cortes. But this was a new time. A time for old faiths to be renewed.

With a snarl the satanic beast turned away and continued its progress at an increased pace, diminishing into the shadow strewn distance. Diaz pressed his eyes closed. When he opened them again, the devil dog was gone. Or maybe it never existed. Regardless, Diaz's forehead was sheathed in sweat.

At this rate you'll be checking into the emergency room before the night's over, he thought. Get a grip.

With one hand he brushed the flashing gallery lights aside like a cloud of gnats and charged across the sidewalk and up the front steps of the edifice.

Double front doors of some burnished metal posed a new obstacle. As Diaz wrestled with the unyielding handle, a couple came up behind him. The man reached past Diaz and pressed a button on the wall of the entrance alcove. With a click the latch released, the doors opened. The couple barged past.

Swept up in their wake, Diaz tumbled like flotsam into the gallery, following the undulating movement of the woman's bare shoulders and pulchritudinous behind. The couple merged into the milling throng and disappeared from view. A cacophonous human sea of wealth, decadence, affectation and eccentricity filled the gallery. Some stood in little cliques, smoking, sipping wine and sharing the latest gossip. Others, singly or in pairs, drifted aimlessly as smoke, stopping from time to time to consider a painting. With a sigh Diaz made his way amid the gaudy crowd.

Of the five painters showing their work, three had used Amanda Smallwood as muse. One had painted her in lush imitation of Lucien Freud, breasts, thighs, crotch and armpits exaggerated in thick strokes of lavender, ocher and moss green. The second cast her as the femme fatale in a lurid nineteen fifties film noir style. In the work of the third artist, Amanda was displayed in a series of pornographic couplings with grinning satyrs amidst crumbling Greek temples and Mediterranean vistas.

Diaz leaned close to one of the latter works, squinting at an unreadable squiggle he assumed to be the artist's signature.

"An interesting position," said a female voice behind him. "Have you ever tried it?"

He looked around into the twilight gray eyes of Consuela Domingue. A mischievous smile crinkled her lips.

"I think it would require someone with acute gymnastic abilities. Not my forte. Besides, it's difficult to teach an old dog new tricks."

"I personally wouldn't mind giving it a try," she said. "Or whatever an old dog might have in mind."

Diaz let the offer expire.

"So, Inspector. I didn't expect to see you here tonight. Are you a collector?"

"The woman in the painting and the murdered woman you discovered in the *jardin* are one and the same. She worked as an artists' model."

"How incredibly bizarre."

Consuela gazed again at the painting.

"Looking at this painting now seems like an act of necrophilia."

A simulacrum of Amanda's corpse lying on the gurney in Moza's clinic appeared in Diaz's head. His throat constricted with an intense dryness, just as a waiter passed bearing a tray of effervescing champagne flutes. Diaz grabbed two, handing one to Consuela, while guzzling the contents of the other.

"Thirsty, Inspector?"

In affirmation Diaz grasped and guzzled a second glass.

"Leo and I waited at our hotel all morning and part of the afternoon for someone from the *Judiciales* to come by and interview us. No one came."

"My apologies for such third world inefficiency. I hope at least you were able to rest and recover from the shock of last night."

"Seeing that girl lying there with empty black holes instead of eyes. Ugh! Who could ever recover from that?"

"I understand. But perhaps, if you're sufficiently rested, after this…" Diaz waved his hand distractedly. "…this spectacle, we could go for a drink."

"Are you trying to pick me up, Inspector?"

"No, no. I meant you and Senor Bremmer. To conduct the interview in the more relaxed venue of a quiet cocktail lounge."

"What a lovely way to end a Friday night – discussing rape and murder over a pear martini. But Leo and I came to the gallery with a friend. I need to find out her plans. I'll catch up with you a little later. Enjoy the art, Inspector. Maybe it will get a rise out of you."

Consuela eased into the crowd, her provocative physicality bursting the seams of a wintergreen sheath dress.

Wandering among the throng, Diaz came upon a pretty young woman with purple hair. A plastic badge affixed to the slop of her breast confirmed she was an employee of the gallery and that her name was Julia. He bowed slightly, to which she responded with a warm smile.

"Inspector Diaz of the San Miguel *Policia Judiciales*."

The smile turned to a frown. But before she could duck away, he took her arm and led her across the room to the largest of the Lucian Freud-like canvases. They stood before it in a state of tense equilibrium.

"I need you to introduce me to the three artists who used this woman as a model." He nodded toward the painting. "She was murdered last night."

Julia's kohl-heavy lashes fluttered at him like small black butterflies in jeopardy. For a moment he thought she was going to faint. Then he realized that it was the adrenalin of excitement, not fear, which coursed through her body.

"How wonderfully *fantastico* and grisly. Of course I'll introduce you."

She swooped him up and guided him to a small bar set up beneath the stairs leading to a balcony area, her perfume dancing little naked pirouettes up Diaz's nose. A tall, strikingly handsome man in his mid-30s came into view, leaning against the bar. His blue almond-shaped eyes scanned the passing scene with studied calculation.

Two harpies, frightening with their two-tone lipstick, teased hair and jiggly push-up boobs, fawned over him as though he might be their next meal.

One of the women commenced relating some tidbit of torrid gossip, while the other buried her tongue in the speaker's ear. With a bored glance, the man picked up a wine bottle from the bar and carelessly began to refill the gossiper's glass. The level of the dark red vintage rose dangerously toward the lip of the glass; then gushed over the edge, splashing the woman's chest.

"Oh, sorry."

In a panic the woman stroked desperately at her ruined dress with a cloth napkin. Her friend laughed.

"Pay Gilberto for the napkin," the man said.

"Brian," interrupted Julia. "I'd like to introduce you to someone."

"You'll excuse me, *senoras*."

Brushing past the aging harpies, or whatever they were, the man named Brian sailed across the room, flashing his teeth at persons he knew. Diaz and Julia followed in his wake. Abruptly he stopped beside the only sculpture on exhibit, an ancient Toltec face of tarnished metal, and swung about like a yacht at anchor. His eyes flashed at Diaz. Diaz met Dillinger's eyes with stainless steel indifference.

"Inspector Diaz of the Judicial Police."

"Brian Dillinger."

Dillinger's grip was paralyzing.

"Any relation to the gangster?"

"He's rumored to be a distant cousin, but I've never checked into it. My family comes from Chicago. Speaking of cops and robbers, I never expected San Miguel's top cop to show up at one of my openings."

"Actually I'm not the top cop, as you put it. But I am here investigating the murder of Amanda Smallwood."

"Horrible!" Dillinger said the word as though commenting on a bad bottle of wine.

"If tonight's exhibition is any indication, she was a rapturous inspiration."

"Hot would be the best description of Amanda Smallwood. She was a total slut. But I'll miss her. She was in love with the idea of artists wanting to transform her raunchy little body into a voluptuous vision of concupiscence."

"What was your relationship with her?"

"I painted her bigger and gaudier than life. The large canvases are mine." He waved his hand proprietarily. "There was nothing else between us. No torrid love trysts, I'm afraid. Not even a handjob. Outside the studio we were oil and water."

Brian smiled at Julia as if to reassure her. She didn't look reassured.

"Did you see her last night?"

"Yes. She came to my birthday party. Then she left with some people."

"Do you remember who they were?"

"A couple of guys I'd never seen before. They must have crashed the party. But they weren't the only ones. Lots of people I didn't know were wandering around my house last night, drinking my booze."

"You were upset by all these freeloaders?"

"Not really. I throw a lot of parties, Inspector. I like parties." Brian indicated the crowded room. "And lots of people who weren't invited always seem to show up."

"I thought painters were all paupers."

"I'm sorry," broke in Julia. "I forgot to mention to Inspector Diaz that you own the *Galeria Rana.*"

"As a painter I'm strictly a dilettante. I'm a businessman. I came to San Miguel eight years ago with some money to invest and I've done very well. The gallery's only a sideline."

"Ah." Diaz raised and lowered his eyebrows in his best imitation of a tall, slender, *Latino* Hercule Poirot.

"And please don't ask me if I know anyone who might have wanted to harm Amanda. Everyone loved her. They all wanted to go to bed with her. Especially the women. But that was a pleasure she gave to very few. Now, unless you have further questions, there are other people I need to talk to."

Before Diaz could respond, Brian bolted perpendicularly across the room. In his path appeared a horse-faced woman attired in black lace melodrama. Catching her up with one arm, he propelled her across the room. As his lips nuzzled her neck, she whinnied.

Diaz gazed quizzically at Julia.

"So, do you think your boss is capable of killing someone?"

"Off the record?"

"Of course. I'd never paint a beautiful woman into a corner."

"In that case, the answer is yes." She gripped Diaz's arm. "But isn't everyone capable of murder at some time or another?"

They climbed the stairs to the balcony and came upon a plump, goateed creature holding court. A grape-colored bowtie sprouted like an exotic bloom from beneath his bearded chin. The roundness of midlife was made amusing by the broad red stripes of his shirt. He took Diaz's hand as though it were a leaf that had drifted down from the sky. His nails were buffed and polished to perfection; his small hands pink and soft. *Profesor* Montalban spoke with a Castilian lisp.

"Such a pleasure to meet you, Inspector Diaz. Perhaps you would consider sitting for me sometime? It would be an honor to paint an authentic police investigator. Do you like my work?"

They turned and looked at several of the *Profesor's* noirish compositions displayed on the wall behind. Dark alleyways and suppressed violence, boobs and lingerie, guns and cigarettes. The last inspired a sudden desire by Diaz to smoke. He placed a Montana between his lips and torched its tip with the flame of his lighter.

"I adore the Italian cinema," said Montelban. Especially the classical period after the war. Do you, Inspector? *Riso Amaro.* Do you know it? Or *La Dolci Vita* or *Divorzio All' Italiana.* So much emotion. And the movie posters. So wonderfully tawdry."

He was still holding Diaz's hand in his sweaty faux grip. Movie posters, thought Diaz. That was the *Profesor's* inspiration.

"But you aren't a fan of the Italian cinema, are you Inspector? Nor of the art of Emilio Montalban." The *Profesor* sighed.

"No. You're here solely because of the grotesque murder of little Amanda. A sweet but unloved child, weak and malleable. Her fey character was perfect for my paintings. And her curves."

A look of wistfulness crept into the *Profesor's* eyes. Surely, Diaz considered, this sadness was for the loss of Amanda the person, not her accoutrements. *Profesor* Montalban didn't strike Diaz as a breast man, at least in the traditional sense.

"What can you tell me about Amanda, *Profesor?*"

"She was one of the lost. Drifting here in San Miguel like a pretty paper hat dropped in the gutter during a downpour. Drugs. Parties. Sex. The warm afternoon sun. She told me she once dreamed of becoming an artist. But she was bereft of talent. So instead she became an artist's wet dream."

"Did she have a serious relationship with any of the artists she posed for?"

"I'm afraid she was just a whore." Montalban flicked his wrist dismissively. "She loved men and women equally. But never anything serious. She played at love. All models are tarts, Inspector. That's why they make such good models."

"Could any of the artists she toyed with have borne her malice?"

"My theory, which I'm sure you're dying to hear, is she was fucked and strangled by a drifter passing through our quaint town. A predator whose satanic path she crossed by pure chance. Who else but a psychopath would have gouged out the little strumpet's eyes?"

Caught off guard by this graphic disclosure, Diaz's mouth opened and closed soundlessly. Such details had not appeared in the newspapers. Julia's eyes blinked in horror. How had Montalban come by this insider information? Had Moza said something injudicious? No. Diaz was sure it was that slimeball, Silva. Making up for his failed shakedown of *senor* Bremmer.

"That circumstance isn't generally known, *Profesor* Montalban."

Montalban looked quizzically at Diaz.

"But I'm afraid it is, Inspector. You've just confirmed the rumor that's been swooping around San Miguel all evening like a blood-sucking little vampire bat."

"Flying or not, I insist you not discuss that detail with anyone further."

"You have my word," said Montalban, holding out his hand again. Diaz shook it, though he knew Montalban's commitment was only pro forma. The cat was out of the fucking bag, so to speak.

Diaz and Julia walked back downstairs in silence. They searched high and low through the thinning crowd, looking for the third Amanda-inspired artist. But Gregory Gregorovich was nowhere to be found.

"I saw him earlier," apologized Julia. "He must have gone off with friends. But you can find him easily enough. He lives with a ceramic artist named Fran Kovacs. She has a studio on *Calle Terrapien*."

"You've been very helpful. And a lovely escort." Then, on a whim: "Perhaps we could go for a drink some time."

She looked at him doubtfully.

"You don't find older men attractive?"

"Sometimes I do," she said. She handed him a business card. "I'll consider your offer. Give me a call."

Diaz was disheartened that the only phone number on the card was for the gallery.

From the crowd's edge Diaz watched Julia stop and talk to a woman in a Chanel-looking suit and her pinstripe-attired husband. What madness had inspired him to ask her for a drink? She must be all of twenty-three. Not much older than the dead woman. Why was he driven to hit on every attractive pair of coconuts he came into contact with? At his age he should be cooling down.

He considered calling Martina. Despite her sometimes belligerent demeanor, they shared a certain simpatico.

"Inspector, you're still here."

It was Consuela. Behind her the sandy-haired Leo Bremmer pitched and yawed like a sailboat in a typhoon.

"We're ready to go for that drink," said Consuela. "Or at least I am. Leo's already completely shit faced." She grimaced.

"I thought you came with a friend."

"Jane Ryder? She got herself picked up tonight by some artist named Gregorovich. So I'm all yours, Inspector Diaz. Every centimeter of me.

in the front garden i've impaled a pig's head on a wooden spike as a warning to them. stay away. dried blood stains the mottled snout. blue bottle flies crawl into the nostrils and across the dead eyes. their proboscises flick in and out as they feed on rotting flesh.

this was my dream.

when i awake from a glancing blow of light across my eyes, they are still here.

they are not a dream.

lying amid sweat-drenched sheets, i hear them whispering just around the corner in the hallway and on the tile roof outside my bedroom window. their words are indistinct. at the edge of my vision they move like shadows.

the metallic lisp of a knife blade being drawn across the oiled surface of a whetstone causes the hairs on the back of my neck to stand at attention.

going into the bathroom i gulp back the scream that wants to burst from my throat. the acid taste of vomit burns my mouth. on the mirror is a child's drawing of a goat, its neck slit open, the blood welling. beneath the drawing the word sacrifice is scrawled in the same cherry red lipstick.

i sit on the edge of the claw-footed tub, fixated by the spaces between the hexagonal floor tiles. my legs won't stop shaking. it's as if they belong to someone else.

an innocent silverfish slithers across the tiles. i

smash it with the heel of my foot. then i grab a hand towel and wipe the message off the mirror surface - and the silverfish muck from the bottom of my foot.

all day i brood about their message. she leaves the house because i'm in an unbearable mood.

at dusk when i fire up the grill to cook dinner, i secretly incinerate the towel with its telltale lipstick stains. later we have a birthday party to go to.

a thick fog rolls in, inundating the town. watching drops of moisture drip from the edge of a tin roof, i imagine a pair of sightless eyes thrown across the flat stones of the courtyard.

in my vision they scurry from the dark corners, fighting over these empty offerings.

Chapter 12

Every bartender in San Miguel made his own version of the perfect margarita, a mystical combination of fresh limejuice, Cointreau and enough triple-distilled blue agave tequila to knock your socks off. The baby-faced waiter at *El Restaurante y Bar Locuelo* set two of them on the glass-topped table between Diaz and Consuela. One was *con sal*, the other *sin*.

Diaz held aloft a half moon of lime. As he pressed his fingers into the lush pulp, a trickle of milky droplets cascaded into his drink. His eyes rested exclusively on Consuela.

They were alone. Leo Bremmer, Consuela's lover, consort, business associate, pimp or whatever, having been poured into the backseat of a taxi and dispatched prepaid back to the hotel. Consuela met Diaz's gaze for a series of long, uncounted seconds. Then drank half her margarita in a single gulp. Her tongue licked the lime spume from her lips.

Across the room a heavyset man with nowhere to go leaned over the bar watching the bartender ply his trade. Otherwise the bar area was deserted. Over the sound system came the sibilant undertow of some avant-garde jazz combo. Somewhere a fountain tinkled.

"I don't smoke, but do you have a cigarette?"

Diaz lit two cigarettes and handed her one. She took a puff, then mashed it into the ashtray, where it smoldered like a burning tire at a riot. When the baby-faced waiter appeared to provide a clean ashtray, she waved him away.

"So, *senor* Chief Inspector, what do you want to know about that horrible night less than 24 hours ago?"

"It's Inspector Diaz." He smiled. "But please call me Hector."

"Since I'm not on a first name basis with my priest, *mi abogado* or *mi ginecologo*, I'm not sure I should be with you."

"As you wish." Diaz raised his palms in a gesture of peace. "Just tell me what you saw or heard or smelled or felt as you passed through the *jardin* last night at 2:00 a.m."

"When we left the restaurant, about one thirty, Leo was very drunk."

"A long standing habit of his."

"Don't be unkind. Some people drink to excess, some fornicate indiscriminately, others shoot heroin. We all have our tragic sides. I'd been drinking too, though not as willfully as Leo. That night he was all over me like a cheap suit."

"Now who's being unkind?"

She sipped her margarita, rolling the piquant concoction over her tongue, exploring its labyrinthine intricacies. Limejuice, with the metallic essence of a copper coin; blue agave tequila like a long, lingering kiss.

"It was miserably cold and damp last night," she said. "I only had on a little strapless thing and a thin shawl. I remember being half frozen and very unhappy. Wishing we'd taken a cab. Just as we came into the *jardin*, we passed a private security guard."

"How do you know he wasn't a policeman?"

"He didn't look like a policeman."

"What did he look like?"

"A security guard."

"No, I mean his physical description."

"I have no idea. He stuck his flashlight in my face – like some Nazi brownshirt. Then Leo tried to grope me. I was so totally pissed off, I ran up the steps into the *jardin*. All I wanted was to be back in my room at the hotel under a pile of blankets."

Diaz motioned the bartender for another round of drinks.

"At the top of the stairs, Leo was after me again. I pushed him off and went into the *jardin*. I remember him yelling. When I looked back, I saw the outline of a man moving down the street behind him."

"Down *Calle San Francisco*?"

"Whatever that street's called."

"How did you know it was a man?"

"His physique. The way he moved. Trust me, it was a man. I do know the differences." She gave Diaz a reproving look. "He was wearing a white shirt or jacket. That's why I could see him so distinctly even in the mist."

"Could you see his face?"

"You must be kidding. He passed by under a single streetlight on the far side of the street beyond Leo. And it was drizzling. Do you think he did it?"

"Who?"

"The man I just told you about."

"I have absolutely no idea."

"Then maybe it was the security guard?"

Diaz lit another Montana, watching her question disappear like the smoke curling up into his eyes, making him squint. Their conversation was going nowhere. The night felt suddenly heavy, pressing down on his brain and gonads. He found Consuela attractive in the same way that an overripe mango offers the promise of unimaginable sweetness. But he didn't know if he had either the mental or physical energy to explore that image in the flesh.

"After that everything gets a little blurry," she said. "There was the body of the girl, or woman, lying in the shadows. Then the horror of her mutilation. I started screaming and couldn't stop. That's when Leo hit me. The creep. Look. I've still got a bruise on my cheek."

She leaned forward, a finger touching the ridge of her cheek, where a stain the size and color of a jumbo martini olive bled through her makeup.

"The next thing I remember is being inside the police station. Because I was finally out of the bone-chilling fog. Then, like some demigod, you swooped down and rescued us from the clutches of that asshole Sergeant Silva."

She smiled wantonly.

"Well," said Diaz. He stood up and drained his glass. "You'll excuse me for a moment?"

The baby-faced waiter directed him to the men's room up the hallway toward the street. Diaz ambled to the reception area, glancing into the main dining room, where a few parties were still masticating away.

Reversing his path, he returned halfway down the corridor. Cattycorner to the men's room entrance was a closed louvered door. From behind it came the muffled sound of men's voices interspersed with outbursts of laughter.

As Diaz paused to enter the men's room, the louvered door opened. A thickly built man in a black suit stepped though the opening. For a brief moment the door stood ajar, revealing nine businessmen around an oblong table, drinks and cigars in hand. Then the bodyguard pulled the door closed.

His below zero eyes froze on Diaz for several seconds, assessing the likelihood that he was a threat. Beneath the bodyguard's left arm was the telltale bulge made by a heavy-caliber weapon.

Rich bastards having a Friday night business meeting to figure out whom to screw next, thought Diaz. He squinted menacingly back at the bodyguard, who was too stupid to flinch. Then he pushed his way into the men's room.

After a lengthy whiz, Diaz stood in front of the mirror. He was not reassured by what he saw. Pushing aside his own anorexic image, he replaced it with a mental snapshot of the men seated around the table in the private room.

Seven of the nine men were older business types, heavy waisted and ruddy complexioned from years of excess. Broadcasting a studied casualness in shirtsleeves and loosened designer ties, they remained distinctly predatory.

Diaz recognized the man at the head of the table as Senator Abraham Limon, one of the most powerful men in the ruling party in the State of Guanajuato. Beside him sat a much younger eighth man whose similarity of features identified him as the off-spring of the *senor* Limon. And surprise, surprise. Next to Limon the younger leaned Brian Dillinger – *numero nueve*. No wonder Dillinger had been successful in his business ventures.

For an instant Diaz thought about barging into the private room and placing them all under arrest for suspicion of crimes to be determined. But it would be a gesture of futility. Not to mention suicidal.

• • •

When Diaz finally returned to the bar, he found Consuela wrapped in a multi-colored Indian shawl, sipping a glass of *agua gaseosa* and joking with the bartender.

"You took your own good time in the *pissoir*," she said. "Did someone get you off?" Then, with a laugh: "And you stuck me with the check."

As Diaz started to fuss about splitting the bill, she turned back to the barman.

"*Buenas noches*, Pedro."

"*Adios, senora.* I hope to see you here again soon."

Diaz scowled at the barman. Not likely.

The street on which Diaz and Consuela stood outside the bar offered, like the majority of streets in San Miguel, the option of going uphill or down. They turned and, like comrades of the revolution, walked arm in arm up the steep slope in the direction of her hotel. Their steps wobbled a little, due as much to the bartender's generosity as the unevenness of the stone pavement.

As they passed a dark doorway, Consuela whispered:

"I need to pee."

Hiking up her dress, she squatted and made on the stones. Her piss splashed the pavement like a drinking fountain stuck in the on position. As she stood up, she ran her hand up Diaz's fly, quickening the sudden tumescence.

"*Oh Dios,*" she breathed as she leaned into him. He put his hands on her naked buttocks. The flesh was smooth and cool. One of her hands was inside his fly, extricating his schlong. She twisted backwards against the wall, one leg cocked behind his.

"Do it now."

For a moment Diaz was almost lost, consumed in the visceral demands of his cock. Then he saw in his mind the empty corpse of Amanda Smallwood lying on a metal shelf, but colder than the metal would ever be. He pushed Consuela's hands away.

"It's been a long day."

Chapter 13

After Consuela stomped up the street as best she could in four-inch stiletto heels, Diaz decided not to go home right away. His mouth, where she had hit him, felt bruised. One of his teeth had sliced his lip open and the front of his shirt was bloody. Or maybe it had been the hard edge of Consuela's ring, with its gold and diamond-eyed image of a skull, that had cut his flesh.

Hard as nails, he thought. Ultimately Diaz was a romantic. He needed more than just a cold fuck.

A cab dropped him in front of the Municipal Cemetery with its looming whitewashed walls. He wended a circuitous trail through the crowded, subdivided gravesites, around miniature wrought iron fences and white oblong low-rise mausoleums. Leaf shadows cast by moonlight danced in the wind that had come up off the semi-arid *compo* sloping to the predatory mountains in the west.

Soon enough he came to his daughter Estella's grave. A coffin-shaped vault surmounted by a heavy cross. The whitewashed surface seemed to pulse in the starlight, sending signals into deep space. Diaz scratched his chin and gazed at the night sky. Its vastness cut him to the bone, filled him with unspecified dread.

He sat on the low mausoleum. It was cold and hard. Bending forward, he rested his elbows on his thighs.

"Estella. Estella." He spoke her name in a barely audible whisper. But he didn't know what to say, or think, next.

"Don't be laying your guilt off on Estella, asshole."

That voice!

Its echo clanged in Diaz's head, a malfunctioning metallic bat slamming back and forth against the sides of a basso profundo cast iron bell.

His eyes pivoted left, then right. In the shadowy depths of the cemetery he could see no one. Where the fuck was Reyna, his ex? Was she down on her knees behind one of the tombs? Kneeling, he had heard through the rumor mill, was a frequent position for her these days. And not to take communion.

He stood up.

"No one invited you. This is between me and Estella."

"She doesn't need to spend any more time with you. If you hadn't taken her to the *jardin* that New Year's Eve…"

"Give it a rest."

"After you destroyed my life?"

So melodramatic. Reyna had been raised on a diet of *Univision telenovelas*.

In the darkness Diaz found it impossible to pinpoint the source of her voice. At times it even seemed to be coming from inside his head.

But that was an old trick of hers.

"Come on out, Reyna," he said. "Get off your knees so I can slap you silly."

"Always the low level violence. That's what your job does to you, Hector. The more violence you see on the streets and in the cellblocks, the more insensitive you become. Then you start to like the violence. You enjoy kicking some guy in the balls because he's dealing weed to gringo hippies to pay the rent. Or jamming someone's head into a wall until his brains turn to guava paste because he looked at you the wrong way during a traffic stop. It's like joining a gay S&M club. Like in that Al Pacino movie. What was it called? *Cruising*. Though you're nothing like Al Pacino. Not even close."

"I'm not gay either," protested Diaz.

A feminist diatribe. Diaz just hoped she wasn't armed, didn't start wildly shooting in his direction. His eyes continued to scan the deepest shadows.

"Okay," said Diaz. "I'm not perfect. But neither are you." He crossed his arms. "Show yourself, Reyna."

"I'm inside you."

"That's funny. Like some kind of demonic possession?"

"No, asshole. Like some deviant fantasy dreamed up by Dr. Sigmund Freud."

"I can't talk to you, Reyna."

"That was always an issue."

"So was your drinking."

The image of a Punch & Judy puppet show materialized in his mind. Two puppets, one unmistakably the simulacrum of Hector Diaz, the other a bodacious Reyna, used sticks to beat each other without mercy.

This is stupid. Reyna lives in Cuernavaca now, Diaz reasoned. That's more than 400 kilometers away. No way is she lurking about in San Miguel's Municipal Cemetery at one o'clock in the morning. This conversation exists only in my loopy brain. Which means I'm finally going totally apeshit.

Or maybe it was just the lingering effects of the bacteria ensconced in his intestines and his exhaustion from lack of sleep. Having acknowledged his psychosis, Diaz was now able to make the delusion disappear:

"Okay," he said. "Go away Reyna. I need to talk to Estella."

The Punch & Judy stage set disappeared in a puff of smoke, exploding stars and exclamation points.

Diaz's forehead was covered in sweat. His underarms drenched. He lit a cigarette and puffed desultorily.

"Estella, sweetheart. If you were alive today you'd be almost nineteen. Almost the same age as the woman killed last night and dumped in the *jardin*. There was no way to trace the random bullet that penetrated your heart that New Year's Eve. But this murder is different. Not accidental but carried out with brutal intent and precision. I'm going to get the bastard who did it. I swear."

"Do what you think is right," Estella replied.

Feeling that he had succeeded in pushing his allotted ball of dung to the top of the hill, Diaz slapped his hands on his knees and rose to a standing position, brushing the flaking whitewash from the ass of his pants. Now he really was going home to bed.

He had a feeling the Amanda Smallwood case would break

soon. Just keep digging, he told himself.

Trudging among the graves, he retraced from memory his intricate entry route. Only once did he end up in a cul de sac and have to rescind his progress.

As he stepped briskly through the arched entrance of the cemetery, Diaz nearly collided with a slow-stepping night pilgrim draped in a filthy sheepskin coat. Baggy rayon trousers, black or Navy blue, covered his lower appendages; handcrafted *huaraches* made from an old truck tire shod his dusty feet.

At that junction a single low-wattage streetlight illuminated the passing scene.

"*Hola*," said the stranger, screeching to a halt and raising his hands in surprise. He blocked Diaz's path up the narrow byway leading from the cemetery to the street.

Diaz decided to bluff: "Out of my way, scumbag!"

"Hold up there, *amigo*," the stranger said. "Don't I know you?"

He backed off several meters, at the same time drawing forth a large caliber handgun from beneath the sheepskin. Diaz identified it as an ancient Colt .45, more suited for a museum display than for committing murder and mayhem. A glint of recognition shown in the *pistolero's* eyes like the sudden flame of a struck match.

"Why if it isn't Hector Diaz the cop. You're out late tonight, *senor* Diaz."

The vagrant waived the pistol adroitly in his hand, a *bandito* escapee from the celluloid world of a spaghetti western.

"Don't you remember me, Hector? You're a cross of pain branded on my brain. I lost my youth and my mind because of you."

The gangbanger's eyes gleamed as though reflecting the fires of perdition. Or so it appeared to Diaz.

This is not going well, Diaz thought.

He considered an abrupt about face, dodging back into the interstices of the graveyard.

At that moment two other figures materialized out of the darkness behind the armed stranger.

Diaz eyed the three.

The first stranger, the one with the gun, had a face like the bottom of someone's shoe. Soft crumbling mouth, worn holes for eyes, nose twisted, broken, flattened. Long scraggly hair. Wispy chin whiskers. A primitive prison tattoo of a rapacious viper entwining around the blade of a dagger covered one side of his throat.

Diaz's mind raced. Who was this slime bucket who knew his name? Then it came to him. Emile. Emile Zato, a sadistic sociopath Diaz had sent to prison seven years before for rape, armed robbery and aggravated assault. Emile and his older brother had accosted an American tourist couple, beaten the husband senseless for thirty dollars and forced the wife to perform double fellatio. The husband had suffered brain damage; the wife was scarred beyond redemption. Diaz had sent Emile's brother straight to Hell with a bullet through his forehead. Now too late he realized he should have done the same to Emile.

The other two drifters were mere ciphers. There was nothing individual about either of them. Nothing whatsoever. Just two lost men dressed in rags, drifting on the night wind. Looking for trouble or death, it didn't matter which.

In daylight they would just be a pair of vagrants afraid of their shadows.

But at this empty hour Diaz knew they too were very dangerous. But Emile was the ringleader. The one who would decide whether Diaz lived or died.

A leer of filthy, decay-ridden ivories crept across Zato's face.

"Yes, my dear. I would say it is way past your bedtime."

Just then a fat oily rat shunted across the cemetery wall at eye level. Directly in front of Diaz and the armed psychopath, the rat stopped, twitching his bristly snout like a vaudeville actor his trademark mustache. Its miniature jaws twisted in a sneer. Its hairless, prehistoric tail poised like a ringmaster's whip.

I need to ease up on the mezcal, thought Diaz.

But Zato's reaction to the rat's appearance was totally unexpected. Emitting a high-pitched scream, he dropped to his knees, as if he had seen Satan himself.

In the wake of Zato's freakout, Diaz dove backwards through the graveyard entrance, his hand grasping for the contoured grip of the Glock holstered beneath his left arm.

The very bad man, recovering quickly from his nightmare visitation, commenced firing wildly.

BLAM!

The rat disintegrated in a haze of blood.

Two more shots were aimed into the darkness that had swallowed Diaz.

BLAM! BLAM!

Scuttling behind a virgin-white tomb, Diaz hugged the earth like a supplicant. In his rush for safety, his wrist struck the tomb's immutable edge, sending the Glock spinning into the night.

Where had it landed? Diaz lay on his stomach behind the brick and stucco barrier of the sepulcher, his hands searching feverishly in the thick shadows, seeking the lost weapon. It was nowhere to be found.

As precious seconds ticked by, he took a series of deep, controlled breaths, assessing his chances. Did the shooter have extra bullets for the old Colt? If not, he had only three shots left. But three shots were more than enough to put Diaz two meters under ground.

I'm out of time, he thought. Even as he lay there contemplating his navel, the three vagrants were closing in. He had to make a run for it. Run like hell.

Without further debate he leaped up and took off higgledy-piggledy through the maze of graves, loose gravel spattering beneath his churning feet.

"Get him!" Emile howled.

Diaz heard running footsteps behind him. Then a sudden scream; the thud of two bodies violently colliding; a gargantuan groan of mortal demise. At the same instant starlight glinted off the oily sheen of his Glock where it lay half in shadow on the path in front of him. Diaz went for it.

"Surrounded by fools!" shouted Zato, in a bad imitation of King Lear on the heath.

The wail of a police car siren ripped apart the night. Someone in the neighborhood must have called about the shots fired.

The imminent approach of the *Policia* sent the felon scrambling over a crumbling adobe wall and shunting down a narrow, garbage-strewn footpath that twisted between high-walled properties.

Re-armed, Diaz sought out the remaining two attackers. One he found dead, impaled on the rusted spike of a cast iron fence surrounding one of the graves. The other rolled on the ground moaning in pain, his nose broken from colliding with his vagabond buddy in the dark.

Beyond the cemetery the flashing red light of the police car blinked on and off like a channel buoy, as Diaz kicked the whimpering drifter into unconsciousness.

When the two *Preventiva* officers, weapons drawn, came down the narrow lane to the cemetery entrance, they found Diaz leaning against the stuccoed wall, smoking a cigarette. The unconscious criminal lay at his feet, blood and mucus dripping from his nose and mouth.

"There's another one in there." Diaz nodded his head in the direction of the arched cemetery entrance. "Impaled himself on a metal fence. Looks dead to me."

"Are you all right, sir?" asked the older of the police officers. His trained eyes absorbed the facts of Diaz's bloodstained shirt, the rips in both knees of his suit trousers.

"Just some late night slimeballs who decided I was an easy mark." Diaz shrugged his shoulders. "Bad call on their part. The third one went over that wall and down the hill. Long gone by now."

"Would you recognize him again, sir?"

"*Absolutamente*," said Diaz. "By his stench alone."

San Miguel had always been such a quiet, peaceful backwater, thought Diaz. Now suddenly it seemed as though the criminals and thugs were gnawing their way out of the woodwork like ravenous wood ants. Where would it end?

An unaccustomed weight hung heavily upon Diaz's soul.

At last it was time to go home to bed.

Chapter 14

Propelled by the vicious forward sweep of a hand, the alarm clock spun across the room, hit the wall with the pinging sound of splintering plastic and rebounded onto the floor. Despite this ill treatment, the alarm continued to buzz like some insect in high lust.

Diaz moaned, as if the day was tugging at his soul, dragging him back from some deep limbo. He lay in a cocoon of sheets and blankets, too self-absorbed to search out and complete the destruction of the nerve-jangling timepiece. Realizing at last that the Japanese alarm clock wouldn't commit hara-kiri on its own, he eased himself sideways over the edge of the bed, hands roving across the cold tiles like a pair of predatory mongooses until they found the mechanical device and subdued it.

Inert amid the disarrayed bedclothes, Diaz remembered his dream from before. Like shuffling a deck of cards, the images realigned themselves in his head.

Hunched beneath a sheltering portico, he gazed across an expanse of azure water. Grit and leaves driven by a gale force wind stung his face. A flight of doves, each with the eyes of Amanda Smallwood, which he had never seen, landed beside the pool. In a panic one by one they jumped into the water and were sucked under. Diaz was powerless to help them. The wind drove the surface veneer of the water in arcs of light and metallic lightlessness. Rain clouds shunted across a blue sky, shifting the color of the swimming pool from azure to black to aquamarine. The dark shape of a swimmer moved in its depths. The figure curled upward and burst the surface near the edge where Diaz crouched, revealing the soft curves of a nude female form. The woman shook her head from side to side, tossing back her wet hair. He didn't recognize the face. Only the reprise of yesterday's horror, for the woman had no eyes. Only bottomless black holes. Rivulets of blood stained the silver-blue water.

Diaz blinked, once, twice, ten times. The dream images scattered to the four corners of his mind. He touched himself. His genitalia had shriveled into a tight, leathery ball.

Throwing back the covers, he stumbled into the bathroom, where he splashed ice-cold water on his face until it made him gasp. His jaw ached. Exploring the soreness, he remembered the full bore slap of Consuela's hand before she stalked into the night. Another failed human contact, he thought. Another debacle between the sexes.

The chill droplets of water on his face drew Diaz back into the world. It was a transition Amanda Smallwood would never make again. Suddenly angry, he considered smashing his fist through the glass of the small window above the sink. Instead, he brushed his teeth vigorously, gargled and then lit the first cigarette of the day. Outside the window palm fronds waved in a light wind. Sunlight shimmered off shards of broken glass embedded in cement along the top of the wall between the garden and the street.

When he came into the main living area of the apartment, he found his father curled up asleep on the leather couch. A blanket had fallen in a wool puddle on the floor.

Since the death of his wife, Alonzo Diaz officially lived with Hector's older brother Valerio. But the relationship between father and elder son was temperamental at best. Hector had given Alonzo a key to his apartment and Alonzo was a frequent refugee on his couch.

The oblong room was sparsely equipped. Black leather sofa, antique table, six blue and gold painted straight-backed chairs. Whitewashed walls, a colorful Indian tapestry suspended on one, an antique crucifix of copper and painted tin on another. Ancient beams striated the ceiling.

In a primitive glass-doored cabinet several ancient clay figures were displayed. Polygenic creations, part human, part animal and part god. A ceremonial mask, adorned with turquoise and red shell, leered like some Mardi Gras demon. Years before during camping trips into the Sierras, Diaz and his paternal grandfather had liberated each of these relics from secret Aztec tombs known to the elder Diaz.

Beside the couch a stack of books had fallen over and lay strewn across the tile floor.

Diaz, standing in the kitchen alcove, clanged metal against metal and opened and closed the refrigerator repeatedly. His father awoke and sat up, rubbing his legs to stimulate the blood. By prior agreement they never discussed Alonzo's relationship with Valerio or the particulars that from time to time drove Alonzo to the sanctuary of Diaz's apartment.

"When did you come in?" asked Diaz.

"Late."

"I'm working today. You can go back to sleep in the bedroom." Alonzo yawned dismissively.

"Will you have a coffee?"

"If there's enough."

"This isn't the Great Depression."

Diaz lit the gas under the Italian style espresso pot. Taking a sharp knife from a drawer, he peeled half a papaya and cut segments onto a plate over which he squeezed limejuice.

"I see you're still sleeping alone," his father commented.

Now it was Diaz's turn to shrug. He lit another cigarette.

"You need a wife. Or at least a live-in girlfriend. You'd work less and live longer. You shouldn't smoke so much either."

"You never listen to my advice, papa. So you haven't any right to give it."

"A father always gives advice to his children – whether they want to hear it or not."

The coffeepot began to steam furiously, as if it might explode, sending shrapnel rampaging through the room. Diaz turned off the flame and poured coffee into two small cups. He set one of them on the table along with the plate of papaya.

"Drink your coffee. And no more advice," he said irritably. "I've got enough to worry about. I need to get dressed and into the station." He walked back into the bedroom, sipping from his own tiny cup.

As Diaz buttoned a starched shirt, his father's voice followed him: "The murder of the American girl must be getting under your skin."

You don't know the half of it, thought Diaz

He stood in the doorway, knotting a gold and turquoise tie. At the table his father looked up, a fork full of papaya halfway to his mouth.

"Is it true that the murderer gouged out her eyes?" his father asked.

"That information is police business," snapped Diaz. "Not for gossiping with your pals."

When he was dressed and had brushed his shoes to remove the mud and dust from the day and night before, Diaz returned to the main room. Alonzo was back on the couch, holding one of the books from the collapsed pile. He waved it in Diaz's direction.

"The Secret History of the Byzantine Emperors. What kind of book is that?"

"It's about the end of the Roman Empire. And not too strangely it often feels like the writer's talking about our own civilization. If you can call this mess a civilization."

"Shouldn't you be spending your time reading *novelas de policia*?"

"It doesn't work that way. My job isn't a novel."

At the apartment door Diaz looked back at his father, who was now wholly absorbed in reading the book he had questioned moments before. Time had made him brittle and easily distracted.

"Don't forget to lock the door when you leave."

When Diaz entered, the *Judiciales* station was silent and full of apprehension. He counted the close-cropped heads of four officers and the ponytail of the intern Felicia. No one looked up in acknowledgment of his arrival.

Surely they couldn't all be hung over. Something was rotten in Norway. Or was it Denmark?

"What's up with everybody?" demanded Diaz. "Don't tell me the Pope's been caught *in flagranto delecti?"*

"Ah, Hector. You're here at last."

The voice coming from the open door to Diaz's office belonged irrefutably to *Don* Cedillo, the rat mayor. Its thick, syrupy sound had the same effect on Diaz as fresh blood in seawater to a passing shark. He crossed the room and entered his office with a surge of adrenalin, ready for the attack. Cedillo was in his favorite power pose: leaning back behind the desk, alligator hide shoes resting on its edge. Their eyes locked with practiced enmity.

"I'd appreciate it if I could have my chair back," said Diaz.

Don Cedillo bounced to a standing position and walked nonchalantly around the desk. "It was the most comfortable place to sit. And since you weren't using it..."

Diaz rounded the desk in the opposite way from Cedillo and took his seat. Ignoring the uncomfortable looking chairs on the visitor's side of the desk, the mayor remained standing, his hands gripped together behind his back.

"To what do I own this imperial visit?"

"I didn't drop by for casual banter, Hector. I have to be in Guanajuato for an important Rotarian luncheon. At two I'm playing golf with the Governor. He'll be very interested to know if the American woman's murderer has been cast in irons."

"An important lunch? I've always considered lunch to be very important. The highlight of the workday."

"The luncheon is beside the point," sputtered Cedillo. "Stringing up the killer of the *norteamericana* woman *es muy importante.* I need to know everything you're doing to flush out this rabid dog."

"At the moment I don't have a suspect, if that's what you're asking. And what's the hurry anyway? *Senorita* Smallwood isn't going anywhere. We should learn patience from the dead."

Diaz lit a cigarette and blew smoke rings toward the open transom. The mayor frowned.

"Someone told me you were out on the town last night."

"Working, you mean. I ruined a perfectly good suit. Everything possible is being done to apprehend the..." Diaz looked at the mayor for inspiration. "How did you say it?...the rabid frog."

"I need details."

"I'm sure your fertile imagination will come up with some entertaining nonsense for the Governor. My office is conducting a police investigation, not a political spin campaign."

"This murder has political implications."

"Isn't that why you get paid bags of *pesos*? To handle the political fallout?"

"You're not making me happy, Hector."

"Since when have I ever made you happy? Perhaps I should ask our intern Felicia to give you a complimentary blowjob. Though it's not part of her job description. Would that make you happy?"

Don Cedillo's cheeks flushed the red of a clown's nose. A muscle in his jaw twitched. Was he about to suffer a fatal aneurysm, abruptly ending a feud that had festered for a lifetime? Anticipation and regret spun in a dance across the gymnasium of Diaz's mind.

Gradually Cedillo's complexion returned to its normal earth tone. The spasm ceased. But hatred remained, a brushfire burning deep in his eyes.

"You always take things too far, Diaz. Some day you'll regret it."

Cedillo spun about and pitched violently out of the office.

"It was only a joke," called Diaz, adding the final public exclamation point to his victory.

Chapter 15

Having dispatched Armando and Felicia (he thought a woman's touch might come in handy) to intercept Bass Smallwood at the Guanajuato airport, Diaz called the delinquent Dr. Moza's clinic.

After five rings a voice as raw and dust choked as a recent landslide answered:

"What is it?"

"Diaz here. You sound like hell."

"Are you expressing a philosophical opinion or just calling to waste my time?"

"You never called me back last night about the dead American girl."

Across the phone line came the dull slap of Dr. Moza's hand against an unyielding object, most probably his forehead.

"My God, what could I have been thinking? That last night I chose to spend five hours attending to the victims of a head on collision on the road to Queretaro, when I could have been chatting with you at midnight about the overripe corpse of a dead tart."

Diaz pictured Nicholas hunched over his desk, eyes pressed closed, forehead cupped into the palm of his hand as if he were suffering some exquisite pain. White shirt as wrinkled as a rhino hide; cuffs bloodstained.

"So what the hell are you doing in the office?" muttered Diaz defensively. "Go home and get some sleep."

"As you've so conveniently forgotten, Hector, I hold a clinic every Saturday morning. It begins momentarily. Even now I can hear the meek and downtrodden wheezing and coughing and dying in my waiting room."

"Far be it for me to keep you from your ministrations. Just tell me if anything unusual turned up in the autopsy."

"As far as I know, nothing."

Diaz sighed. "What does that mean?"

"It means the medical examiner in our illustrious state capital hasn't gotten around to cutting open the body yet."

"How is that possible?" blurted Diaz in frustration.

"I spoke with Dr. Gupta, the chief examiner. Like everyone else, they're overworked and underpaid. His priority is the corpse of a certain bus driver, one of eight people killed when the bus he was driving missed a curve and tried to fly without wings. Everyone wants to know whether he was high on methamphetamine or mezcal. Next in line are the bodies of two people who died painfully several hours after eating lunch in a private room at a certain very expensive Guanajuato bordello. One was a sixteen-year-old gangster, the other a career priest with sodomitic predilections. No one's betting on botulism as the culprit. But Dr. Gupta promised he would personally attend to the Smallwood dissection."

"When does Doctor Gupta think he might get to our lowly case?"

"Your lowly case, *mi amigo*, not ours. Maybe today, if he's working this afternoon. Though he mentioned something about a golf game with the Governor. My guess would be Monday, if nothing more important comes up."

"No wonder we're still considered a third world country."

"Relax. Take some deep breaths or a naked yoga class. You seem to be the only one obsessing on the sex murder of some obscure foreigner. What you need is a steady girlfriend."

"That's exactly what my father said."

"Food for thought, no?"

"When I want your advice as a sex therapist, I'll ask for it." Then, after a pause, during which Diaz considered with malevolence a black spider archly walking across his desk dragging a dead fly like a suitcase: "Call me as soon as you hear from Gupta."

"*Jawohl mein Fuhrer.*"

"And don't forget to put on your hair shirt before opening the clinic."

When Diaz emerged from his office, the station was deserted. Only the mechanical lives of circling ceiling fans and radiating computer terminals bore witness to prior human habitation.

Where was everyone? And why was it that he and Cedillo were the only ones fixated on Amanda's murder? With Cedillo the answer was easy. The potential panic in the streets by tourists and expats, as word spread about the girl's vicious death, was both an economic and a political threat. But how to explain his own single-mindedness? Fertile beauty cut short by some demented human flaw? But Amanda's casual existence among the *artistas* and slackers of San Miguel was already a wasted life. Was her young death then a reminder he was running out of time to redeem his own soul?

Forget about your half-assed soul, thought Diaz. Just get on with the fucking investigation.

Flipping through the San Miguel telephone directory, he found the address of Fran Kovacs, the friend and helpmate of the elusive Gregory Gregorovich. Since no one had returned to the station by the time Diaz was ready to leave, he left a hand written note of his whereabouts taped to Ortiz's computer terminal.

Diaz barged his way purposefully through the *jardin* amid families in their holiday best strolling along the paths or crowding around the numerous vendors of grilled pork and chicken, sweet drinks and every variety of *dulce*. Each weekend brought forth another religious festival with its drinking, rutting and opportunities for mayhem. The cheap tricks of a magician dressed in bishop's robes, thought Diaz.

Turning up *Calle Terrapien*, he left the burgeoning crowd behind. Like most of the streets in the center of San Miguel, it was narrow, steep and paved with a riprap of irregular stones. Diaz bounded up its incline like a goat. The entrance of No. 83 was a narrow, wooden door painted a glossy turquoise. He rang the bell. Shortly the metal cover of a miniature eye-level window slid open. A single, Cyclopean eye contemplated Diaz with suspicion, as a muffled female voice inquired as to his business.

"Inspector Diaz of the *Policia Judiciales*. I'm looking for an artist named Gregory Gregorovich. I understand he resides here."

"Used to," responded the voice.

"It would be easier for both of us if you'd let me in off the street and we could talk face to face."

The peephole window slid shut. Then the latch clicked and the door opened inward onto a dazzlingly white courtyard splashed with the reds and pinks of potted geraniums.

The woman who held out her hand in formal greeting was not beautiful. But this unlucky toss of the dice was mocked by the energy that sprang from the pair of greenish-yellow eyes considering Diaz. Her long, narrow face complemented the angularity of her slim figure, draped in a floral patterned cotton sundress. Her high set breasts were modest, but not in a negative sense. Tawny hair was cut in careless, bristly layers.

She was someone, thought Diaz, who had survived and prospered by her own will – a flower among stones.

"Fran Kovacs," she said, as Diaz shook her hand. "I was just making tea."

She led the way across the courtyard and through a glass door into a high-ceilinged room painted the same stark white as the walls of the courtyard. Daylight gushed through floor-to-ceiling plate glass panels. Along the back wall pottery sculptures were arrayed on pedestals and in wall niches. A low table was set with an English china teapot and a single cup and saucer.

Fran stepped down a hallway and returned with a second cup and saucer. She and Diaz faced each other on twin white leather sofas. From her demanding eyes, his gaze wandered to the back of the room.

"This space is both a living area and a gallery for my work," she said, pouring tea into one of the cups and saucers and handing it to him. He took a sip. Oolong, a dark and twiggy brew that he hadn't tasted since his student days. Back then, for a brief time he'd dated a half-Chinese woman who, whenever they made love, afterwards served oolong tea and fortune cookies. None of the predictions had come true.

Pushing aside this unexpected recollection, Diaz spoke:

"Julia at the *Galeria Rana* gave me your name."

"She said I was harboring Gregory, did she? Or perhaps she gave a more primitive description of our relationship."

"She just mentioned that he lived here."

"And how did you interpret that?"

"No particular way."

"Not that Gregory and I were fuck buddies?" There was incipient anger, or bitterness, in her tone.

Diaz shrugged. "It's not anything special one way or the other."

She didn't smile. "So why are you so interested in Gregory?"

"I'm investigating the death of an American woman who lived here in San Miguel. Amanda Smallwood. You may have read about her murder." Diaz nodded toward a copy of *Atencion* that lay on the coffee table between them. "*Senor* Gregorovich used her as a model."

Now truly, thought Diaz, there was bitterness in the ripples of emotion that creased the brow and twisted the lips of the woman sitting across from him.

"Yes, Amanda was one of Gregory's little sluts. He collected them. But she was the only one who never put out for him. Though he wasn't shy about asking."

Her cup and saucer clicked together like a set of clenched teeth, as she set them on the table.

"One would never imagine that about her. From his paintings of her. That she didn't put out, I mean."

"I'm afraid I haven't seen Gregory's most recent work – the real paintings, not the stuff he did for the tourists. He worked in a shed at the back of my property and was as secretive about it as the KGB. 'Bad luck before a show to let anyone see my paintings,' he said. He had an ego as big as a second rate politician. Since I was screwing him, I figured I was entitled to the first glimpse of his genius. But if I came anywhere near his workspace, he'd tell me to get lost. Even now I haven't been back there."

"Even now?"

"Oh. Didn't I mention it before? Gregory no longer lives here. Not since last Thursday night. We went to a party and he behaved like the asshole he's always been. I was just too stupid before to do anything about it. Finally that night I locked him out. I haven't seen him since."

She abruptly opened a decorative pottery box on the table and took out a cigarette. Diaz took this as a sign that it was okay for him to smoke. He spent several seconds fumbling in his pockets for a crushed pack of Montana's. Fran waited impatiently for him to produce his lighter, a glossy chrome Zippo. Then blew a cloud of yellow smoke ceiling-ward and leaned back, rolling her shoulders and thrusting her breasts forward like a pair of high strung beagle puppies.

Diaz watched Fran's erotic stretch with fatalistic dismay. The woman might as well be stark naked, he thought.

"But surely you attended *senor* Gregorovich's opening at the *Galeria Rana*?" he said.

"Why would I? Before last Thursday I was just some stupid schoolgirl swept off her feet by the dangerous *artiste* from L.A. with a name out of Dostoyevsky. Luckily the little whore I caught him with that night snapped me out of my daydream."

"When did you and Mr. Gregorovich come to San Miguel?"

"It wasn't like that."

Fran stubbed out her cigarette and leaned back, suddenly more at ease. "I bet you were born in San Miguel. Am I right, Inspector?"

Diaz shrugged.

"And you probably don't care much for all these expats moving here, buying houses, opening businesses. But I've only had one piece of luck in my life. I had a moderately rich, childless aunt who was very fond of me. When she died her estate was sufficient for me to move here four years ago, buy this place and restore it into what you see. For me living here is a dream. Otherwise my life has been pretty much of a fucking disaster."

Diaz grew suddenly impatient. He didn't have time for a lonely thirty-five-year-old American woman living too well in old Mexico, who felt dolorously sorry for herself because she had just caught her live-in boyfriend cheating on her. However intriguing, now was not the time for playing out the erotic possibilities of an otherwise empty Saturday. Not while the body of a young woman lay dead and unrevenged.

Bounding up, he paced to the far end of the room to inspect the ceramic sculptures on display.

"These are yours?"

"Yes," she called out to him.

Surprisingly, he liked what he saw – the curving, intersecting surfaces, the blending of shades of earth and heaven. He turned back in her direction.

"Your work is very striking. Sensuous."

"Thank you."

He realized he had been thinking the same about her ever since the moment when she stood back from the door of No. 83 to let him enter. He lit another cigarette to refocus on the reason he was there.

"Tell me about Gregory Gregorovich."

"Not much to tell. About seven months ago he appeared at my doorstep like a stray cat. Jeans, a torn Ramones T-shirt and a sly smile on his lips. Someone told him I had some extra space he might be able to use as a studio. I knew immediately who he was. He was rather famous for a while in L.A. Before he became infamous for screwing a fourteen-year-old actress. I showed him the shed in the back and he liked it. Moved in that afternoon. Slept there on an old mattress. Two months later he moved into my bedroom. He was very charming. And if you must know, he was a damn good lay. Of course that was part of his reputation. I should have known better."

Diaz raised his hands questioningly. "But you said he doesn't live here now."

"The other part of his reputation is that he'll sleep with just about anything female he comes across, including a ripe papaya. Thursday night when I found him doing high fives in bed with a naked teenager, I lost it."

We're going in circles, thought Diaz. Though the concept of a rambunctious underage tartlet had a certain cachet.

"Do you know where he is now?"

"Why would I? Probably mooching off the little *puta* he seduced the other night. Or sleeping in Jeffrey Dillinger's cabana. Jeffrey owns the gallery where Gregory shows his work, if you don't know that already. Or who knows, maybe he's left town. Though I doubt it. He was planning his big artistic comeback through Jeffrey and his connections."

"I'd like to see his studio, if it's not too much trouble."

"Why not."

When Fran stood, Diaz found himself staring directly at her swollen nipples pressing against the soft fabric of her dress. Diverting his gaze, he fixated momentarily on a tuft of black hair emerging tarantula-like from Fran's armpit. What was it with *gringa* women and body hair? he wondered, quickly dropping his eyes to the floor, where he counted ten mauve-painted toes annexed to long, tapering feet. It occurred to him that he had always found women's bare feet to be highly provocative. It further occurred to him for the second time that morning that under her dress Fran Kovacs was, in all likelihood, entirely and utterly naked.

"Follow me," she said.

Suppressing these concupiscent considerations, he followed as Fran went outside and across the courtyard. Above the potted geraniums a pair of butterflies flickered like misplaced quotation marks.

She led the way down a narrow passage, which surprisingly opened out into another sun-dazzled courtyard, this one filled almost entirely by an azure swimming pool. A lush banana palm ballooned in one corner. A portico with lounge furniture ran along one side of the pool. The scene seemed vaguely familiar to Diaz. He ignored the resulting sense of unease. His left nostril itched. He ignored that too.

At the far end of the pool Fran pushed open a high metal gate. Beyond, a black Land Rover SUV sat in a gravel parking area. A squat metal-roofed adobe building with rotting window casements formed one side of the parking space. Stuccoed walls topped by jagged glass fragments and another metal gate decorated with razor wire completed the enclosure in typical Mexican fashion. Was it to keep the desperate out or the fearful in?

Removing a set of keys from the pocket of her dress, Fran unlocked the padlock that secured the shed door. She reached into the dark interior and flicked a toggle switch. Motioned for Diaz to enter.

Bare bulbs on ancient wiring illuminated the space within. A long antique table covered in daubs and splashes of paint. Tubs and jars and cans of paint arrayed haphazardly on table and floor. Brushes erupting like weeds from an assortment of glass jars. Empty liquor bottles lay strewn about like passed out drunks. A typewriter, lonely and dust covered, occupied a corner of the table. A white sheet had been nailed to one wall; in front of it sat a single wooden chair like a prop for some existential play. Behind the table a stack of canvases leaned, faces turned toward the wall.

A large, partially completed painting stood shockingly on an easel in the center of the room. In it Amanda's dishabille was rendered with the tawdry realism of a Penthouse photo shoot, as a giant purple-veined prick threatened from the foreground.

As Fran Kovacs starred at the libidinous transmogrification of Amanda Smallwood from flesh to paint, her face erupted in a snarl of loathing. Lunging forward, she grabbed a mat knife from the table and slashed viciously at the painting. Dark, ugly cuts erupted in its surface.

Fran's madness caught Diaz off guard. Too late he reached out and grasped the wrist holding the blade aloft for another strike. His other arm curved across Fran's chest, pulling her backwards toward him. She struggled, her body heaving against him, testing his strength. They twisted back and forth for several seconds, two dancers in a neurotic tango.

"Easy," he said. "Easy now." The pressure he applied to her wrist was unrelenting. The mat knife clattered to the tile floor. Then he released her. She twisted to face him.

"Fuck you!"

"I was afraid you might hurt yourself."

In the next instant the savageness drained from her. She half smiled.

"Yeah, sure," she said. She moved to the doorway. "Look around to your heart's content. I'll be by the pool."

Diaz poked and prodded amid the detritus of Gregorovich's studio. But found nothing of interest besides a pair of burgundy-colored lace panties and a package of condoms. He slipped both into his jacket pocket. The stack of canvases behind the table contained a series of clichéd scenes of rustic Mexican life. It was strange how banal the creative process turned out to be, thought Diaz. At least Gregorovich had taken precautions against unwanted pregnancies and the spread of sexually transmitted diseases.

Before leaving the studio Diaz called Felicia on his cellphone. Yes, they had picked up Bass Smallwood at the airport. Yes, he had identified Amanda's body at the morgue in Guanajuato. They had checked Bass in at the hotel in San Miguel, where he had gone immediately to the bar and started drinking.

Diaz gave Felicia the address on *Calle Terrapien* and told her to pick him up in ten minutes.

He found Fran Kovacs lying on a chaise by the swimming pool, her eyes closed, her legs slightly apart. In the warm sunlight her dress had slipped upward almost to her waist. She wasn't wearing panties. It occurred to him he might offer her the pair he had found in the studio. But the implications of such a proposal were too complex to deal with.

Her white skin gleamed with a veneer of sweat. Diaz wanted to touch it, but restrained himself. A wad of phlegm filled the back of his throat. He coughed. Her eyes opened halfway. As she looked up at him with vague interest, she lifted her hips and casually adjusted the hemline of her dress downward to a more modest position.

"One final question."

"I can only hope."

"Do you think Gregory Gregorovich could have killed Amanda Smallwood?"

Her eyes were wide open now. She pushed herself up on her elbows.

"Gregory? Kill someone? He might screw them to death. But murder and mutilate them? No. He didn't have that kind of temperament. I should know. My father was an untalented plumber and a drunk. When I was eleven, he beat my mother to death with a length of lead pipe."

The sudden violent image slammed into Diaz's brain like the blow of a steel-toed boot.

Chapter 16

The Indian sitting in the cab of the stolen Dodge Ram waited impatiently for something to happen. His drug-enhanced temperament was, as always, on the edge of a meltdown. His fingers drummed the dashboard like a downpour on a tin roof. A burn scar in the form of an ancient hieroglyph disfigured one cheek. All who had been able to decipher it were dead, a revelation at the moment of extinction.

Cattycorner from where the pick-up was parked against the high stone curb was the turquoise door of No. 83 *Calle Terrapien*. Muddy runoff from Thursday night's drizzle and fog had pooled in low spots in the stone paved street.

Five minutes after the Indian's arrival, a vaguely official looking dark blue sedan bounced down the cobblestones of *Calle Terrapien* at a dangerous rate of speed and came to a stop in front of the turquoise door.

The Indian sat up, his attention riveted, wired. Each second of time took on the slow motion freefall of a plasma drip into the arm of a crash victim.

Two laborers staggered down the steep incline of the street, passing a pint of rum between them. The heftier of the two men, wearing a plaid cowboy shirt with fake pearl buttons and stained black pants, took a final slug and held the empty bottle aloft.

"Let's get another one of these," he said.

"You drank it all, you dirty *cabron*!" Seizing the bottle, the second drunk hurled it across the street in disgust. It shattered on the front fender of the Ram.

The two drunks gaped in disbelief. Then they saw the Indian, his head and shoulders framed in the cab window. His eyes stared at them with illimitable malevolence. Like a silent scream, the idea that they were about to die penetrated the haze of their drunkenness.

"Sorry," mumbled one, his hands half raised in apology or to ward off the devil's gaze.

At that moment, the turquoise door of No. 83 opened inward and Diaz emerged, ducking his head to avoid the low doorframe.

The Indian's attention instantly refocused on Diaz's slim and carefully attired figure. There was no mistaking Inspector Hector Diaz of the San Miguel *Judiciales*. That was the name whispered over the telephone as the Indian, nearly comatose, watched the play of dawn light and shadow across the whitewashed ceiling. He had lain in that bare room all night gripped by psychotic insomnia, waiting for the call.

Now his foot pushed in the clutch and he eased the gearshift into first. Feeling beneath the beige windbreaker tossed across the seat beside him, his hand caressed the hardness of the .357 Colt Python resting there.

Diaz came down the two short steps to the sidewalk and leaned into the open passenger window of the navy blue police car. From behind the wheel Corporal Felicia Goya gave him a quick smile.

"Anything?" she asked.

"*Nada*."

Diaz rolled his eyes. "All *gringos* are *loco*. But I'd like to find this artist named Gregorovich. He's a wild card. Doesn't live here anymore since his girlfriend the owner caught him in bed with a tart. He's somewhere just under the radar. How's Smallwood?"

"Bad. A long day of drinking ahead would be my guess. When I left the hotel, Armando was trying to coax him out of the bar where he's been slamming back Scotch for the past hour."

"I'd better talk to him before he becomes unconscious."

Seated in the passenger seat, Diaz hooked the seat belt closed.

"Don't drive too fast," he said. "My insides are a little off today."

Felicia raised a knowing eyebrow. It was the left one, out of Diaz's line of sight. She revved the engine and with a miniature screech of tires pulled away from the curb.

Edging into motion, the Ram jolted to the middle of the street, its wide tires and heavy-duty shocks riding roughshod over the cobblestones, three metric tons of steel and chrome bearing down on the subcompact police car. His skin tingling from some allergic reaction to existence, the Indian hunched over the wheel, the Colt Python coiled in one hand. His blood soared like a taloned hawk riding an updraft.

The Ram loomed above the police vehicle. Twisting the steering wheel hard right, then left, the Indian forced one side of the pick-up to leap onto the high sidewalk. At this precarious angle the Indian had a clear field of vision encompassing Diaz's head and right shoulder. Without hesitation he fired off a shot.

Seconds before, Felicia's darting eyes had seen the Ram, a surging shark in the rearview mirror. *Mi Dios*! Some drunk-out-of-his-mind *paisano*! screamed inside her head. Instinctively she veered the police vehicle crazily to the left, throwing Diaz against the dash. The rolling sound waves of the exploding bullet, the spider web disintegration of the glass in the rear passenger window and the spiral of adrenalin corkscrewing through Felicia's blood were events so close together as to be simultaneous. Diaz's hands flew up to ward off the flying glass. Felicia bit through her bottom lip, tasting blood. As her former life as a rally driver took control, her features set into hardscrabble concentration. The car leaped forward, responding to a jolt of gas.

"Fuck, fuck, fuck!" The Indian, indeed out of his mind, blasted away at the police car as it sped helter-skelter down the incline. The Ram, in hot pursuit, shimmied wildly, its wheels squealing like hogs in a slaughterhouse. Two women burdened with string bags filled with the day's shopping dove for cover in a shallow doorway. A wizened old man lost his prized dentures as he gaped at the careening pick-up.

"Keep your head down," commanded Felicia. She was in ice

cool control. The back window imploded in a cascading torrent of glass wasps, one of which stung a lesion bright with blood across the gazelle-like curve of her throat. A second bullet destroyed the AM/FM radio inset in the dashboard. "Got to get out of the line of fire."

Diaz leaned partway out the passenger-side window trying to get a shot off. An impossible task to achieve with the police cruiser bucking and jolting down the steep declivity at full bore wild-assed speed.

Ahead the opening of a narrow alleyway appeared, a fissure in the blank façades of the street. Felicia went for it, pumping the brakes, downshifting with vivacity. The car balked at the sudden, wrenching change of direction. A law of physics unequivocally prevailed, bringing molded steel and stone wall into bone-jarring contact. Amid a shower of sparks and the scream of tearing metal, the car drove into the shadowy cut through.

In a rage the Indian accelerated past the alley. It was far too narrow for the Ram to enter. With reckless abandon he squeezed off a bevy of final shots through the open passenger window. They ricocheted harmlessly, embedding themselves in soft adobe.

As they jolted to a stop ten meters up the alley, Diaz burst from the car, 9mm at the ready. He edged toward the main street. Felicia took up a firing position across the trunk of the car.

When Diaz reached the intersection, the pick-up was gone. The street empty. The primitive drum rhythms of the festival drifted up from San Miguel's *el centro*.

Felicia came up behind him.

"It would seem you've severely pissed someone off," she said.

Chapter 17

The left side of the police car was hopelessly scraped and scarred. One front headlamp dangled from its wires like the exposed viscera of a robot's eye. But none of the tires were losing air. Wounded, yes. But not fatally.

As Felicia drew up in the porte cochere of *El Palacio Real*, the four star hotel where Bass Smallwood was being held in protective custody, the head bellman gave the car a disapproving once over. Diaz flashed his badge and walked into the lobby without a word. Its marble finishes shown like newly spit-polished boots. A waterfall and clumps of ferns lent a pseudo-tropical air.

Felicia caught up to Diaz at the elevators. She seemed distressed.

"Get used to it. When you're a cop, lots of people want you dead," volunteered Diaz. "The chances of catching that bastard or even finding the truck is next to nil. By midnight the Ram'll be cut into piece parts scattered for sale across half the auto junkyards in Leon."

"It's not that," she said. "The concierge kept insisting I park the car in the very back of in the garage."

"Fuck the concierge."

"I did," she said. "He used to be my boyfriend."

The elevator arrived and they rode in silence to the third floor. Diaz grappled with Felicia's revelation. A cigarette smoldered between his lips, despite the no smoking sign above the elevator controls.

When they walked into the room, Bass Smallwood, all seventy-four *gringo* inches and two-hundred sixty *gringo* pounds of him,

JONATHAN WOODS • 111

lay stretched to the four corners of the king-sized bed. He was naked except for black socks and a pair of boxers decorated with yellow smiley-faces. Under the glare of the overhead light, his body glistened with sweat.

The acrid reek of vomit hung in the air. A room-service cart, strewn with the remains of a steak and its accompaniments, was angled into a corner. Two flies locked in copulatory abandon clung to the gnawed steak bone. In the fetid airspace a third fly, shiny green and evil, looped and barrel rolled like a World War I bi-plane at an armory show.

A *telenovela* was playing on the television but without sound.

"What's going on here?" demanded Diaz.

Armando appeared through the sliding glass door from the balcony, a fretful look distorting his face. "After all the liquor, he insisted on eating lunch. Then he threw up. Now I'm not feeling very good," he told Diaz. "Maybe he brought a virus from *Tejas*."

"Don't be ridiculous," said Diaz. There was no way he was letting Armando off the hook this afternoon so he could slip away to his beloved Carmen. "Dump Smallwood in the shower," he commanded. "Order some herbal tea from room service. Then get him dressed. I'll be on the balcony."

Armando's pulling and prodding of the vast, inert bulk that was Bass Smallwood elicited a deep moan. Smallwood leaned over the side of the bed and started to gag. Then lost his equilibrium and rolled off the bed, pulling Armando down with him.

"Help me out here, Felicia," begged Armando from somewhere beneath Smallwood.

Disgusted, she sat on the end of the bed and turned up the TV sound. On the tube a man sporting a wastrel mustache and a woman in a skimpy outfit were deep in argument. Next instant they were dry humping across a conveniently placed couch. Cut to commercial.

Diaz reemerged from the balcony, shaking his head. The three of them managed to drag and cajole Smallwood into the tiled shower stall, where they left him beneath a pounding stream of cold water.

Task accomplished, Diaz told Felicia to take the afternoon

off. After all, she'd saved his ass, as well as her own. A cool, no-nonsense performance by San Miguel's first female *Judiciales*.

Sometime later Bass roused himself from the tile floor of the shower and, wrapped in a way-too-small hotel robe, came and sat wordlessly on the balcony next to Diaz and Armando. Diaz poured a cup of chamomile tea and set it in front of him. Bass stared into it but neither hope nor any other salutary vision arose from its jaundiced depths.

In the garden below a rampage of blood-orange day lilies caught Diaz's eye.

"I'm sorry," said Diaz. "But I need to ask you some questions."

Bass gave no reaction. Diaz lit a Montana. Bass's nostrils dilated at the smell of burning Turkish.

"Give me one of those," he demanded. "And get rid of this cat piss." He flung the teacup and its contents over the balcony railing. "What I want is a Goddamn drink!"

While Diaz offered calming sentiments, Armando summoned room service again, this time bearing a bottle of Johnnie Walker Black and three glasses. The teapot and cup-less saucer were removed.

"I understand your daughter came to San Miguel a year ago," said Diaz. "Why?"

"She was unhappy. She wanted a new life."

"A love affair turned sour?"

Bass looked at Diaz with sudden enmity. "Who the hell are you?"

"Diaz. Inspector of police. I'm investigating your daughter's murder."

Confusion reigned in Bass's eyes. Then the fog lifted momentarily. "Oh, right."

"You were talking about Amanda."

"Yeah. So, I guess it was a year or so ago, the guy she was seeing took off with some barmaid. Or something like that. And her mother had already trashed whatever happiness might have existed in our little family."

"How's that?"

"Alice got an itch. Guy living in a seven thousand square foot McMansion overlooking a mud-bottom lake said he could scratch it. Kept his 35-foot cabin cruiser in the same lake. Alice moved out and took up residence in the cabin cruiser. On July 4th she got drunk during a party, fell overboard and drown. After that everything went to hell."

Bass drained the whiskey in his glass, then poured it half full again. He swirled the dark liquor into a vortex. Hoping perhaps to drown in its maelstrom depths. Diaz pondered how he had felt when Reyna left him. There had been a sense of relief, not disaster. Lightness, not fucked-up-ness. He didn't want to hear any more about Bass Smallwood's marital screw-ups. It was time to stir up the mud at the bottom of the pond.

"So your wife moves into the big house with the lake view. Then your daughter's boyfriend splits. Is that when she decided she was a lesbian?"

The question sailed into oblivion. Bass had moved far away. A tear stuttered down his unshaven cheek. Diaz had to get the interrogation back on track.

"I understand you still run an art gallery in Dallas?"

After a long moment, Bass's eyes came back into focus.

"What else would I do? Rob fucking banks? Hustling art is all I know."

"Did you know Amanda was working as an artist's model in San Miguel?" asked Diaz.

"She did that in Dallas."

"In the nude?"

"Since she turned eighteen Amanda's pretty much done whatever she felt like doing."

"And you didn't object?"

"I didn't want to lose a daughter too."

You did anyway, thought Diaz.

Smallwood looked bleak. Diaz was sure there was a secret hidden somewhere. In families there were always secrets. You just needed to find the right incantation to draw them out, like extracting venom from a snakebite. If Ortiz were here, thought Diaz, he and Bass would have gotten into a fight. Blood would have been spilled on Ortiz's Hollywood cop shirt and tie, ruining them beyond redemption.

The whiskey bottle was already a third empty. Armando bent over his notebook, scribbling furiously. Maybe I should send him to a shorthand class, thought Diaz.

"One day," said Bass, "Amanda just disappeared. A week later I got a postcard from L.A. A few months after that, another postcard came. With a foreign stamp. From this shit hole."

"Did she know an artist named Gregorovich when she was in L.A?"

Bass pursed his lips and blew a loud raspberry. The alcohol was having strange effects.

"What was she doing in San Miguel?"

"Same thing as in Dallas – hanging out, modeling when she needed cash. And whatever else young women do these days."

"This was when you got ill?"

"What do you mean, got ill?"

"Amanda's roommate said Amanda flew back to Dallas a lot because you were terminal. On your last legs."

"Well, the roommate got it wrong. I've got a business to run. That's when Amanda came up with the idea I should promote works by some of the artists she knew in San Miguel. Why not, I said. She brought up a couple of paintings on consignment. I sold them right off the bat. To a new client. So I told her to bring more. By the end…"

Bass's voice broke. He drew his legs up to his chest, wrapped his hands around them and bent his head between his knees, becoming a giant human ball of misery. The metal chair groaned as he rocked back and forth.

"If I'd made her come back to Dallas," he moaned. "She'd still be alive."

The ball exploded. Bass burst to his feet, a bereft giant standing at the rail. His too small robe parted; his cowboy cock hung limp as a windsock in a dead calm. The cast iron balustrade shook under the torment of his thick cowboy hands, as if he intended to rip it loose from its cement moorings. Holy shit! thought Diaz. He's going to throw himself off the balcony.

"I've come to take my daughter home," Bass yelled. At the hotel guests lolling by the pool below. At the empty sky. At the pointless universe. He struggled to shake off the twin weights of Armando and Diaz restraining his arms.

"I just want to take her home. Bury her in Texas where she was born."

"Of course," said Diaz soothingly. "We can go right now to make the arrangements. But you need to put on some clothes."

Bass grew suddenly calm.

"If you're lying, I'll kill you," he said.

"Somebody already tried that twice in the last twenty-four hours," said Diaz. "So good luck."

They drifted back into the room and Bass began to dress.

Further questioning would have to wait, considered Diaz. But he was sure Bass knew things about Amanda that no one else did – things that would lead Diaz deeper into her life in San Miguel. Which was where he needed to go.

Chapter 18

Using the telephone by the bed, Diaz called Dr. M. Valdemario, San Miguel's most distinguished undertaker – and a distant cousin. Manuel agreed to see them in half an hour.

Leaving the hotel room, Bass, Diaz and Armando passed through the lobby and the porte cochere, then across a small, shaded plaza overhung by eucalyptus trees where folk artists exhibited their work on weekend mornings. It was empty now except for a dog asleep in the dry fountain. As far as Diaz could remember, water had never flowed from its brass fittings – a typical Mexican failure to reach closure. An iguana scuttled through dry leaves.

From there, heavy with emotion, they trudged into San Miguel's precipitous and stony streets.

It was mid-afternoon; siesta time was ending. Shop doors swung open. Children still half asleep watched passing tourists with heavy eyes. Cars and pickup trucks again filled the narrow streets, forcing pedestrians to walk single file, choking the thin mountain air with gasoline fumes.

The odor of grilling meat wafted through the bead-curtained doorway of a family-run *taqueria*. A naked child, his tiny penis as pointed as a wasp's stinger, ran into the street. Brakes squealed. A woman screamed. The child, unhurt, began to wail at his sudden notoriety.

Approaching the colonial *el centro*, the two cops and the grieving father were sucked like debris into the vortex of the religious festival that had commenced that morning. Nearly naked peasants danced in feathered costumes. Little girls, glorious in their christening dresses, skipped rope and screamed. Families strolled, ate, laughed and argued. Madwomen in rags crouched in doorways, hands raised in supplication. *Caballeros* and politicians preened astride nervous, prancing horses. Indian mothers in hand-loomed dresses balanced babies and sacks of trinkets for sale on their hips. Drunks and tourists collided and cursed. Beggars and thieves watched and waited. The entire populous of the campo and the town cascaded through the walkways of the *Jardin Principal* and its adjacent streets.

Amid this ebb and flow the three passed in single file, almost unnoticed. Diaz and Armando like ravens in their dark suits. Bass some errant clown in a garish yellow and black houndstooth jacket that hung across his wide shoulders like a discarded candy bar wrapper.

At last they entered the Stygian gloom of the colonnaded *plazoleta* where the mortuary establishment passed down to Dr. M. Valdemario had resided for five generations. Chicken bone thin and *elegante* in starched white shirt, lavender tie and black, velvet-collared suit, the Doctor, an apparition from a bygone age, emerged at the clanging of a copper bell above the door. He grasped Bass's hand, nodding his head and whispering some incomprehensible condolence.

At one end of the crypt-like room in which they stood, a tableau of Victorian chairs and a sofa provided the setting for muted consultations about the business details of burying the dead. A whalebone inlaid desk circa 1851 sat to one side, reserved for signing the obligatory contractual documents.

The price was payable in full, in cash, in advance. There were no exceptions. Those who couldn't meet these conditions were sent packing to the fly-by-night undertakers who came and went in the new town at the bottom of the hill.

The bulk of the vaulted space served as a showroom of funereal accoutrements. Coffins were lined up in two rows, ranging from pedestrian pine to hand-waxed Mexican oak to the brilliant shine of the finest Malaysian teak. Overlapping folds of black satin lined each oblong box, catching the light and absorbing it into nothingness. Handles and fittings ranged from solid brass to chrome veneer to gunmetal steel.

"Something simple but…meaningful," murmured Bass, as the Doctor led him down the room, lauding one attribute of each offering like a fruit seller his bananas, mangos, papayas and figs.

"Don't want to look chintzy," confirmed Bass over his shoulder to Diaz. "Not with my ex's family nosing around. Always looking for another good reason why it was okay for her to run off with that yachtsman fuck."

Diaz followed behind, amazed at the variety of containers for packaging the dead. Across the room sat Armando, his face draped in worry. Diaz wondered why he didn't just call Carmen on his cellphone. Maybe he enjoyed fretting about the possibility of another miscarriage. Or was he trying to put a guilt trip on Diaz for making him work on Saturday afternoon?

Using Diaz as an interpreter, Bass chose a dark and dreary but expensive coffin. Dr. M. Valdemario would take custody of the body as soon as it was released from the Guanajuato morgue. Arrangements would be made for its prompt transport to Dallas. "It" was the operative word. Amanda Smallwood was no longer a person, just an empty carrion husk. Her soul wandering in limbo.

When the paperwork was completed and signed, Smallwood proffered an AmEx card.

"*Solamente* cash."

The knuckles of Bass's clenched fists bled white with fury. Diaz ground his teeth in anticipation of a scene.

"You find it difficult to collect from the dead, do you, you little bastard?" snapped Bass.

Diaz yelled for Armando. Together they eased Bass to a seat on the sofa. Drawing Manuel into a gloomy corner, Diaz apologized. The death of a child. An ill-mannered *gringo*. Etc.

Manuel nodded, but still insisted on cash. A bottle of brandy was produced. Successive shots were poured and consumed by Bass, whose mood shifted from anger to maudlin despondency to catalepsy.

Roused by several slaps to the cheek, Bass stumbled the rounds of the ATMs with Diaz's help until sufficient funds spat forth. The deal signed, the cash delivered, they began the bleak trek back to the hotel.

Grief had sucked the spirit out of this huge *norteamericano*, thought Diaz. When Diaz's father Victor died, how would Diaz feel? There was a natural simpatico between them. But Victor's death would be in the natural order of things. It would not be the same as losing a child. As having a child murdered! Diaz knew what that felt like.

In the *jardin* the *fiesta* that had been building up all day like a billowing thunderhead was in full dervish motion. Indians in full Aztec regalia, others dressed as Satans or death heads, still others all but naked except for elaborate body painting, twirled and twisted to pounding drumbeats. Fire swallowers swallowed fire; fortunetellers foretold; magicians pulled coins from the ears of children. Onlookers straddled every space along the stone balustrades of the *jardin* or leaned in the shaded porticoes that circled the grand plaza.

The cafés and restaurants with views overlooking the plaza were packed to the gills. Flower-covered wooden arches stood before the main cathedral, guarded by the peasants who had constructed them. Inside, the priests murmured prayers blessed by the Vatican, even as the stone vaults echoed with the boom of pagan drumbeats from the streets.

At one corner of the plaza, a café sat above street level like a stage. A front table suddenly became empty. Grasping the railing, Bass heaved himself up and took one of the vacated seats. A frenzy of Latin agitation erupted between the staff and several parties who had been patiently waiting for a table. Bass refused to budge.

Today I'm a babysitter, thought Diaz. Tomorrow I'll go back to being a cop. He slipped a hundred pesos to the café manager, a longstanding acquaintance and a socialist. Other tables were found for the most vocal of the preempted customers. *Dos cervezas* and a double Scotch were ordered. Bass leaned forward in his chair, absorbed in the drama of the Saturnalia.

"Never seen anything like this before. Not even at a Cowboys game."

"*Si. Es muy interesante.*" replied Diaz noncommittally. A dark, beetle-shaped premonition kept flying against the screen door of his mind. He needed to get Bass back to the hotel and heavily sedated.

Instead he leaned back and sipped his pilsner.

At the next table he observed an attractive fortyish woman. Blond hair, straw hat and wearing a tiny yellow dress that accentuated her curvaceously full figure. She spoke fluent Spanish to the waiter but with a foreign accent.

Diaz sighed then glanced at the younger man in a bedraggled linen jacket sitting next to her. His lips wandered shamelessly along the arc of her neck; his hand tripped the light fantastic between her thighs. When the woman noticed Diaz watching, she gave a careless laugh and pushed the man away. The man pouted like some down-at-heels aristocrat evicted from his triple-mortgaged *estancia* by a peasant uprising.

Diaz considered offering the woman a smile of some sort, but when he sought her eyes she looked straight through him, as if he was invisible. He stood.

"Going to take a piss. Be right back."

At the back of the café, Diaz pushed open the door to the men's room and stood at an ancient coffin-shaped urinal, cracked and rust stained but still serving its noble purpose. He added his stream to the greater flood of human waste drowning the world.

When Diaz emerged from the dank *pissoir*, the table where he had left Bass and Armando was empty. He glanced toward the bar. Nothing. Suddenly apprehensive, Diaz hurried forward to the railing and scanned the crowd quadrant by quadrant. Smallwood's massive form was nowhere to be seen. Nor Armando's plump Alfred Hitchcockish profile. The waiters had seen nothing. One minute they were there, the next – poof!

Hesitation devoured valuable seconds. Finally, Diaz walked briskly up a side street in the direction of the hotel, pushing his way roughly through a group of querulous alcohol-mean Indians. Curses were hurled after him. He twisted around, his hand reaching for his Glock, anticipating trouble.

Just then, three dancers in gaudy, animalistic masks, their bare arms, legs and bodies painted with primitive petroglyphs, materialized from nowhere and surrounded Diaz. Ancient chanting bubbled from their lips, blending with the laughter of shaken bells and the solo beat of a handheld drum. Diaz recognized them as anthropomorphic Aztec god-images. One, a buffoonish toad, held Diaz's wrist aloft, while a jaguar demigoddess, her bare breasts mottled in ocher and black, tied around it a bracelet of colored threads. Growing up, he remembered his grandfather doing the same thing each time before they set out on a trip into the Sierra backcountry. Protection from devils and servants of the underworld lord *Mictlantecuhtle*, his grandfather had said. Each thread one of the circles of the cosmos.

Then, almost before they had arrived, the three dancers whirled away down the street toward the *jardin*. In a moment they were lost in the milling revelers. Only the interwoven threads remained as evidence of their existence. Diaz raised his eyebrows in perplexity.

At the next intersection a uniformed officer waved ineffectually at snarled traffic trying to go two ways down a street only wide enough to accommodate a single lane. Diaz flashed his ID.

"Have you seen a huge *gringo* walking this way wearing a black and yellow checked jacket? Or a police inspector in a dark blue suit?"

The policeman looked at Diaz as if he was tripping on peyote.

"Why would I pay attention to someone walking by? I've got enough problems with these fucking cars. Every driver is drunk. I should place them all under arrest."

Diaz walked another block then turned back toward the *zocalo*. Maybe Smallwood just wanted to buy some peanuts or a souvenir. He and Armando would be back at the café table, speculating on Diaz's long absence. Wondering whether he might have slipped and cracked his head on a urinal.

But back at the epicenter of the festival, their former café table was occupied by a group of melancholy German tourists flaunting expensive digital cameras. Diaz felt on the brink of some unnamable disaster.

At the café steps he came face to face with Consuela Domingue, dressed to kill in a white chiffon strapless sundress as tight and dreamlike as a second skin. Her ironic gaze held him in thrall.

"Inspector. I hope you made it home all right last night. After we parted company so abruptly."

"*No problemo.* Though I have a little stiffness in my face. I must have slept wrong."

"You're lucky to be alive."

Diaz blinked.

"I thought you were leaving this morning for Mexico City."

"Leo wanted to stay for the *fiesta*."

She seemed neither happy nor the opposite.

"We're just meeting up with my friend Jane," said Consuela. "She and that Russian painter are just up there in the café."

Adrenalin exploded in Diaz's bloodstream.

"Perhaps you would like to come for a drink?" asked Consuela. "We can discuss whether anything can be retrieved from last night."

Diaz was much too excited about at last finding the elusive *senor* Gregorovich to focus on what Consuela was saying. He took her arm distractedly.

"I'd very much like to meet Jane."

"I'm sure you would. Like all the other stud bulls."

Consuela laughed while Diaz pretended not to be looking at her capacious boobs nestled in white. Tucking her arm in his, she started up the steps. At the top she surveyed the tables.

"Well, shit." Consuela's forehead beetled. "They're gone. You know, I actually had the feeling they didn't want to see Leo and me."

There was only one empty table. The one next to where Diaz and Bass and Armando had been sitting. The one occupied by the blonde and her persistent lover.

"Is your friend Jane a blonde wearing a yellow dress and a straw hat?"

"How did you know?"

Diaz wondered why fate kept giving him the finger. He flashed Consuela a wan smile. Maybe he should have slept with her last night after all. A heady balm for tattered nerves.

He imagined her nose pressed into his *culo*, as the tip of her tongue tickled the crinkled rim of his anis. Next moment in his mind's eye she squatted over him, her memorable breasts low hanging fruit.

Diaz sighed inwardly. She was probably in a swingers' group, he thought. Way too dangerous for a small town cop.

But at least now he knew what Gregory Gregorovich looked like. It was only a matter of time before they had a chat.

Chapter 19

Consuela's fingers gently touched Diaz's cheek.

"Don't look so unhappy. All Mexican men have a thing for blond northerners. But it rarely works out. Come and have a drink with us anyway."

He shook his head. What he needed to do was find Bass Smallwood. Get things back under control.

"Got to go."

Avoiding Consuela's proffered lips, Diaz blew kisses past either cheek and wished her a safe journey back to Mexico City. His hands held her sumptuous body at a decorous distance. Looking past her, he saw Leo maneuvering his way unsteadily up the café steps. Diaz rushed by him with a nod.

Wandering the streets in the hope of finding Bass and Armando seemed quixotic at best. At worst a total waste of time. And Armando wasn't answering his fucking cell phone! A more organized search was needed. Diaz headed back to the *Judiciales* station.

When Diaz walked in, Armando leaped up from his desk, dropping the crime comic book he had been reading onto the floor. Contrition and worry etched his face. A puppy caught peeing on the carpet. Before Diaz could formulate an official reaction, Armando blurted out his excuses.

"Without warning Smallwood jumped up and vaulted over the railing into the crowd. He was gone before I could even put down my glass. I…"

"You mean before you could get off your ass. You screwed up, Armando. Why didn't you call me?"

Sergeants Roberto Ortiz and Garcia Sanchez, who had come

up behind Armando, edged away, eyeing their chances of slipping down the hallway to the unisex bathroom. Unisex since the arrival of Felicia.

Armando's walnut complexion took on a reddish hue. His voice quavered. "Dead battery. Forgot to charge it last night."

Even as they backed away in slow motion, Diaz became aware of Roberto and Garcia.

"*Amigos*." Diaz's long fingers gripped Garcia's shoulder. "Congratulations! I'm assigning the three of you for the duration, or at least for what's left of today and tonight, to the task of finding Bass Smallwood, who's gone native and is no doubt lying wasted in some AIDS and roach infested *taberna*. I want hourly reports on your progress, whether or not I answer my phone – and keep it brief."

After the three officers had departed on their mission, the police station was as deserted as a whorehouse on Sunday morning. The machinegun-toting sentry had long since gone off duty. The overhead lights blazed down on empty desks and dead computer screens. Diaz wondered whether someone would dare to rip off the *Judiciales's* computers if left unattended. Nothing, however unseemly, was impossible in the present dark age, he decided. Switching off the lights to save energy and wear and tear on his sleep-deprived eyeballs, Diaz sat in his darkened office, smoking. His feet hurt and his head throbbed. Slowly his eyelids collapsed.

A noise jerked him back into wakefulness. His cigarette butt still smoldered between two fingers. What had disturbed him? His eyes tapped the overlapping layers of shadow like blind Pew the rutted road of his demise.

Someone was standing in the doorway of his office! An impossible silhouette – black on black. Diaz felt for the .25 caliber snub-nosed pistol clipped to the underside of his desk.

"Who the fuck's there?"

At the same moment the florescent lights flooded the room. A man in Cuban style olive drab fatigues stood in the doorway, gazing ironically at Diaz, his eyes as blank and unknowable as the hidden channels of a sacred Mayan *cenote* in the Yucatan. Sunken cheeks. Nonexistent lips to pass judgment on the world. A sun burnt hand passed across a shaved skull.

"Who the hell are you?" demanded Diaz.

"You never returned my call."

A pulse of apprehension twitched through one of Diaz's fingers. To dispel this, he sat up straight and, one-handedly, flicked open his Zippo and lit a fresh cigarette. His other hand extracted the Saturday night special from its under-desk holster and rested it in his lap beneath the desk.

"I'm sorry. I didn't catch your name."

"Lieutenant Morales. I'm with the Feds."

"The phone message yesterday."

"Brilliant."

"You drove all the way from Guanajuato because I didn't return your call? I hope there weren't too many drunks on the road. San Miguel and the entire *compo* are stoned on religion, cheap *tequila* and *pulque*."

"*Es no problemo.*"

"If your message had even hinted at its urgency, I might have saved you a trip."

Lieutenant Morales' hands rested heavily in the pockets of his fatigues. His voice had a rasping undertow, like an old jazz recording:

"As a kid, in wintertime when the nights came early, I used to sneak onto the roof of the work shed in our back yard to watch my sister undress by candlelight in her room. She was fifteen and already a woman."

As Morales spoke, Diaz's eyes wandered to the far corners of the room, then back again to the shaved head with its sheen of sweat. Who was this guy? Was this a test to see whether Diaz would reveal himself as a secret pedophile? Was *Don* Cedillo dropping hints in the state capital that Diaz was a pervert? Divorced seven years and still not remarried.

"I hope you didn't drive all this way just to make a confession. In any case you need to see a priest. I'm not qualified to give absolution."

Morales resumed his story as though Diaz hadn't spoken.

"One night my sister saw me on the roof and told our father. He beat me to a bloody pulp. Then dragged me to see the local priest, who said I was guilty of a mortal sin. In the end I was sent to live with my father's brother, who ran a shoe factory in Nuevo Laredo. My father's brother was a sadist. I worked in his factory for fourteen-hours a days. At night I slept in the dirt yard with his dogs and chickens. I lost two fingers in the shoe presses before I worked up the nerve to run away."

Diaz blinked. This guy Morales was ripe for satire.

"And despite such trials, here you are, a respected officer in the Federal Police."

"You haven't been listening, *mi amigo*. Too busy being the stand-up comic." Morales' voice was a ragged whisper.

"Oh? Were you trying to tell me some elemental truth? Shed some light on my dark, ironic soul?"

"There are forbidden things, Hector. When you become involved in them, bad things happen to you."

Diaz hated it when people he didn't know used his first name, as if they'd been pals for years.

"What exactly is your point?"

"The Federal Police in Guanajuato are involved in some very sensitive investigations. We don't want you jeopardizing them."

"I don't have any idea what you're talking about."

A mean smile edged Morales' lips. "Come on, Hector. Pretending to be a dumbass doesn't play with me. I'm talking about Amanda Smallwood's death. Ease up on it, *amigo*. Let it go."

Morales held up his right hand. Where the index and middle fingers should have been were two stubs of white scar tissue.

This grotesque disfigurement jolted Diaz backwards in time to the night his daughter was killed by a random bullet fired off by a drunken New Year's Eve reveler. He remembered her resting in his arms, a look of incomprehension and fear in her eyes as blood from the gunshot wound bubbled between her lips. Then her eyes rolled back and she was gone.

Rage gripped Diaz's *cojones* like the teeth of a fight-trained Rottweiler. He knew he was going to do something stupid, but he didn't care. In a single violent motion he rose out of his chair and catapulted across the desk. Morales grunted in surprise and pain as Diaz slammed into him. Diaz's forearm pressed hard across his throat; Morales' head snapped back hard against the doorframe. The nickel-plated .25 caliber pistol appeared in Diaz's other hand, its ugly snout distending Morales' nostril.

"Amanda Smallwood was brutally murdered. She didn't deserve her death. I intend to find her killer. You can stick your droll stories and piquant threats up your ass, Lieutenant. And don't ever call me *amigo* again."

Diaz removed the .45 caliber weapon from the holster on Morales' hip. The ejected ammunition clip clattered on the desktop. When Diaz released the Federal police officer's throat, he bent double gulping for breath. Diaz half pulled, half dragged him to the station door.

Outside Morales stopped and messaged his neck. Looking at Diaz, his face caught in the light above the door was a grain-less veneer empty of emotion. Then he turned and walked away, his hobnail paratrooper boots tapping out a declining tattoo on the hard pavement.

Diaz watched him disappear up the dark street. If there's one thing I'm good at, Diaz thought, it's making enemies.

Chapter 20

Bass Smallwood awoke to the reek of his own vomit splashed down the front of his shirt and pants.

His skull was wedged into the apex of three intersecting planes, two walls and a floor, in a narrow passage leading to a fetid *pissoir*. His brain car-jacked.

Struggling to his feet, he made his way to a parsimonious doorway at one end of the passageway. Beyond was a squat-ceilinged room sweet with the vices of alcohol, tobacco smoke, weed and human lust. A bar of low character. The space was filled with a haphazard explosion of rough-hewn tables. Dead or passed out, a ragged *mestizo* sprawled across one of them. Swing doors led to the street. Above and below them daylight seeped in like a slow release poison.

It took Smallwood several ponderous moments to remember that he was in some hick town in Mexico where he had come to identify the corpse of his only child. To realize that his genes had reached an abrupt dead end.

Standing outside the *cantina*, he took inventory in the ozone-distorted sunlight of early morning. A stumblebum. Clothes stained and wrinkled, face smudged with filth, a ring of dirt around each sock-less ankle. How had he lost his socks?

Two hard Indian women walked by, looking through him as if he were a peyote induced hallucination. Patting his trousers, Smallwood confirmed that by some miracle he still had his wallet. His head was a pounding dead zone.

He recalled his meeting with Dr. Valdemario the undertaker, an asshole as arch and arrogant as a bullfighter. The arrangements for shipping Amanda's corpse back to Dallas had been made. Bass had done all he could for her. There was no reason to stay longer in this diabolical town. He walked through empty, early morning streets until, by a fortunate turn, he came upon the hotel.

The drowsing desk clerk showed no surprise at Smallwood's early morning return or his destitute appearance. In his room Bass showered and put on clean clothes. Then fell asleep for half an hour. A message to call Diaz, handed to him by the desk clerk, lay crumpled and disregarded on the bureau.

At five minutes after nine when Bass Smallwood appeared at the front entrance of the hotel, the bellman waved over a for-hire car that had been waiting patiently across the street since before midnight. The bellman, having previously received a 100-*peso* gratuity from the driver, put Smallwood's single bag in the trunk and helped him into the back seat.

A Texas Rangers baseball cap covered Smallwood's buzz cut scalp. As the car pulled away, bound for the Guanajuato International Airport, Bass regretted not obtaining a bottle from the bar.

From San Miguel the two-lane highway to the airport passed through 80 kilometers of lonely, semi-arid countryside before brushing the edge of the suburban sprawl of the state capital and then turning south through the airport industrial zone. Rocky escarpments rose to the left, then right. Broad, windswept valleys filled with emptiness offered slim purchase to thorn trees and stunted broad-leaf oaks.

Transient life was intermittent. A man in dusty clothes and a *sombrero* led a donkey down a narrow dirt track. A large unknown bird flew across the road and disappeared into a cactus thicket.

The driver of the hired car wore a blue checked shirt and a mustache. His hair was carefully greased and combed. Rounding a curve, he suddenly pulled the car to the side of the road and brought it to a stop.

Smallwood's brow creased. Was it a flat? There had been no telltale shimmy, no thumping sound of a deflated tire.

The driver's eyes did a somersault in the rear view mirror. Smallwood glanced over his shoulder as an ancient VW Bug came out of nowhere and pulled to a stop behind them.

"A friend of yours?" asked Bass.

The sole occupant of the second car was a certain psychopathic Indian known for his deadly gaze. He sat utterly still, humming a ditty remembered from childhood, then suddenly shoved open his door, leaped out and rushed forward. Desert winds and bad karma had deeply scoured his dark complexion. The amphetamine glint of his eyes radiated despair.

In three steps the Indian stood beside Bass' hired car. Instead of leaning down to talk to the driver as Bass had expected, he wrenched open the passenger door and pointed a small caliber automatic at Smallwood. Its chill snout pressed against Smallwood's temple as the Indian climbed into the car. Afraid, Smallwood twisted his bulk toward the far corner of the back seat. But there was nowhere to hide.

"*Adelante,*" commanded the Indian.

The car lurched back onto the pavement. Smallwood quivered in an emotional limbo, the reality of imminent death shifting in and out of focus around him. What the fuck was happening?

A tourist suddenly fallen into the hands of third world kidnappers, Bass emptied his pockets, offering cash, credit cards, a handful of worthless Mexican coins and a plastic dispenser of dental floss. A burn scar ravaged the Indian's face, the dead-white skin shimmering with cabalistic meanings just beyond Smallwood's comprehension.

The hired car fishtailed around a curve and with a squeal of brakes turned sharply onto a dirt road, deep ruts on either side of an axle-killer spine of hard packed earth. Stones clanged off the oil pan as the car jolted and bounced up the hillside then slid to a dusty halt out of sight of the highway.

The driver alighted, scurried to the far side of the car and threw open the door against which Smallwood cowered. At the same moment the homicidal Indian pressed the pistol more firmly into Smallwood's blanched flesh.

Deprived of support from behind and prodded by fear, Smallwood tumbled backwards onto the hardscrabble earth.

"Please," he stammered, holding supplicating hands toward the Indian, whose eyes shimmered with fool's gold. "Whatever you want, I promise it's yours."

For a moment in time Smallwood saw his daughter struggling against unknown fingers pressing deep into her throat. Her desperation to live rising like a mist from the deep waters of her eyes. A final breath sighed between her lips.

In the same instant the Indian pulled the trigger. The bullet ricocheted off Smallwood's cheekbone and fatally pierced his brain. Smallwood never heard the gunshot. His mind was too busy absorbing the purple flood of extinction. He sank back onto the ground, lifeless.

The Indian, jumping up and down in a spasm of nerves, fired the pistol twice more into Smallwood's chest. A waste of ammunition, a redundancy of death.

After the Indian calmed down, he and the driver hefted the dead weight of Smallwood's body through a landscape of tangled brush and wild grasses and heaved it into the depths of a circuitous ravine. Unbuttoning his fly, the Indian urinated over the edge of the *barranca*. As he buttoned up, he saw Smallwood's Rangers cap lying in the dirt. Picking it up, with a twist of his wrist he sailed it into oblivion.

It was as if Bass Smallwood had never existed.

they lied. they said one would be enough. but now they want another. i knew, once they had a taste, there would be no turning back.

first they whined and wheedled, until i couldn't think straight. then they threatened violence. that's when i agreed to bring them the first two legged goat.

foolishly i thought if i met their demand, they would be satisfied.

but even as they feasted and read the entrails, they laughed at me. sated, they fell asleep by the pool in the shade of the banana palm.

but soon enough they demanded another. their cosmic yen for blood vibrating in my brain.

Chapter 21

A framed photograph stood at attention on one corner of Diaz's desk. His mother in a soft summer dress counterfeited from a Barbara Stanwyck melodrama. A beatific smile on her face. In pleated *guayabera* and straw porkpie hat, his father scowled into the camera. Behind them, a gaudy, chrome-toothed 1955 Chevrolet. The picture was snapped the day they left on their honeymoon – a road trip to Houston and Galveston. Three children and thirty-seven years later, his mother was dead of pancreatic cancer.

Diaz smoked two cigarettes but neither Ortiz nor Ruiz nor Sanchez called. He suspected they were holed up in a cozy *bodega* playing cards and drinking *cervezas*.

Reaching into his jacket pocket to check his cellphone, his fingers engaged the lace filigree of the raspberry colored panties he had taken from Gregorovich's studio. He pulled them out and held them to his nose. Dust and mildew.

Twirling them around and around on two fingers, Diaz considered delivering them to Dr. Nicholas Moza for analysis by the lab in Guanajuato. But it could take days or even weeks to get the results. And at best what would the lab analysis prove? That Amanda Smallwood had left a pair of undies behind in Gregorovich's lair. And where would Diaz be if it turned out they didn't even belong to Amanda? Could these be the panties of a murderess?

For a moment he dangled them over the wastebasket. Then changed his mind and stuffed them into the bottom drawer of his desk behind an out of date compendium on criminal law.

On his way out, Diaz stopped in the men's room to wash his hands. Since as usual there were no paper towels in the dispenser, he used his cloth handkerchief to dry his fingers. He was careful to lock the front doors of the station, fumbling with the key, back turned to the street.

A shoe scraped on stone. Diaz whirled, expecting Morales to come barreling down upon him, seething with revenge after lying in wait for the past hour. But it was only a topsy-turvy drunk who had wandered away from the *fiesta*.

Diaz walked through dark streets, heading away from the sounds of revelry in the *jardin*. When he unlocked his apartment door and flicked on the light, it felt like the abode of a stranger. What was he doing here? He wanted to be somewhere crowded and raucous – where he could forget about the dead girl and his quaint sense of obligation towards her. A place where people pressed three deep along the bar. The bartender breaking a sweat as he hurried back and forth filling drink orders, frowning at a lipstick-stained glass that someone had put back in the overhead rack.

Ortiz would be there, accompanied by the tattooed model from the *Instituto*, her voice hoarse and provocative from too many clove cigarettes. And Quevedo, strung out by too many hours of surveillance. And perhaps Felicia as well, tagging along, trying to be one of the guys. Each officer buying a round. The model running her hand against Diaz's crotch, vinyl fingernail extensions rasping on the zipper teeth, while Ortiz was distracted telling an elaborate dirty joke involving a platinum blonde, a penguin and a priest.

Diaz longed to be far away from thoughts of dead girls and missing fathers. Far away from the echo of empty rooms.

With a sigh Diaz entered his apartment and threw the dead-bolt. He took a long shower until the hot water ran out. Dressed in jeans and a sweatshirt, he lay on his couch, sipping a tumbler of his favorite small still mezcal over ice, eyes closed, savoring the smoky taste.

Several hours later Diaz awoke to the insistent clamor of his cell phone. The Secret History thudded to the floor. By his trusty Rolex it was twenty minutes after one. He vaguely recalled being in a bar, drinking with his fellow *Judiciales*. A fragment of a dream? Or a group portrait caught in a cell phone photo op?

Ortiz's voice whined over the wireless connection. They were hungry and exhausted. And without hope. Their futile search had taken them through 30 bars, *cantinas*, *bodegas*, lounges, private drinking clubs and *pulque* joints, each one overflowing with a multitude of drunks, lushes and lowlifes. They had trekked back to the hotel three times to no avail. Bass Smallwood had fallen through a crack in the universe.

"Okay, okay," said Diaz. "I want Armando at the hotel first thing tomorrow morning. If Bass has shown back up, he's to sit on him until I get there. Is that understood?"

Diaz could hear Ortiz repeating his instructions off-line.

"Oh, Ortiz…"

"*Si.*"

"Aren't you on duty tomorrow?"

"*Si.*"

"Well with three quarters of San Miguel hung over, it should be pretty quiet. Have a restful Sunday."

"Thanks, Hector," said Ortiz. "You too."

Diaz was always suspicious when Ortiz assumed the pose of obsequious camaraderie. Was it just sarcasm or was he setting Diaz up for some impossible request, like a raise or a week's vacation?

"Did you want to say something else?"

Dead silence reigned. Ortiz was obviously saving his supplication for a more intimate moment.

"After eleven I'll be at my sister's if anything comes up," said Diaz. "We'll start fresh on Monday."

Cutting the connection, Diaz went into the bedroom and put on a pair of cotton pajamas against the winter chill. For the next three hours he lay in the dark, his mind spinning through the events of the last two days. Two images returned again and again. One was of Fran Kovacs's hate distorted face as she savaged Gregorovich's painting with a knife. In the second Fran lay in listless semi-nudity by her pool. At least I'm not obsessing about the dead girl any more, thought Diaz.

It was almost noon when Diaz awoke, the salt taste of pond scum on his lips. He splashed water on his face, dressed quickly and hurried out of the apartment. His sister Olivia would be furious if he was late for lunch. She was the goddess of punctuality.

Elisa, the oldest daughter, age ten, answered Diaz's knock. He scooped her up in his arms and charged down the hallway, as she squealed with delight. Olivia, standing at the stove, looked up at this brazen cacophony and smiled.

Diaz set Elisa down and gave Olivia a brotherly half hug. She was the exact image of their mother in the photograph on his desk, though more serious. Black hair was parted in the middle and pulled harshly back. Milk chocolate eyes viewed the world with suspicion.

"You're actually on time."

Diaz grimaced.

"I've been attending procrastinators anonymous."

"I think you just got lucky."

A large iron pot simmered on the back burner. Steam, piquant with cumin, garlic and tomatoes, wafted ceiling-ward. Diaz lifted the lid and sniffed.

"Maximino will be here any minute. He took Bianca to the park."

Maximino, Olivia's husband, was an insurance adjustor. Diaz was sure he was on the take. He always had plenty of cash. But who wouldn't be tempted, with all the expats and their oversized SUVs that they drove too fast? Diaz never looked too close. Maximino was good with the two girls. And Olivia seemed generally happy.

"How about a drink?" said Diaz.

"Coke or orange Fanta?"

"That's it?"

"You know I don't keep alcohol in the house. It sets a bad example."

That meant Maximino did his drinking elsewhere. Diaz thought Olivia was taking a risk enforcing such a harsh position. In San Miguel's numerous bars and *cantinas* there were always women ready to provide companionship at an individual or group rate.

Before Diaz could retort, Maximino and Bianca arrived. During lunch Diaz sipped his Fanta and said little.

Afterwards he and Maximino went outside to smoke. Olivia

didn't allow smoking in the house either. They had little to say to each other. Later Diaz read a story to Bianca. Elisa pretended she was too old to be read to. But she listened from across the room.

After the story Diaz said it was time to leave. But Olivia insisted on showing him the new compost pile she had started in a corner of the back garden. Egg shells, lime rinds, a layer of humus. But what lurked beneath? wondered Diaz. The same worms that feasted on the flesh of the dead.

He made a face.

"Don't you believe in progress?" Olivia demanded. "Everything biodegradable in the house goes back into the earth. That's more worthwhile than spending your time consorting with gangsters, prostitutes and killers."

"It's a matter of perspective. Someone has to protect the small businessman and avenge the wrongfully slain. Prostitutes are a fact of life, like confession and taxes."

Olivia didn't appear convinced.

"You should get married again, Hector. It would mellow your outlook. And you won't catch a social disease."

"I need to get going."

"I suppose you're working overtime on the murder of that *norteamericano* girl. I'm glad you found time for us. The girls really like you." She leaned close and kissed him on the cheek. He smelled peppermint on her breath. "Stay out of trouble, Hector."

"Tell Maximino I'll call him to go for a drink."

Before she could protest this nefarious suggestion, he strode out the side gate and across the road to his aging Wrangler.

Diaz downshifted to second to maintain his momentum up the cobblestoned incline to the colonial *centro* of San Miguel. Moments later he jerked the wheel wildly to avoid an Indian sleeping in the gutter. A casualty of the *fiesta* or a lost soul?

Speaking of lost souls, Diaz realized he hadn't heard from Armando. Had Bass never returned to the hotel? Or had Armando dropped the ball again?

Angrily Diaz stomped the accelerator and made a detour in

the direction of the hotel where they had stashed Bass. When he arrived, the clerk on duty told him, based on the hotel's computer records, *senor* Smallwood had checked out early Sunday morning. Beyond that he knew *nada*, having just started his shift half an hour ago.

It's time for a serious chat with Armando, Diaz resolved. In the meantime someone had to move the murder investigation forward.

When they got the graveyard shift desk clerk on the phone, all he could add was that Bass had gotten into the back seat of a dark sedan parked across the street from the hotel. A dead end.

But Diaz had another idea.

Ten minutes later he parked in the cul de sac ending at Brian Dillinger's conspicuous residence. It was a modern industrial-looking affair of concrete and burnished wood with an unexpectedly colorful abstract stained glass window above the door. Because of the narrowness of the lane on which the house stood, Diaz was obligated to park his Wrangler with two wheels resting on the sidewalk, tilting the vehicle at a precarious angle. The day was falling toward evening. Childish colors lit a filament of clouds.

Dillinger himself answered the door, wearing a Green Day T-shirt and sweatpants. His hair was a jumble. He blocked the doorway, a look of pique corrugating his forehead.

"Inspector. What an awkward hour to be dropping by. Can't this wait until tomorrow?"

"I just need to clarify a few things from our earlier conversation."

"Of course. I'll come to your office. Shall we say ten o'clock on Monday?"

"This will only take a few minutes."

They stared at each other. Diaz wondered if this was what was referred to as a Mexican standoff. Then Dillinger blinked.

"All right. Come in."

Dillinger led the way down a hallway and through French doors into a high ceilinged room. He closed the doors behind them. Glass-fronted cabinets filled the walls except for one of Dillinger's lush nude paintings.

Two leather chairs in a mock Deco style filled the foreground of the room. Opposite them resided a heavy Victorian desk, and beyond it a computer table overflowing with expensive electronics.

Dillinger motioned to one of the chairs. Diaz remained standing.

"A comfortable set up, *senor* Dillinger. Your business interests must be doing very well."

In response Dillinger asked laconically: "Drink?"

"Mezcal, if you have it."

Dillinger stepped to a miniature bar between two cabinets.

"I think you'll find this interesting. It's from a nameless mountain village outside Oaxaca." He handed Diaz a hand-blown shot glass filled with a leather-colored liquor. Diaz took a sip.

"Very smooth." Then, as an afterthought: "I'll expect a case in my office first thing Monday."

Diaz smiled at his flirtation with *mordida*. When Dillinger failed to respond, Diaz leaned over and peered into the nearest glass cabinet. It was filled to overflowing with gewgaws and curiosities. Ivory and silver snuff boxes. Cast iron piggy banks. Animal skulls. Feathered and beaded Indian gear. Silver cigarette cases engraved with the initials of their original owners. An obsidian-bladed Aztec sacrificial knife. Two old typewriters, one of which might have been used by Hemingway, the other by Leonardo De Vinci. A collection of exotic moths pinned in a display case. And last but not least, a Daffy Duck lunchbox.

"I see you're a packrat, Dillinger."

"Just whatever interests me wandering through the flea markets and antique shops. A form of entertainment." After a pause: "Can we get to the Q&A sometime before midnight? I have other obligations."

Diaz lowered himself into a chair. Now only Dillinger remained standing.

"First…" Diaz's voice trailed off. Behind Dillinger a woman's disembodied face peered through the glass of one of the French doors. Red lips, high cheekbones, a hard rural beauty. Then she was gone.

Dillinger's wife? Diaz didn't think Dillinger was inclined toward family life. A girlfriend, then? Or just a Sunday afternoon hooker? Dillinger seemed the type for that sort of diversion.

"Inspector?"

"Oh, sorry. What I wanted to ask you was... That is, the other night you said the *Galeria Rana* was just a sideline of yours. I was wondering what business you're in."

"Did I say that?" Then with irritation: "That's what you came by to clarify?"

"*Si.*"

For a moment Dillinger's eyes blazed like a grass fire whipped by the wind. But his anger just as quickly dissipated.

"Leisure. My business is leisure. For *gringos* and rich *mexicanos* alike. I own two hotels and three restaurants in San Miguel." He named them, including the restaurant where Diaz and Consuela had sipped margaritas. All were on the luxury end.

"I hope the *gringa* murder hasn't resulted in a downturn in business."

"Not yet. But I'm counting on a quick arrest before there's another killing."

"You think there will be another? What makes you so sure?"

"The cruelty of it. It would seem to be the handiwork of a serial killer. A drifter."

"Handiwork. A nice turn of phrase."

When Dillinger didn't respond, Diaz laughed harshly.

"Next question," said Dillinger.

"I need the name of someone who can vouch for your whereabouts between midnight and two a.m. on Thursday night."

Angrily, Dillinger strode across the room, then spun around leaning against the edge of the Victorian desk. In his hands, twisting this way and that, was an evil looking Nazi dagger bearing the insignia of the Waffen-SS.

"I was at my own birthday party. There were dozens of people."

"Of course there were. But it would have been very easy for you to slip away for half an hour. Especially late in the evening when everyone was stoned out of their minds. It takes less than two minutes to strangle someone. That leaves twenty-eight minutes to drive Amanda Smallwood's body down the hill and dump her in the *jardin*."

"Just two minutes? Did you use a stopwatch, Inspector?" Dillinger set the Nazi dagger on the desk, then nervously picked it up again. "Amanda left my party before midnight. I'm sure of that because the band was still playing when she waved goodbye. The last set ended at twelve-fifteen."

"The other night you said Amanda left with two men you'd never seen before. Now you're sure she left before midnight. Just give me the name of somebody who'll vouch for you. Any name will do."

"Two men? Did I say that? Maybe I was thinking of someone else. No. I'm sure I saw Amanda leave with Gregory. Gregory Gregorovich, the artist."

Fran Kovacs had a distinctly different recollection, thought Diaz. An unquenchable need washed over him to find the elusive Russian artist sooner rather than later.

"I know of *senor* Gregorovich," replied Diaz. He finished his mezcal and set the glass on the table between them. "Since you've changed the facts, *senor* Dillinger, let me suggest another hypothesis. Seeing Gregorovich leave that night with Amanda aroused great jealousy in you. That some ne'er-do-well artist could fuck the most desirable *ingénue* in San Miguel. She posed nude for you but wouldn't suck you off. You followed them in your SUV. When, surprisingly, they parted company, you accosted Amanda. The rest is history. Is that perhaps a viable scenario?"

Cool as a cucumber Dillinger said:

"Pulp fiction worthy of Raymond Chandler."

Without warning he drove the point of the Nazi dagger fiercely into the beautifully veneered surface of the desk. Diaz sat erect, his hands raised palm up before him.

"I apologize if I've upset you."

"I'll see you in Hell, Diaz."

Dillinger walked out, leaving the glass French doors wide open.

Diaz showed himself out. He was elated he'd gotten under Dillinger's skin. Exactly what the prick deserved.

Chapter 22

As he climbed behind the wheel of the Wrangler, Diaz realized he had an erection. A hard-on for Brian Dillinger, he thought with a self-satisfied smile.

Need to get this attended to, he thought.

Extracting his cell phone from his jacket pocket, he dialed Martina's number. After several rings, the call spiraled to voice mail. Shit!

But since their relationship was less than casual, even nonexistent, what right did he have to expect her to be waiting by the phone on the odd occasion when a goatish yen tickled his *cojones*.

In the west blood red spears of light streaked from the setting sun, impaling a ridge of high clouds, transforming them into the four horsemen of the apocalypse riding forth to rape and pillage.

Somewhere nearby a rooster crowed. Another out of synch citizen. Crowing at sunsets.

Whom else could he call?

He ran the cursor through his phone's address book. This is really out of date, he thought. Using his thumb, he proceeded to delete names linked to ancient history.

Wendy he remembered as a hard-charging waif-thin tennis player, who over time grew to like drinking far more than serving aces. A *gringa* nut case living for free in a rambling San Miguel *estancia* (including red clay tennis court) owned by her step uncle whom she occasionally screwed. Her penchant for a quart of Stoli a day had ultimately come between her and Diaz.

Then there was Alejandra, a cash only professional. No whips, chains or handcuffs, no knives or olive oil rubs. The rest was up to your nerve. She lived in Cuernavaca now. Diaz wondered if she knew Reyna. Maybe they turned tricks together. Or compared predilections on the morning after over con leche sipped in the shade of a eucalyptus tree.

Felicia's number scrolled into view. Don't go there, he thought. At the same instant his thumb, seemingly possessed of a life of its own, depressed the green connect button.

She answered on the second ring.

"Goya."

"Hola. How's it going?"

"Okay, I guess."

"Anything new in our investigation?"

"I wouldn't know, sir..." In the pause, Diaz imagined shadows of puzzlement deepening across her face. "I mean," she stammered, "...you'd know before I would...about anything important."

"Actually that's not always true. Sometimes I'm the last to know."

Was he admitting to a trust problem in the department? Or just bumbling incompetence?

"I just interviewed Brian Dillinger for the second time," he volunteered. "He's the gallery owner whose artists used Amanda as a model."

"I know who he is," she said coolly. Then added: "It's Sunday evening. Don't you ever give it a rest?"

"Actually, that's why I called. If you're not busy we could meet for a drink."

"And talk about the 'CASE', you mean?" Her voice added caps and quote marks. Her irony was as subtle as a rocket-propelled grenade.

"Just come and have a drink. Maybe get something to eat. Get to know each other better."

"Are you sure that's a good idea? You're the one who has to make the final recommendation for my employment by the Judicial Police. I wouldn't want anyone to imagine..."

That you fucked your way up the chain of command. Diaz completed the thought.

"Heaven forefend," he said, "This is only an opportunity for team building. Or may the devil strike me dead."

"I think I'll pass."

"But I hate to see you waste a good Sunday evening." Was he laying it on too thick?

"I really have things I need to do. I'll see you Monday morning."

The connection went dead.

I'm an idiot, Diaz thought. He tossed the phone on the passenger seat. Felicia was absolutely, incontrovertibly right to reject his suggestion of a rendezvous. It was an invitation to a beheading, Aztec style.

Cranking up the engine, Diaz drove the Wrangler up the steeply inclined streets toward the highest point of the town. Near the bullring resided a small *bodega* he sometimes patronized. They made an excellent fish stew. And always had on hand several small-batch mezcals for sipping into the late hours.

Paco, the owner of *Tio* Pete's, stood by the cash register wiping his thick, doughy hands on a none-too-clean apron. A veneer of sweat oozed across his bald dome. When sufficient sweat accumulated on the precipice of his brow, a fat droplet would roll slalom-like down the moguls of his forehead, ending on the tip of his nose. There the droplet hung suspended like an Olympic diver until gravity plunged it into the bowl of fish stew or other delicacy he was delivering to a customer.

Diaz eased onto a barstool.

"Inspector. A pleasure to see you. What can I get you?"

Diaz ordered a *cerveza* and a dish of *chicharrones* over which he squeezed the juice from several wedges of lime, then dusted with chili powder.

"So...how's the law and order business? A bit dicey from everything I read."

Diaz shrugged. It was a day of shrugging. Everything seemed vague, out of focus. A landscape seen through the near-sighted eyes of a person who has misplaced his glasses.

Playful laughter arose from a shadowy back corner of the *bodega*. Glancing in that direction, Diaz saw two people, one petite, the other tall and wide shouldered, rise from a plank table. The male of the species appeared to be groping at the female, who pushed him aggressively away.

A damsel in distress? Diaz's nerve ends quickened.

"Stop!" commanded the damsel. The troll tottered backwards, tripped over the bench behind him, crashed in a heap. Beauty stepped triumphant from darkness into light and strolled toward Diaz, who bore witness to the jiggle and jive of her carefree and languorous knockers and the knowing smile of her lips. A rhinestone brooch pinned at the center of the low-scooped neckline of her little black dress shimmered like an advertisement for salacious pleasures.

Hers was a face Diaz had observed in close detail on more than one occasion, as she moaned beneath his thrusting boyish buttocks. Each pore; each blemish; each acne scar. Truly she was a wonderful fuck, he thought. But her name eluded him. Alicia? Or was it Alita? He was so bad with names.

"Well, if it isn't the gloomy Hector Diaz," she said. "Still haven't stuck your head in a gas oven?"

"It would appear not."

They hugged. Her breasts pressing against him seemed to have lives of their own, like naughty pink-nosed albino rabbits.

"Let me buy you a drink," he said.

In the meantime the fallen lout, having regained his feet, walked to the front door and outside. But not before eviscerating Diaz with his straight razor eyes. "I'll see you later, Alita," he mumbled under his breath.

"What an asshole," Alita said, settling her buns on the stool next to Diaz.

"That sounded like a threat," said Diaz. "Maybe you need police protection."

"Oh, Hector." She grabbed his face in her two hands, pulled him toward her and kissed him with verve, smooshing her lips against his. Just as abruptly she released him and took a meaningful sip of her usual rum and coke, which Paco had set on the bar in front of her.

"So…how's it going, Alita?"

"Life sucks, then you die."

"I know what you mean."

Diaz crunched on a *chicharrone*. Paco polished a parabolic glass. Like a smoked ham time hang suspended. Through *Tio* Pete's front door the night crept in like a buck-toothed rodent.

"Solved any good cases lately?" Alita asked.

"Things are a bit confused at the moment."

"So nothing has changed since last time we dilly-dallied." She put her hand on his knee and squeezed. This piquant gesture sent a shiver deep into Diaz's fundamentals. Ever so casually he took another sip of his beer.

"I guess you could say that." Diaz was suddenly depressed. "Do you want to get something to eat?"

"Why not," Alita replied. "That's all I do these days: eat and fuck." She gave Diaz a lustful grin. "Paco makes a fish stew to die for."

"I'm not in a dying mood. More of a blood dripping steak mood."

"In that case we'll have to go elsewhere."

In no time they sat side by side in Diaz's Wrangler, bucking and bouncing over the irregular cobblestones. If it wasn't for the need to keep the town "authentic" for the tourists, thought Diaz, we'd have decently paved streets. Not these dry streambeds that eviscerate your vehicle and shake your organs loose.

As they drove down a sloping street past shops selling antiques and high-end home furnishings, Diaz's hand strayed without objection from the rugged gearshift to the smooth plain of Alita's thigh.

Suddenly something in the window of a passing shop caught Diaz's eye. No fuckin' way, José, he thought, as he slammed on the brakes. The Wrangler stopped on a dime, tossing them roughly against their seatbelts.

"Jesus, Hector! You trying to kill us? I'm too old to die."

But he was already scrambling out of the Jeep, striding back up the street to stand staring into the window of an antique and bric-a-brac shop.

In the center of the window display, a sculpture two-thirds of a meter tall portrayed in hyper-realistic detail three comely young women from the chest up. Of course they were naked, sporting preposterous tits and come hither smiles. The medium was ceramic in a high-gloss pearl glaze.

There could be no doubt that Amanda Smallwood had been the inspiration for the woman in the center of the trio. Diaz would remember her face to his dying day.

The three fates, he thought. Or the three whores of Babylon.

The initials C.V. were etched in one corner of the sculpture.

The store was pitch black inside. The door locked. A sign announced it would reopen on Monday at 1:00 p.m. Across the upper portion of the glass window in gold leaf it read: Syd's Collectibles.

Syd is one of those androgynous names, thought Diaz. Why would anyone call their kid Syd?

Claro, there had to be a way to get to Syd, whoever she or he might be, sooner than one o'clock the next day to find out the name and address of the artist whose initials were C.V. He would put Felicia on it.

Alita came up and stood watching as Diaz shook the unyielding door handle a second time.

"I'd say they're closed for the night. What's the deal anyway? Forget to buy your girlfriend a birthday present?"

"It's a long story," said Diaz.

They trudged back to the Jeep, climbed aboard and drove on. Diaz wasn't hungry any more. For that matter, his interest in a Sunday evening frolic, with all the emotions and emoting that entailed even with an old and amenable acquaintance, had evaporated. He was back to obsessing about Amanda Smallwood's murderer. A new avenue of inquiry had opened before him. He felt like Conan Doyle's Professor Challenger when he ascended above the clouds into a lost world, a throwback to one million B.C. Well, he thought, maybe that was a bit of an exaggeration. The initials C.V. were not as startling as discovering a place where dinosaurs still roamed the earth.

As luck would have it, as Diaz drove unenthusiastically around the next corner he saw, loping across the little plaza in front of the Church of San Francisco, the drifter Emile Zato. The vagrant sociopath still wore the same filthy sheepskin coat. His hair, the bleached yellow of dried straw mixed with sheep dung, hung listlessly across his forehead.

Was it possible that Zato had murdered Amanda Smallwood? A chance encounter on a dark, fogbound street? The idea ricocheted like a trapped wasp against the window glass of Diaz's mind.

As Diaz bore down on him in the Jeep, Zato turned his head and looked squarely at Diaz, piercing him with his feral eyes.

Diaz would have hit him, stuck him down in the street, except the drifter flipped into amphetamine overdrive. Bending low, arms pumping, he sprinted around a low parapet and down a precipitous byway, coat streaming behind like the molting skin of a viper. Diaz pulled up short at the top of the incline and looked across at Alita.

"You need to get out of the Jeep. I've got to go after that animal. He's wanted for attempted murder of a police officer."

Alita, not sure whether to be offended or frightened, started to climb hesitantly from the Wrangler.

"Hurry!" urged Diaz.

Even as she lowered one foot to the pavement, he slammed on the gas and drove pell-mell down the ragged slope. The scumbag had already turned another corner. Squinting against the encroaching darkness, Diaz spun the Jeep after him. Illuminated by the Jeep's headlights, parked cars and pickups lined one side of the deserted street down which he sped. As Diaz surveyed the way ahead, nothing moved except the black shadow of a fleeing *gato*. Terrorized by the roar of the Jeep's engine as Diaz downshifted, the beast, a witch's familiar, leaped to the top of an adobe wall. It turned and hissed at Diaz, its yellow eyes glaring like flares, before it disappeared down the other side of the wall. The fugitive drifter had similarly vanished.

Diaz barreled around two more corners but Emile Zato had slipped away into some crevice of the night.

Sooner or later you'll be mine, Diaz assured the gangbanger's ghost.

When he got back to the corner where he'd jettisoned Alita, she was gone. He thought about checking the bars in the area. Then opted for sleep.

Back at his apartment Diaz took half a Lunesta and a shot of mezcal. He lay on his bed in his boxers waiting for sleep to come. He still had a hard-on.

Chapter 23

Monday morning reminded Diaz of cleaning day when he was growing up, a whirling commotion of contradictory behaviors going nowhere fast. The cause, an attempted robbery around 5 a.m. two blocks from the *zocalo*. Unexpectedly the intended victim was armed. By the time the sleazeballs realized their mistake, one of them was dead. The other, butt shot, fled limping into the night.

The press was all over the story like a hooker on a flaccid cock. Trying to link the aborted holdup to the Amanda Smallwood murder. After all, in each case someone had died.

"No. No. No. Absolutely no connection," barked Diaz for the umpteenth time into the mouthpiece of his phone. He slammed it down. Felicia waited, her athletic body rigid on the edge of a chair in front of his desk. She wore a fitted blue-gray pants suit and an innocent white blouse with several rows of pleats down the front.

"Relentless," said Diaz. He shook his head.

Felicia, unsure whether to smile or frown, did neither.

"We know Smallwood hired a car yesterday morning outside his hotel. Probably to take him to Guanajuato International. Call the airlines and find out if he got on a plane back to Dallas. Or anyplace else."

Diaz had already dialed Smallwood's home in Dallas three times. Each time the receiver rang and rang, until he cut the connection. Who in this day and age didn't have an answering machine or voicemail?

"And send Ortiz in."

"He's not here yet."

"Well, where the hell is he?"

"Maybe he's not feeling well," she suggested.

"Then he should have called in sick." Diaz glowered. "Since he's off malingering somewhere, you'll have to fill in. Get the telephone number and address of Smallwood's art gallery in Dallas. Then find out whether Smallwood showed up this morning to unlock the door. If he's there, I need to talk to him."

On her way out of the office, her back to Diaz, Felicia made an ugly face, her tongue protruding witch-wise between pink-hibiscus-tinted lips.

"Wait," Diaz called.

She turned, all smiles. "Yes, sir."

"I've got another, perhaps more interesting, assignment for you. There's a shop on *Calle Frida Kahlo* called Syd's Collectibles. I want you to find Syd and have him here by eleven o'clock, along with the sculpture of three woman in Syd's window."

"Collecting art are we now, chief?"

"Hector. And it's called evidence."

"Hector." She rolled the word around in her mouth like a piece of hard candy. Then: "What's the deal with Syd?"

"The artist who made the sculpture I want you to take custody of used Amanda Smallwood as his model. We need to find the artist."

"You think he did it?"

"I have not a clue, Felicia. Maybe Smallwood was killed by a witches' coven. The artist whose initials are C.V. is a 'person of interest.'" He'd heard the term used on TV on some *gringo* cop show.

Felicia turned to leave.

"By eleven," Diaz said. Felicia resumed her witch face as she strolled purposefully out and across the main precinct room.

Diaz lit the fifth Montana of the morning. His mouth felt like a construction site.

The tap-tap of Armando's knuckles on the doorframe didn't make him feel any better. Armando's usual apologetically grinning face eased into the doorway. Like obsidian pinballs, his eyes ricocheted from object to object, avoiding looking directly at Diaz. "About Sunday morning…"

"We'll leave that discussion for later. Right now I want you to find the car and driver that picked up Bass Smallwood at his hotel Sunday morning. I want the driver sitting in my office by noon. If Carmen calls you, tell her to take an antacid and put her feet up."

Even as these last words irretrievably left Diaz's lips, a bad feeling settled in his gut. What was it about Armando and Carmen? How had they been transformed from an under-performing, over-weight cop and his controlling, passive-aggressive wife into the kind of couple featured on morning talk show television direct from *Mexico D.F.*? Thank God the media hadn't actually discovered them. It was bad enough that they'd become the tincture of true romance to the relationship-starved veterans of San Miguel's *Policia Judiciales*.

"I'm on it, boss."

In a flash Armando was gone. Diaz sat perfectly still, his thumb playing distractedly with his talismanic Zippo, easing the metal cap open and closed, its chrome plating partially worn away long ago by this repetitive motion. Diaz's mind looped like a Mobius strip.

Where were they in solving the Amanda Smallwood murder? Everyone had gone missing. Bass Smallwood. Gregory Gregorovich. Even Ortiz. Gregorovich had to be somewhere close by, shacked up with the fading blonde Diaz had seen him with in the café. The notorious Jane Ryder. They needed to check the cheap hotels and rooming houses. Or had the lovers fled to some x-rated beach resort in the Yucatan?

Then there was Dillinger. Hanging out with the Senator and company. He talked a good story. *Gringo* entrepreneur who'd made good south of the *Rio Grande*. But in Mexico everyone had silent partners, whether they wanted them or not.

And was it merely a coincidence that Dillinger and Bass Smallwood owned art galleries on different sides of the border?

Diaz didn't believe in coincidence – the bugaboo of the existential West. Only in the corruptibility of the human soul. And sometimes in dreams and apparitions.

And finally, who was C.V.? He kept thinking the letters stood for *curriculum vitae*. How idiotic was that!

His mind felt like a clogged drain. Sludge, hairs, nail clippings.

He needed a breath of fresh air to clear his head. And the autopsy report on Amanda Smallwood.

Felicia was on the phone when Diaz walked past and said: "I'm going to the Wonder Bar." Her eyes rotated up at him. "For a coffee," he added defensively. "When Ortiz shows up, send him over."

Outside the day was overcast and cool. Diaz was glad he'd decided, while staring morosely out his apartment window at seven a.m., to wear a wool suit. After the previous night's adventures, he'd suffered another bout of the runs and gone to bed with his asshole throbbing. He hoped there wasn't an amoeba running roughshod through his plumbing.

Just the scent of the coffee rising from the espresso cup Felix, the Wonder Bar's owner, set in front of him revived Diaz's interest in life…and death. He waved away the proffered brandy bottle and took the first sip. Aaaah.

Felix wiped his hands on a bar towel. Pouring himself a shot of brandy, he drank it down in a single gulp. His bushy mustache, which looked like it had been glued on with rubber cement, retained a few dark beads of the raw liquor, which his pink tongue judiciously collected.

Left-handedly Diaz dialed Dr. Moza's clinic on his cell phone. The serendipity of the opposing thumb was an incredible breakthrough, Diaz thought. Imagine what we could do if we had a prehensile tail. He motioned for Felix to pour brandy into the half-empty espresso cup.

Moza answered on the second ring.

"*Que hay de nuevo*, Nicholas?"

"You seem to have survived another weekend," came the brusque retort. "I saw on the news several of your compatriots in Mexico City were gunned down in a fire fight Saturday night. Picked the wrong side in a drug turf war."

"You've made it through another one as well. In fact, you're positively upbeat this morning. Get laid by any chance?"

"That information is between me and my pederastic priest, assuming, hypothetically, that I were to attend confession. A practice run for my inevitable demise."

"I'm sorry I asked."

"Don't be."

Without waiting for instructions from Diaz, Felix set in front of him another espresso, this time brimming with liquor. Diaz downed it *muy rapido*. But, thought Diaz, bitterness creeping into the corners of his mouth, it was never the same as the first cup. His experience with women was not dissimilar. He remembered he was on the phone with Moza.

"Any word from your pathology pals in Guanajuato?"

"They're not my pals," Moza retorted. "But as a matter of fact, Dr. Gupta phoned me this morning. He spent time on Sunday afternoon with the Smallwood corpse. The little slut was higher than a kite when she died. Scag. Shit. Scat. Mexican brown. Whatever you want to call it."

"But there weren't any needle marks."

"Most women don't like needles. Until they're beyond caring. But smoking or snorting the stuff gets you to the same place."

"What else did Gupta have to say?"

"*Nada.*"

"So."

"So. The fact that your little wet dream had a skag habit doesn't change the fact she was brutally murdered and disfigured."

No, it certainly doesn't, thought Diaz.

"If that's it, I've got other business to attend to."

Moza disconnected, leaving Diaz to order a third coffee and carry it outside. A kid in baggy bright-orange hip-hop shorts buttonholed him for a shoeshine. They quibbled over the price for an appropriate length of time.

As the kid went to work, rolling up Diaz's cuffs, daubing on polish with his stained fingers, the clouds dissipated, revealing a blue infinity. Sunlight warmed Diaz's cheeks. He tilted his face at an ergonomic angle and closed his eyes.

Nicholas's new information didn't seem to amount to much. Amanda's roommate slash lover hadn't mentioned drugs. But then, why would she to a cop? And drugs, including heroin, were just part of the life among San Miguel's demimonde.

The shoeshine urchin began vigorously buffing each shoe,

shaking Diaz out of his reverie. When Diaz opened his eyes, the sun slanting off the new shine on his black oxfords dazzled him.

Someone was coming up the narrow one-way street on which the Wonder Bar resided. As the figure approached, Diaz made out not Ortiz's stalwart bulk but the willowy figure of Fran Kovacs, sheathed in tight black jeans and an embroidered white shirt. Through the shirt's sheer tracery, the dark circles of her nipples lay like pirate coins on white Caribbean sand. Momentarily Diaz wondered whether a charge of public indecency would hold up in court. Then rejected the idea in favor of the *status quo*.

"Inspector Diaz." She smiled chastely. "Here you are, just as the young woman at your office said you would be. You look like a sly tomcat soaking up the sun."

"Actually most of my ancestors worshiped the toad as a tutelary genus. A few the coyote. Both night creatures."

She gave him a what-the-fuck-are-you-talking-about look.

"Forget it. I'm glad you were able to find me. Are you here to tell me that *senor* Gregorovich has returned, begging for forgiveness? A call to my cellphone would have been a lot easier than tracking me down in person."

"If Gregory was back, there'd be no need for me to contact the police. He'd be writhing in agony, his *escroto* pinned to the wall with a paring knife.

Diaz felt instantly distressed by this image.

"It's best not to confess your revenge fantasies to the police. They might take you seriously."

"But I want you to take me seriously, Inspector."

"Yes, of course. In that case, will you come for a coffee or a drink?"

"If you twist my arm."

Did she really want him to do that? he wondered.

Diaz slipped the shoeshine boy a few coins. It was more than they had agreed upon, but the boy said nothing. Diaz held open the door of the Wonder Bar and coaxed Fran inside, his long fingered hand ungainly on her narrow waist. He felt slightly flushed by her propinquity. They sat on opposite sides of a booth. Against his better judgment, he ordered another coffee. She a glass of fresh squeezed orange juice, with a shot of vodka added. He met her forthright gaze. Except for a yin-yang pendant of ivory and polished onyx, she wore no jewelry. At last he spoke:

"If *senor* Gregorovich hasn't reappeared, why are you here?"

"I wanted you to see this." She leaned forward, digging her hand into the front pocket of her jeans. Her breasts, pressing against the fabric of her blouse, fulfilled their promise. Diaz tried to remain *tranquilo*. People were drifting into the bar for an early lunch. She handed him a folded and crumpled piece of paper.

"It's a letter from Gregory. I found it pushed under my door this morning."

Diaz unfolded the cheap bond and began to read the typed document:

dear fran

i know you'll hate me forever. but i never believed i would fall in love again either. i don't mean the little number you found me with at gregory's. i'm sorry about that. but i've found someone different from all the rest.

if you haven't already torn this letter to shreds, i just wanted to tell you about the happiness i've found. from out of nowhere. if this can happen to an asshole like me, there's hope for everyone.

i know your life will turn lucky now that i'm out of it.

xxx

Below the x's a name was scrawled in ink, the only readable portion of which was a capital G. It was a signature that Diaz had seen before. He looked up and met Fran's blazing eyes.

"He's right about the asshole part," she said.

"Naturally you're upset."

"I can look after myself, Inspector. It's the woman he's with now that I'm afraid for. What if he decides to kill her, like he did that slatternly little model."

"Those are serious accusations, *senora*. What facts do you have to support them?"

"Finding the letter started me thinking about that night. After I wouldn't let Gregory back into the house, I'm sure he must have gone to Amanda's. When he told her I'd thrown him out, she would have laughed in his face. She hated men, liked to humiliate them. Spreading her legs but never allowing anyone to touch."

Her lips became harsh parallel lines.

"I'm sure he flew into a rage and killed her. Don't they say once you've killed, once you've tasted the power of life and death, it becomes like a drug?"

"The other day you had a very different opinion of *senor* Gregorovich's psychological capabilities for murder. Perhaps you still pine for him."

"You're a swine, Inspector."

"Just doing my job." Diaz refolded the letter and slipped it into his pocket. "I want very much to have a chat with *senor* Gregorovich. As soon as we can find him."

"A chat?" Her laugh was brittle. "But what about the woman he's with now? What if…?" Her hands were shaking.

"You're under a lot of stress, *senora*."

After a moment, satisfied that Fran was not going to collapse or bolt for the ladies room, Diaz rose.

"Thank you for having a drink with me. But now I need to get back to work. *Pronto*."

She smiled like a Madonna.

"Please come by my studio for a cup of tea, Inspector. Or a drink. Whatever you like. I promise not to be so boring."

It was an offer he knew he couldn't refuse.

Chapter 24

Felicia spent an hour on the telephone and left the *Judiciales* station at 10:00 a.m. She was running late but she still had an hour to meet Diaz's deadline. And besides, Diaz had gone off to the Wonder Bar, allegedly for a coffee, so what the hell was the big rush?

By the time she left the office, Felicia was sure, as far as one can be sure about anything in this life, that Bass Smallwood had not boarded a flight out of Guanajuato International since he had disappeared on Saturday afternoon.

The day, which had started out cold and overcast, had turned pleasantly mild with a sky the color of blue milk, so she stopped for a coffee and pastry at Victor's.

"How's it going," asked Rafael, who was working the espresso machine. He'd been in love with Felicia since the days when she was a rally driver and he had worked in the pit crew of a rival driver.

Her face contorted into that of an asymmetrical gargoyle. She wolfed down the sugar-studded pastry twist and finished her espresso in two quick sips. Her eyes studied the passing scene, measuring the criminal proclivities of each passer-by on her internal crime-o-meter.

"Got to go," she said, raising her hand in a pathetic excuse for a wave. Given the slightest encouragement, Rafael became a stalker.

Cutting cross the *jardin*, with its strolling tourists and lolling, perennially opportunistic ne'er do wells, she walked determinedly the ten-minutes through narrow seesaw streets required to reach *Calle Frida Kahlo*. It was an old *calle*, recently renamed.

Syd's Collectibles was locked up tight. Felicia observed the soft-core porn statuette of Amanda and her two friends. Stacked, she thought. In life the little tart had no doubt achieved a certain cachet among a cross section of San Miguel's male population. Somehow in death she had achieved sainthood, at least in the eyes of Inspector Diaz. Hector.

Fuck it! she thought. Not my problem. On the other hand, if Diaz had some sort of a nervous breakdown, her official swearing in as a Corporal in the *Judiciales* could be held up indefinitely. Stop worrying and just do your job, she told herself.

So, Sydney, where are you?

A *tabaquero* two storefronts down, offering cheap hand-rolled cigars, cigarettes, lottery tickets, postcards, Hall's throat lozenges and, if you were a *gringo*, under the counter tabs of Ecstasy, looked like a good place to start asking around.

"Cheroot, please."

She gazed into the face of the cigar seller. He was at least a hundred and five years old. Or so he appeared to her. In which case, she thought, to him I must look about fifteen.

"And a box of matches."

She counted out the sum he named and placed the money in his outstretched hand before he would relinquish to her the cheroot and the *cajita de fosforos*.

After she got the cheroot going, she ordered an orange Fanta. Sipping orange nectar fit for the gods and puffing on the goat dung infused cheroot, she asked: "Where can I find Syd?"

"Syd doesn't open 'til one."

"I know that. But I need to talk to him right away."

"If you're looking for work, I can tell you you won't make any points contacting her at home."

"You're telling me Syd is a woman?"

"Syd's not sure."

"Regardless. I need to speak to her."

"Are you a customer? Syd always pays me a little commission if I bring him a customer."

"Yeah, sure. I'm a customer. When I see Syd I'll tell her you found me wandering the streets." Felicia handed the ancient tobacco vendor a 100-*peso* note. The cigar seller held the legal tender up to the light, assessing its genuineness. Satisfied, he snapped the bill to smooth out its wrinkles and tucked it into his shirt pocket.

"Syd Diamante lives out of a rented room two blocks from here." He gave an address.

"Lousy cigar," Felicia said, dropping the cheroot in the gutter where it smoldered like a politically incorrect thought. She set the empty Fanta can on the counter and walked away.

"Fuck you, lady. And Syd doesn't like visitors, especially before noon."

Five minutes later, she arrived in front of a two story mango-colored apartment house. Random navy blue tiles and tropical green doors provided additional gaudy details. No. 94 *Calle Edgar Poe* was at best eclectic, at worst a monument to exquisite bad taste.

In Apartment 1-A the soap opera sound track coming out of the TV ricocheted off the walls and ceiling like an argument with itself. The door to 1-A was wide open. Since there was no bell, Felicia knocked on the frame of the doorway and glanced around its edge into the murky interior. A ceiling fan on high blew a torrent of air into her face.

A woman in a slinky rayon robe lolled in front of an old school cathode ray tube TV, tossing back shots of some dark colored liquor. A single florescent light from the bathroom cast the space in bands of chiaroscuro.

"Syd Diamante?"

The seated woman turned her head to glance in the direction of the front door. "Syd ain't here."

"Don't kid me," Felicia replied. "You're Syd. You match the description to a T."

She stepped forcefully into the room.

"Did I say you could come in here?"

"Police officer."

"In that case by all means come in; make yourself at home. How about a drink?"

Standing, Syd, big brown eyes aflutter, was a beautiful young man with the incipient bristles of a dark beard peppered across his cheeks and chin like wire implants and wearing a scrunched and slightly cockeyed blond wig. His lips were painted with the identical shade of red made famous by Marilyn Monroe. His slim body was draped in a fake leopard skin robe. As he bowed drunkenly toward Felicia, the blond wig tumbled to the floor where it lay unmoving like an albino monkey that had suffered a fatal aneurism.

"Oops," said the young man apologetically. "Call me Syd. I like your outfit." Then: "Are you packing?"

"Packing?"

"A weapon."

"I'm here about the artist who made the ceramic statuette of the three tarts displayed in your store window. I need his name and where I can find him."

"Oh, that one. You'd be surprised how many tourists buy tasteless crap like that."

"I'm sure." Felicia's words were impatient, one fingernail tap-tapping on the surface of a small tile-inlaid side table. "Just tell me the name of the fucking artist!"

Syd looked put out by her intensity.

"If you must know, it's Cy Vega. Cy Munoz Vega. He jerks off in an old palacio at the top of *Calle Obispo*."

"Okay. Let's go. We'll swing by your shop to pick up the sculpture on the way to s*enor* Vega's."

"No. No. No. You don't understand. I'm getting drunk this morning. I can't possibly go anywhere. I've given you the name and address. That's enough." Syd held aloft the bottle of liquor, which was Havana Club rum. "How about a drink?"

"Put some clothes on. You're coming with me. You're a material witness in a murder investigation. Besides, I have no idea what Cy Vega looks like."

With a moan Syd flopped backward full length across the caramel-colored leather sofa, throwing one arm dramatically across his face in a gesture of hopelessness. The fake leopard robe swept open revealing Syd's well-exercised physique and outsized dangly dick.

Felicia blinked. This is impossible, she thought. Then realized she had an intense need to pee, having forgotten to use the restroom before leaving the station.

"Where's you toilet?"

As she spoke she espied beyond the galley kitchen a half open door leading to a dank tiled closet-like space from which a heavy odor of urine wafted. Striding across the ghastly kitchen with its piles of filthy dishes, she entered the bathroom and closed the door. Pee molecules and mold spoors assaulted her nose. The tiny room contained an ancient shitter and a pedestal sink cluttered with jars and tubes of crèmes and make-up. Pulling down her slacks and aubergine thong, Felicia squatted over the toilet and urinated. There was neither toilet paper nor Kleenex, so she splashed some water on her crotch from the sink.

With a sigh of relief she flushed and stood gazing into the sink mirror, which was crazed and grease spotted. Did she have the right eyes for a cop? she wondered. Were they cold blooded and threatening enough? Or just bitchy?

Retrieving her cell phone from her shoulder-strapped gray macramé purse, she thumbed the speed dial key for Hector. Waiting for the chain of numbers to activate, she looked again at her mug, decided she needed to use a darker, more menacing eye shadow.

"Diaz."

"How many drinks have you had?"

A silence as thick and heavy as the curtains of a World War II era burlesque theater descended. Then Diaz's voice boomed across the ether:

"I told you eleven o'clock in my office! You're forty-five minutes late. Where the hell are you?"

"The sculptor's name is Cy Munoz Vega. Meet me at his *palacio* in 15 minutes."

"*Palacio*? What *palacio*?"

"I'll see you over there." Felicia disconnected the call without waiting for a further response. When Diaz immediately called back, she let it roll to voicemail and instead texted him the address of Vega's residence.

Diaz could be very intimidating.

When she opened the bathroom door, Syd was on his knees puking into a brass spittoon. She ran cold water on a hand towel and pressed it to his forehead.

"I just spoke to my boss. He says you have to come with me. So let's go macho-man." Syd moaned.

Grabbing the collar of his robe, Felicia dragged him to his feet and spun him around like a top. Arm wrenched behind his back, she marched him into the bedroom. Under threat of more excruciating pain, he dressed quickly in a plum-colored cotton shirt, tapered waist length black pigskin jacket and excruciatingly tight black jeans that left no doubt as to the size of his weenie, rubbed spiking gel in his short dusty brown hair and lit a cigarette. "Take me, I'm yours."

"Funny."

As they left Syd's apartment, a cab came down *Calle Edgar Poe*. Felicia flagged it down, and she and Syd slid snugly into the back seat. The cab driver rolled his eyes when Felicia flashed her police badge. It would take months of time and reams of paperwork to get paid for this fare.

It was a short hop to Syd's Collectables. Felicia dragged Syd out of the cab, leaving its rear door wide open, and up the three steps to the shop door. Syd obligingly unlocked the deadbolt and disabled the alarm system. Felicia had to stand on a small stepstool to reach over the barrier that separated the display window from the main salesroom. Leaning down, she placed a hand under a breast at either side of the sculpture and lifted. The ceramic sculpture was surprisingly light. So light that she was taken by surprise and nearly flew backward off the stepstool. Somehow she maintained her balance, pitching and yawing like an exotic dancer caught in a typhoon.

"Whoa," cautioned Syd. "Go easy with the merchandise."

He put a hand on Felicia's calf then helped her climb down from the stool as she clutched the stacked triumvirate of tarts to her own not insubstantial chest.

"We need to put the work in a box with lots of Styrofoam noodles around it," said Syd. "And don't I get some kind of receipt before you disappear out the door with my property?"

"Fuck the small print. We have to get to Cy Vega's before my boss does."

"OK," said Syd. "You take the girls down to the cab. I'll lock up."

Felicia eased past him through the front door and began to descend the three stone steps to the sidewalk.

At that moment, after a protracted internal debate, the cab driver decided to cut his loses.

Straining over the seatback as far as he could, he grasped the handle of the open rear passenger door. With a yank, he rachetted the door closed, at the same time pressing hard on the gas. With a screech the cab blasted forward.

"Hey!" yelled Felicia. "Wait."

But it was too little, too late.

The cab was already rounding the next corner.

I should have given him a few *pesos*, she thought, even as her foot slid off the edge of the second step. Next instant she was in freefall, grabbing wildly for support, a railing, a proffered hand, a passing grandmother. But none were available.

The ceramic trinity, suddenly as free as three nymphs shedding their undies at the nudist camp entrance, flew briefly upward, then plummeted precipitously. At the nadir of its descent, the sculpture slammed into the unyielding stones of *Calle Frida Kahlo* and shattered into a hundred jagged pieces.

"Shit!" Felicia said.

Chapter 25

When Felicia called, Diaz was submerged in a pool of emotional exhaustion precipitated by watching Fran Kovaks sashay up the street and disappear around a corner. He leaned on the Wonder Bar's mahogany countertop sipping a short whiskey to tamp down his libido.

Fran Kovaks had fingered *senor* Gregorovich as the murderer of Amanda Smallwood. But had no proof. Was acting out of jealousy. On the other hand Gregorovich remained an elusive and enigmatic piece of the puzzle.

Then came Felicia's call. And her first question out of the gate: "How many drinks have you had?" Her inquiry hung in the air like an unholy fart. Where did she get off poking around in his personal life?

After he'd yelled at her, she came through with the name of the newly discovered artist inspired by Amanda Smallwood's bodacious puppies. There seemed to be an endless stream of them – inspired artists that was.

Cy. What kind of name was that? Short for Cynthia? Or from the Welsh, Cynbal, meaning warrior chief? Or a diminutive version of Cyclops?

"Meet me at his *palacio* in fifteen minutes," she had said. Then the line went dead. A minor cell network hiccup or the inevitable breakdown of the world's infrastructure?

When he pressed the dial back button, his call dead-ended in Felicia's voice mail. What a pain in the ass.

He sucked down the last vestige of whiskey in his glass and

asked Felix the owner to bring over the phone book. Would Cy Vega be listed?

At that moment his phone announced the arrival of a text message. An address across town. In the normal course Diaz would have called his driver. Traveled up to the precious *palacio* in style. Except that Felicia was his driver.

"Call me a cab, asswipe," he said to Felix.

From time to time Diaz was subject to lapses of despair and existential ennui. But at the moment he merely felt belligerent. Pissed off in a generic sort of way. Luckily for his crack crime team, Diaz was already wearing his service weapon, so he didn't need to go by the station and rattle their cages.

After an interminable wait, a horn honked from curbside.

Picking up his change from the bar, Diaz left behind a pair of tarnished coins. A paltry sum. They stared back at him like the eyes of the possessed, bringing to mind the scarifying painting of a witches' coven by that other, more famous Goya. He'd seen it at the Prado during his first and only trip to Spain a couple of years ago.

The taxi horn sounded again.

Diaz burst from the dimness of the Wonder Bar, roiled across the sidewalk to the rear passenger door of the white and green taxi, jerked it open and sprawled across the cigar ash singed seat.

"Palacio St. Jude," he ordered. Then realized the driver was a pimply 16 year old, with about as much knowledge of old San Miguel as the Premier of Uzbekistan.

"Hey, pops, you got a street address for that?"

Diaz gave it to him. Along with a ten-*peso* coin bearing the image of an eagle ripping apart a ruthless rattlesnake.

"This is police business."

"Whatever you say. You think there'll be a shoot out?"

"What are you talking about?"

"You know, like in that Robert Rodriguez movie *El Mariachi.*"

"You like movies?" asked Diaz.

"Sometimes."

"That's the way I feel about them too. I didn't think much of *El Mariachi*. Too unrealistic."

They squealed around a corner, the laws of physics tossing Diaz sideways.

"Hey! Slow down."

The driver glanced in his rearview mirror.

"You must like those highbrow cop movies like *L.A. Confidential*."

Diaz didn't feel like getting into a lengthy critical discussion about the cinema with a juvenile delinquent. He consulted his watch. They were going to be late. But this could be the big breakthrough in the investigation. Cy Vega could be Amanda Smallwood's killer. Stumbling across the sculpture in the shop window was like being dealt a one-eyed Jack. But don't get your hopes up, Diaz told himself. Leads, like life, had a way of fizzling out like an uncorked bottle of champagne the morning after.

They drove up the final, precipitous blocks to a T-intersection above which squatted *Palacio St. Jude*. From that locus, the ancient multi-storied structure had an unblemished view of San Miguel, the placid *Laja Rio* and the wide valleys spread out below. Across the street from the main entrance to the *palacio*, Felicia and an obviously gay person in a body sculpting leather jacket sat at a rickety-looking café table outside a snack bar. It was the only table.

"Okay. This is good," Diaz said to the driver, who came down hard on the brakes, further adjusting the geography of Diaz's organs.

"You want me to wait?"

"As a driver, you're full of shit," said Diaz. He said this after he was out of the cab, standing with his hand on the door handle, about to slam it closed. After the taxi pulled away, Diaz ambled across the street and stood looking down at Felicia and the delicate young man. They looked up at him. The young man was drinking a sugary Coca Cola. Felicia a *Coca Light*.

"Well," said Diaz. "I see we're having a little down time."

"Actually, it's lunchtime," said Felicia. "They're preparing three orders of *tacos carnitos adobo*." She motioned toward Syd: "This is Syd. Syd, Inspector Diaz."

"You don't look too good, Syd. Maybe you should start taking a vitamin supplement."

"Syd has an early morning drinking issue," Felicia explained.

At that moment the snack bar's *mestiza* owner and star chef walked barefoot to the table carrying a tray of sizzling *tacos*, *pico de gallo* and fire-roasted tomato *salsa*. Diaz suddenly realized he was starving.

He sat on the steps and, leaning forward, wolfed down three fully loaded *tacos*, excess *salsa* and *pico de gallo* dribbling to the pavement. Felicia ate more cautiously but managed to put away three *tacos* herself. Syd, looking nauseous, sipped his Coke and avoided eye contact with the food.

"I feel like shit," he said. "Are you sure I need to be here?"

In response Diaz stood up, brushed off the front of his trousers, and said with vehemence: "So what the fuck are we waiting for!?"

While Felicia wiped her fingers with a fresh *serviette* and Syd, caught off guard by Diaz's aggressive tone, sprayed Coke from nose and mouth, Diaz glanced down to make sure his zipper was closed. Felicia leaned over and bounced her open palm up and down on Syd's back. She did this several times, pushing Syd's face closer and closer to the tin-covered table top with its bright Corona beer logos.

"Easy there, citizen."

In the next instant she twisted his ear painfully. Part of her new tough cop persona.

"Ow!" Syd pulled away from her pincers and rubbed his ear. Diaz put some money on the table and together the three of them crossed the street and confronted *Palacio St. Jude*. Felicia rang the bell.

A dark-hued Indian woman in a magenta blouse opened the person-sized door inset in the wide wooden gates of the villa's entrance.

"Police business," said Diaz, holding up his badge. "We're here to see Cy Munoz Vega."

"No can disturb *senor* Vega."

"Of course we can. I'm Inspector Diaz of the *Policia Judiciales*. This is my associate Corporal Goya." He didn't bother to introduce Syd. Fuck Syd.

When the Indian tried to close the door in their faces, Diaz pushed forcefully through, knocking the woman on her ass, tumbling over like a planter of bougainvillea.

They stood in a courtyard that was more than 250 years old. The villa loomed on three sides, made of stucco over adobe brinks, decorative stonework and marble stairs. A moss-covered baroque fountain dominated the courtyard, where a quartet of putti pissed streams of water into the fountain's pool. Above them a conquistador clutched provocatively at a scantily clad Aztec princess. In the sea green depths of the fountain's pool, fat goldfish swaggered.

Felicia helped the servant to her feet.

"Take us to *senor* Vega *pronto*," she urged.

They followed the domestic, her face set in a gloomy scowl, up three wide steps and into a living room done in early-*caballero*: horsehair covered furniture, zebra-striped cowhide rugs, elaborate wrought iron floor lamps. A luminous 19th Century tropical landscape painting hung above the deep-set fireplace. Diaz thought it looked like a Frederic Church. Could it possibly be an original?

Beyond was a shadowy dining room and to the left a small chapel, its doors open wide to reveal a primitive crucified Christ, hand-painted in cerulean blue, blood red and gold leaf as shiny as the eye of God. A half dozen candles flickered in front of the godhead. A small plate of food as an offering sat to one side. Best to cover all the bases.

The unhappy servant led them up a staircase, its marble steps grooved by endless repetitions. At the top landing, she knocked hesitantly on a pair of ancient doors studded with ironwork.

"Come in, goddamn it! Come in. Come in."

Diaz pushed open the doors to a huge loft partially open to the sky.

Two-thirds of the way across the barn-like space, a giant figure in rustic tweeds rose from behind a flimsy and ornate desk, a hand-painted piece of French froufrou perhaps as old as the villa itself. In one fist he fumbled a heavy, burl-handled cane. A ragged beard tried unsuccessfully to camouflage a sallow, unhealthy complexion. Flint eyes stared out from deep *barrancas* of bone and flesh. A tragic mouth boomed in deep bass:

"What assholes are these come to plague me at this critical hour?"

"Excuse us, " said Diaz.

"That's *senor* Vega," Syd interjected.

"You find me at an epiphanic moment, as I am about to read the entrails. I must ask you to leave before your foreign vibes fuck up the interpretive essence."

Vega came forward blocking their view of the desk, but not before Diaz observed a large dead-appearing pigeon lying on its side on a layer of newspaper spread across the desktop. Bloody viscera leaked from a ragged tear in the bird's belly. Was this an activity forbidden under the criminal code? wondered Diaz.

He and Vega danced around each other, feigning left, then right, until Diaz finally scooted past Vega and darted forward to a conversation pit in the open-air portion of the room. Wrought-iron lounge chairs with floral-patterned pillows formed a quadrangle surrounding a low table. Diaz sat in one of the chairs, from whence he looked up at the towering figure.

"*Senor* Vega, I presume."

Vega wiped his vast mitt of a hand across his face as if he couldn't believe this was happening. Hoping that, if he closed his eyes, turned around three times, spat into the wind and drank the urine of a rare upland toad, everything would return to the unsullied dharmic state that had existed before the arrival of these asshole interlopers.

"We're investigating a murder," Diaz continued. "The trail led here."

"Murder. Yes, of course you are. The great legacy of the 20th Century: murder by the millions. Ethnic cleansing." Vega turned and looked at the maid or cook or whatever she was. "Paloma. You may go back to work. This is not a problem."

Paloma smiled bitterly, turned and walked away.

"And please bring us coffee," Vega called after her. His eyes rolled from Diaz to Syd to Felicia. They stayed on Felicia. "Coffee for four."

Felicia stared him down.

"I'll have a *Coca Light*," she said.

"Bravo!"

"*Senor* Vega," said Diaz, "I understand that you are an artist? A sculptor to be specific?"

"I am a god, Inspector. I was an artist in a former life."

"Of course you are," Diaz replied mildly. The man was insane!

"Syd here sells your stuff, doesn't he?" asked Felicia, nodding at the mute, still standing figure of Syd. "Created by your former self, I mean."

"For pocket money. Sometimes my monthly disability check doesn't quite cover my per diem expenses."

Well, you could always sell the Church painting for a few million dollars, thought Diaz. Then again, maybe it was just a good copy.

"And you used Amanda Smallwood as a model?" continued Felicia.

"I always use the most robust females available. But I never remember names."

"She's the one in the middle of your piece in Syd's window."

"Oh, that one." Vega's eyes grew large with some perhaps prurient recollection.

"She was murdered last Thursday."

"I read the papers."

Just then Paloma arrived with a tray cluttered by three steaming *cafes con leches* and a can of *Coca Zero* with a straw. "No *Coca Light*," she said apologetically. Setting the tray on the coffee table, she faded away again.

"And where were you last Thursday, *senor* Vega?" Diaz asked.

"Obviously I was here."

"Working on a new sculpture involving the deceased woman?"

"Why not."

Diaz was on the edge of his seat. He fiddled with his coffee cup but didn't pick it up.

"Is it okay if I leave now?" Syd asked. He was the only one still standing.

Felicia impaled him with her gaze. He took a seat and began spooning sugar into one of the coffees. Diaz continued:

"Amanda Smallwood was modeling for you last Thursday night, wasn't she?" asked Diaz.

"I believe it was afternoon. My studio looks west and the light is magical on winter afternoons."

"So she wasn't here when you killed her?"

"What?"

"I mean later that evening when you killed her, you did it someplace else. Not at your studio."

"She left at five. Said she had an appointment. And I was just getting the left nipple down too." Vega, holding his arms dramatically aloft, looked up at the sky where a jet fighter painted a trail of white tracer clouds. "Now there was a beautiful woman, a creature of Greek mythology."

"Is that why you killed her?"

"Because she was beautiful? What a sick mind you have, Inspector. She was a gift from the gods."

"Maybe it was just an accident that you broke her neck."

"Please don't put words in my mouth. I told you she left at five. Paloma will confirm my recollection."

"I'm sure she will."

At that moment a scream shredded the afternoon.

Vega was instantly on his feet.

Another scream and he was running, a thundering water buffalo.

Syd dove for the floor. Felicia placed her hand on top of her holstered Glock and looked to Diaz for direction. Diaz stood possessed by quizzicality, not prepared to dash off willy-nilly in Vega's wake. Caution in the face of unknown adversity had kept him alive during more than twenty years of police work.

Like the running back on a draw play, Vega swerved around furniture, pots of orange and purple bougainvillea, and a wildly blooming Christmas cactus and bounded up a set of narrow, railingless stairs leading to the third and smallest floor of *Palacio St. Jude*.

Diaz turned to Felicia.

"What's up there?" he barked.

"Not a clue," she said, shrugging her shoulders. "Fuck pad maybe?"

Coarseness in a woman is a definite turn-on, thought Diaz.

Two gunshots rang out from the floor above. A torrent of sound swept down the stairway up which Vega had disappeared seconds before. Diaz drew his weapon and hunkered down behind the overstuffed chairs. Felicia followed suit.

Then came the thud of something heavy (like a body) falling on the room above.

"Shit!" ejaculated Diaz.

As he started up the stairs, Paloma staggered into view at the top of the stairwell. Her torn blouse revealed a thin, brown, not-unattractive shoulder and shaved armpit. Her eyes were glazed, exuding the drugged quality of a captive Indian princess atop an Aztec temple waiting for her heart to be ripped from her chest with an obsidian knife. Or the blank expression of someone going into shock.

"*Senor* Vega is shot!" she blurted.

Diving forward from the top step, Diaz tackled the dazed and staggering Paloma, catapulting her to the floor and out of harm's way. He rolled free of her, came up on his stomach and elbows, weapon extended at arm's length.

From behind him a *huarache*-clad foot swept down, striking the 9mm from his grasp, sending it skittering across the tile floor. The swinging steel barrel of a large caliber revolver just missed crushing the side of Diaz's head.

Catching the shadow of movement above, Felicia fired a shot, throwing the assailant into a panic. Instead of the gun barrel, the side of one of the *pistolero's* humble *huaraches* caught the edge of Diaz's chin, even as the intruder turned and bolted for the opposite side of the room.

Diaz rolled sideways, his head buzzing, waves of black spiders assaulting his vision. After a five count, he eased himself onto hands and knees, shaking his head like a dog to clear out the pain. Son of a bitch was his only thought. He had recognized his attacker as Emile Zato.

While Diaz recovered his equilibrium, the escaping felon sprinted across the studio space toward a beehive kiln constructed at the far end of the room. Jamming his ancient Colt .45 into the belt of his grease-smeared trousers, he leaped onto the balustrade to one side of the kiln. A meter below the studio railing, a crumbling rampart from the adjacent building arched over a dank courtyard to connect with the outside wall of *Palacio St. Jude*. Dracula-like, Zato swung over the rail and without hesitation dropped to this connecting wall. Loose brickwork sloughed away, crashing to the ground two floors below. The triggerman wobbled on loose debris, hands out flung for balance. His vile, street-stained sheepskin coat spread open to either side like hellish batwings.

Felicia reached the top of the stairs in time to see the fleeing assailant make his vampire leap from the balustrade. Her eyes scanned the room. The studio space was crowded with worktables, ceramic molds, tools, bags of clay, paint and brushes, partially covered by a corrugated iron roof. Near the kiln, a rack held carefully stacked lengths of hardwood for the firings. Cy Vega lay sprawled in the midst of all this, surrounded by the inevitable pool of blood, his face a roadmap of death.

With a groan Diaz struggled to his feet and staggered toward the precipice from which the street scum had disappeared into thin air.

Behind him Felicia made an executive decision and, without a word, turned and bounded back down the stairs two steps at a time. She descended the second set of stairs to the living room at an even faster pace, making a flying leap from a halfway point. Skating across the slick tiled floor, she recovered her balance, raced into the villa's courtyard.

Above and to the right she saw the wall from the neighboring structure where it arched like a flying buttress before connecting to an outside wall of the *palacio*. The killer was making his teetering way across the top of that archway. Felicia raised her weapon and took aim. But the target suddenly dropped from view, making his escape into the intricacies of the adjoining building. Diaz's face appeared high above, gazing forlornly over the stone railing at the long, potentially fatal drop.

Re-holstering her pistol, Felicia burst through the street entrance of *Palacio St. Jude* and stood surveying the front elevations of the buildings along the block. The building next to the villa was an old warehouse or other industrial structure, abandoned and boarded up. A narrow alley cut behind it.

She sprinted to the corner and, holding her weapon at chest height, glanced around the angle of the wall and up the rank, intestinal passageway. It curved upwards in a sharp incline to a series of primitive steps. These in turn climbed precipitously to a rectangle of sky between high blank walls. The quarry was nowhere in sight.

Had he already emerged and sped up those steps to safety? Or was he still making his way through the gloomy interior of the warehouse?

Felicia edged around the corner and moved cautiously up the slope of the alley, her body brushing the wall. Her foot struck something soft and yielding. A sundered rat confronted her, its jaw clenched in rigor mortis, its single visible eye hazy with death.

Movement made her jerk her eyes upward. Two meters above the alley pavement the dark figure of the fugitive flickered into view in the mouth of an arched opening in the building's veneer. He hovered on the lip, surveying the alley to the left and right.

Felicia froze, hugged the wall like a lover.

The fugitive leaped outward, his body uncoiling like a video game figure, arms raised for balance, sheepskin coat spread wide. He landed with the heavy thump of body weight compelled by gravity.

Felicia stepped away from the wall, her weapon held tautly forward.

"Freeze, motherfucker!"

The *pistolero* turned, sought to raise his arm against the counterweight of his heavy revolver.

Too late. Too slow.

Felicia's Glock barked twice, its greedy bullets easily finding their mark. The scumbag drifter spun backwards, dead. She stood looking down at him, his face a horrific mask of greed, hate, lust and lunacy. Jaw clasped in a pit-bull snarl, eyes empty of light.

Felicia frisked the cadaver, but found nothing but a handful of .45 shells, some unidentifiable pills and a crumpled pornographic picture. She hefted the assassin's pistol from where it lay like an afterthought amid the detritus covering the alley's pavement, then turned and walked back the way she had come.

• • •

Inside *Palacio St. Jude*, chaos chomped at the bit. A medic was applying salve to Paloma's chin where it had struck the tile floor after Diaz tackled her. A white sheet sailed through the air and settled over the earthly remains of Cy Munoz Vega. The twin shots of the assassin had damaged his organs beyond repair. Diaz sat erect in a straight-backed chair surveying the scene with a pissed off expression. Sergeant Armando Ruiz had arrived and was nosing around in the periphery. No doubt looking for something of value he could discretely rip off, thought Diaz.

A second medic kept fussing over Diaz. He kept waving her away.

"Not now. I'm thinking."

Diaz stared at the sheet-covered hillock that had been C.V. Maybe we should read your entrails, he thought.

From the stairway Felicia walked toward him, drinking from the can of *Coca Zero*.

"The gangbanger is toast," she said. "Are you okay, Hector?"

"Do I look okay? Do I sound okay? The same bastard tried to kill me the other night at the cemetery. It has all the earmarks of a conspiracy."

"What do you mean?"

"Here we are very likely on the verge of closing in on Amanda Smallwood's killer, when a criminal I sent to prison years ago assassinates a major suspect before he can confess or name names."

"Sounds like a way out theory to me," said Felicia. "Besides, Vega said he had an alibi."

Diaz frowned.

"You need to think outside the box, Goya."

"Yes, sir."

"By the way, what's happened to Vega's smutty statuette?"

"You're not going to believe this, Hector…"

Felicia's cheeks had flushed the bright red of a perfect Romano tomato.

• • •

By four p.m. Diaz knew the following:

1. The driver of the car Bass Smallwood had hired outside his hotel on Sunday morning was not sitting in Diaz's office by lunchtime. Nor was he likely to appear there anytime soon. Further interrogation of the night clerk revealed that the driver, a nameless Mexican everyman, had slipped him 500 *pesos* and whispered Bass's name. The description of the car hadn't changed: a dark-colored nondescript American sedan. License plate unknown.

2. Unless he'd used a forged passport, in the preceding 48 hours Bass Smallwood hadn't boarded a plane at Guanajuato International for Dallas, Miami, Mexico City, Tegucigalpa or anywhere else.

3. There was still no answer at Bass's home phone. The answering machine at the Smallwood Gallery ran out of recording space at two p.m. No one called back. Bass had disappeared off the face of the planet.

4. Despite Diaz's efforts at thinking outside the box, the Amanda Smallwood investigation was headed for the shitter.

At five minutes after six Diaz tossed an overnight bag into the back seat of the backup dark blue unmarked police sedan and climbed into the front passenger seat. Felicia's hands rested assuredly on the steering wheel. She waited until Diaz clipped his seatbelt closed then eased the car into gear and pressed vehemently on the accelerator. The car tore down *Calle Canal*, moved with alacrity through a maze of back streets and jolted over a speed bump onto the open road to Guanajuato.

Diaz leaned his head back and shut his eyes. In a moment he was asleep.

Forty-nine minutes and seventeen seconds later Felicia parked the car at Guanajuato International Airport. They locked their weapons in the trunk. The last flight to Dallas left at 8:05 p.m. Since he was hungry, Diaz partook of two greasy beef tacos at a fast-food stand in the upstairs departure lounge. Felicia nursed a light beer and wondered about her relationship with Diaz, professional and otherwise.

Chapter 26

It was midnight by the time Diaz and Felicia cleared customs and immigration at D/FW Airport, picked up the rental car and drove the two miles to the Double Suites Inn. Lightning lashed the cloud-banked horizon. A chill wind rippled the dry prairie grass of winter.

"Two rooms," said Diaz to the flamboyantly made-up receptionist. No doubt the clerk had tarried too long in some transvestite nightclub, leaving no time to apply cold cream to wipe away his makeup. He clicked the computer mouse repeatedly, searching through the room database. "No need for them to be together," added Diaz.

The clerk cocked a mulberry-colored eyebrow. He understood the separate rooms gambit.

"I have two rooms on the third floor, directly across from each other."

"Fine." Diaz handed over his credit card. The clerk took it between thumb and forefinger and swiped it through the digital reader. His eyes looked with appraisement past Diaz's shoulder. Felicia, behind Diaz, was falling asleep on her feet, oblivious to the fact that she had been adjudged a working girl of exceptional quality.

Twenty minutes later Diaz lay naked on cool sheets, a burning cigarette between his lips. He wondered if Felicia was also lying awake in the darkness of the room across the hall, alone and perhaps a little destitute.

In fact, Felicia was sound asleep, left hand tucked under her chin, one foot hanging outside the covers. The fingers of her right hand were still damp and redolent from an indelicate romp moments before through the fragrant fissure of her vulva.

Diaz remained awake, the characters of the last few days bounding back and forth in his mind until their identities became confused, their features transposed one to the other, like a child's game. When the rodent-colored light of predawn seeped into the room, he showered, shaved and dressed. His body looked emaciated. He needed to eat more and smoke less. The starched collar of a fresh white shirt bit into the flesh of his neck. He felt weary.

In the lobby he sat reading the papers and drinking weak coffee until Felicia appeared. Her complexion was fresh and unadorned with make-up except the tropical colored lipstick. Her manner was upbeat. They studied a roadmap of Dallas, plotting their course from the Double Suites to Smallwood's gallery on Elm Street. Felicia sipped orange juice from a Styrofoam cup. Dressed in a pearl gray pantsuit and off-white, scoop necked blouse, she looked like a corporate fashion maven.

Her racecar driving skills were no match for the gridlock of the Dallas rush hour. With a sigh she edged the rental car forward meter by meter until they found an exit from the expressway. On the side streets they made better time. At last she turned onto Elm and pulled to the curb in front of a line of single story, brick and glass storefronts. Above one of them a white sign with black lettering read: Smallwood Gallery. Felicia glanced at Diaz, who was looking wild-eyed from lack of sleep.

"What do you think we're going to find?"

"Hopefully Bass Smallwood."

"But there's no record of him flying back to Dallas."

A nerve twitched in Diaz's cheek.

From the car they walked to the gallery front. Horizontal blinds were drawn tightly closed across the plate glass window. The door was locked. The other stores appeared to be empty or also closed. No one was about.

Diaz cut up an alley. Behind the row of stores, they came into a sinister, weed-infested vacant area. Amid brambles a rusting metal barrel squatted like a post-industrial Buddha. Broken glass like piranha teeth glinted in the sunlight.

Metal fire doors stared blankly from a graffiti-tagged brick wall. One door stood ajar.

"That one's to the gallery," said Diaz. By rote, his hand went under his left arm, reaching for the Glock. Which wasn't there.

At the half open door Diaz peered into a dusky corridor ending in blackness. He felt Felicia's hand grip his elbow.

"Hello?" he called.

No reply, not even an echo, came from inside. He cursed silently, then entered the hallway, feeling along the wall for a light switch. A half-visible doorway opened to the right. He flicked on the light. A toilet and washbowl.

The next doorway opened to an office. Gunmetal gray filing cabinets. A desk. Amid a sea of papers floated a dirty coffee mug, a photo of Bass and Amanda in a tarnished frame, a telephone and an answering machine on which a tiny red light blinked like a feeble beacon. The sole wall decoration was a calendar. Ms. February, a full-breasted woman in black lace panties, sprawled like a deer carcass across the hood of a Dodge Viper.

At the end of the hallway, another on/off switch. A burst of light illuminated the gallery. A scene of chaos. Paintings strewn helter-skelter across the floor, broken and torn. Canvases ripped away from their underlying wooden skeletons. Wooden frames shattered into sharp-edged fragments.

"Holy shit!" said Felicia.

"You can say that again," said Diaz.

He scanned the room for bodies. None was apparent. Stepping into the oblong, white space, his eyes flitted here and there over the ruined artwork. He crouched down; his hand touched a twisted canvas showing a Mexican peasant leading a burro across a landscape of cactus and flowering mesquite.

The signature, unreadable except for the initial G, was identical to the one on the Gregorovich letter Fran Kovacs had given him. The style and clichéd subject of the painting were similar to the stack of paintings Diaz had found in Gregorovich's studio.

Amanda Smallwood, artist's provocateur and wayward daughter. Gregory Gregorovich, penurious painter and fornicator. Bass Smallwood, gallery owner and failed husband. An odd assortment of travelers thrown together in the same waiting room.

And more and more it was looking as though Amanda wasn't the only one that had checked out from among the living.

Diaz turned the damaged painting over. It had been ripped free of its rectangular wooden stretchers. These were unusually thick, and each section had been split apart with a knife or other sharp instrument to reveal empty hollow interiors.

It didn't take a genius to imagine what might have resided there.

Without warning ice-cold metal touched Diaz's skull just behind his ear. A chill washed like a riptide up Diaz's spin. Was this the end?

"Don't…fucking…breathe," a voice said. Each word sank like a dead weight into Diaz's brain. "Lie face down on the floor, hands on top of your head."

When Diaz obliged, a knee wrenched brutally into his back. His hands were jerked behind him and the hard edges of handcuffs lashed into his wrists. Where the hell was Felicia?

"I'm a police officer," said Diaz.

"Right." The voice growled. "And I'm Dirty Harry."

A hand leveraged Diaz to his knees. A bull-necked man in a cheap ill-fitting navy blazer came into view. A fat-knuckled hand leveled a large revolver in Diaz's face. As the initial squall of adrenalin subsided, the man's face came into focus. A wide, deeply creased forehead. Pale blue eyes as opaque and mysterious as quartz crystals. Cheeks superficially denuded of whiskers. An expensive set of dentures clenched in a rictal snarl.

"OK, pal. You've had your fun tearin' this place up. Now who the fuck are you?"

"I told you. I'm a police officer. From San Miguel de Allende in Mexico. I flew up to Dallas last night. We're looking into the disappearance of Bass Smallwood, the gallery owner." After a pause: "And you are?"

"Detective Bruccoli, Dallas Police."

Diaz guessed late fifties, in a holding pattern for a full pension.

The muffled swoosh of a flushed toilet interrupted their exchange. A door squeaked open. Fearful that Felicia might be shot accidentally, Diaz spoke up:

"That would be the other officer traveling with me."

"Don't make a sound," hissed Bruccoli.

He scooted up against the rear wall of the gallery, next to the opening of the passageway leading to the back office and the shitter. Felicia walked back into the gallery, then stopped short at the sight of Diaz on his knees. A sudden religious epiphany? His eyes blinked wildly. If this was intended as a warning, it came too late.

Bruccoli's hand clenched deep into Felicia's shoulder. He twisted her around and bounced her against the wall. Revolver barrel resting against her forehead, his other hand patted her down, running inside the lapels of her suit, across breasts and under armpits, then down each side to her waist. A caress to the crotch, a squeeze to each buttock, before continuing down pant legs to ankle boots. During this episode, Bruccoli glanced repeatedly over his shoulder to be sure Diaz remained in his penitent's pose.

Satisfied that Felicia was unarmed, Bruccoli stepped back, holding a leather card case and her passport, which he had taken from a jacket pocket. The gun barrel pressing against Felicia's forehead had left an angry red mark. Her eyes flashed on and off with the message: Burn in Hell!

"Let me guess. You're also a police officer from Mexico?"

Unspeaking, Felicia watched him, looking for an opening.

Bruccoli glanced at her passport; then opened the card case. On top was Felicia's *Judiciales* photo ID. Bruccoli's lips twisted with indecision. Then he pulled Diaz to a standing position and found his police identity card in his wallet.

The tension in the room subsided. Bruccoli holstered his weapon, spun Diaz around and unlocked the handcuffs. Felicia still looked like she was ready to knee Bruccoli in the jewels. Or break each finger of the hand that had groped her.

"Okay, I'll take the chance you really are Mexican cops. But you'd better have a damn good explanation for being here."

Bruccoli stood at a cautious distance, weapon held at his side.

In his impeccable English Diaz told Bruccoli about Amanda's murder, Bass Smallwood's sad arrival in San Miguel and his complete disappearance.

"Something urged me to come to Dallas," said Diaz. "We drove over to the gallery this morning from our hotel by the airport. The rear door was open. We walked in and found this."

"Obviously someone has a hard-on for modern art."

Diaz picked up the shattered Gregorovich painting and showed Bruccoli where the frame had been hollowed out.

"I think your crime lab people will be interested in what was hidden inside. My guess is heroin."

"So that's what this mess is about. Someone looking for a shipment of Mexican brown?"

Diaz raised an eyebrow.

"Well, damn! I'm right in the middle of breakfast when the gallery's assistant manager calls my cell. She knows me because I show up at openings for a free drink or two. She's in a panic; says there's been a break-in. Now you're telling me the gallery's part of some international drug cartel network?"

"Something like that," said Diaz. "I don't know anything for sure. It was just an idea I had. About the heroin, I mean."

"What about Bass Smallwood?"

"I hoped we'd find him here. But I didn't really think it was likely. I'm very worried about *senor* Smallwood's soul."

Chapter 27

Jane Ryder, *au naturel*, felt the rough edges of the pillow-less rattan chaise bite into her flesh. The rest of the tacky furniture in the living room portion of their suite at The Pines was piled in a corner. Across the room, Gregory Gregorovich, dressed in sagging boxers, feverishly applied paint to canvas. When she tried to shift her body away from the discomfort, Gregorovich called out:

"Don't move."

Lowering her buttocks once more against the harsh, spiny surface of the rough-hewn rattan lounger, she had a brief, stomach-churning revelation she was being used. But so what. She was in love. Totally smitten, and lecherous with hope.

The scattered newspaper pages at her feet bore Monday's date. But for Jane time was stationary. Or as though somehow she had side-stepped time's domain entirely.

For the last two and a half days she and Gregorovich had been holed up at The Pines balling like randy Rumanian rabbits with no recollection of yesterday or concept of tomorrow. Gregorovich's sexual predilections turned out to be rather dull and pedestrian. It was up to Jane to suggest variations and extravaganzas on a theme. She initiated a doctor nurse role playing session that sent them both into copulatory hysterics. And her impersonation of Teddy Roosevelt with riding crop ascending San Juan Hill spurred Gregorovich to rarified heights of raunchiness.

Gregorovich's bankruptcy, except for a seemingly endless supply of jizz, meant Jane paid for their room and board. She kept expecting to wake up and find Gregorovich had absconded with her cash and credit cards. But always he was there, ready for another ferocious fuck session, their ancient spring mattress squeaking like an old Chrysler La Baron riding pell-mell down the yellow brick road.

Now at mid-morning on Monday, Gregorovich, destitute, vision-driven artist and copious copulator, stood back to contemplate the emerging image of Jane Ryder on the rectangle of canvas propped upright against a chair back. At his feet sprawled two cheap sports bags and an old typewriter that he'd liberated from his studio on a midnight raid. One of the nylon bags was unzipped, spewing brushes and tubes of paint across the floor like the guts of a sacrificial goat. Jane felt a sudden desire to examine those entrails, to see what troubles they foretold. After all, she thought, it was just a matter of time before their madcap affair crashed and burned.

Gregorovich glanced at his cheesy digital wristwatch.

"Shit. I'm late for my meeting with Dillinger. Need to find out how the show went. How many of my paintings were sold."

Gregorovich clambered into a pair of paint-spattered jeans. Rummaging in the other sports bag, he found a clean T-shirt and slipped it on. Jane decided it was safe to eject herself from the painful pincers and spiky edges of the downtrodden rattan settee. As she stood, Gregorovich swooped down upon her, covering her nakedness with kisses.

"I'll be back as soon as I can."

Then he was gone.

Left to her own devices for the first time in two and a half days, Jane fidgeted and lolled. Read the newspaper; then crumpled it and the remains of their takeout lunch into the wastebasket. The bed creaked when she flounced onto it. Four walls stared back at her.

Slipping into the yellow sundress she had bought on Saturday on the way to the *fiesta*, she left the suite, her goal to buy a cheap thriller to while away the time. The empty hallway echoed with her ruminations and doubts.

Soon she was adrift in the narrow streets of San Miguel's *el centro*, her original purpose forgotten. In front of a whitewashed church she came upon three Indian women knitting away the afternoon on a stone bench. High on something, two teenagers lay in a doorway laughing at the world. A dead pigeon decomposed in the gutter.

Each of these encounters reinforced Jane's sense of impending disaster.

God knows my life's as dull as dishwater, she thought. But did humping a complete stranger provide a *raison d'etre*? More likely she would end up with some incurable sexual disease.

Gnawing on these thoughts, Jane found herself back at The Pines. Gregorovich hadn't returned, but the door to the room was unlocked. Nothing seemed to be missing. The bed was made and fresh towels hung in the bathroom. The maid must have forgotten to lock the door.

Sitting on the floor sipping tequila from the bottle, she stared at Gregorovich's painting of her in all her weedy, tarnished, naked glory. What would old Niles say if he saw the painting? Probably break into that snorting, cynical laugh of his.

Night descended. And with it gloom and loneliness and despair. What the hell had become of her Russian lover? she wondered. What was he up to? Smoking quantities of debilitating pot with his artist pals? Or more likely groping another pair of boobs in some down at the heels *bodega*?

Who was Gregory Gregorovich? And what secrets did he have?

A bare bulb burning in a shadeless ceiling fixture cast its harsh yellow light on Gregory's two sports bags slumped in the corner. Jane eyed them with sudden curiosity.

poor fran. it's true I never really loved her. but I still owe her big time. she took me in when i was in desperate straits. saved me from the streets.

when i first hear them whispering her name, i think they're joking.

then they start leaving me notes. in my sock drawer. scrunched up in the toe of a shoe. scrawled in chalk on an adobe wall. fran. fran. fran. i throw the pieces of paper away, wash off the chalk marks. but their whispering grows louder and louder, rising to a crescendo.

i offer others. a slut i met at a party. a lonely blonde past her prime.

no, they say. fran's the one we want.

in the end i have no choice. they follow me everywhere, demanding i get on with it. their words echo inside my head. i can't sleep. or hear myself think.

in the end i do what they demand.

Chapter 28

In due course a forensics team from the Dallas PD arrived at the Smallwood Gallery and confirmed Diaz's surmise. The hollowed out canvas stretchers had contained extremely pure Mexican skag.

The gallery's assistant manager, a petite woman with auburn hair, arrived and stood frozen in the doorway, gaping at the wreckage. Then she began to shake violently. A shot from a cognac bottle found in the back office had a restorative effect. She sat puffing aimlessly on a cigarette and talking nonstop in a Southern drawl Diaz found impossible to understand.

Felicia, bored, wandered about looking at the artwork strewn across the floor, occasionally moving a painting with her foot to get a better view.

All this took up a major chunk of time.

Afterwards Bruccoli insisted on taking them for a late lunch at a revolving restaurant high above the city atop a cement column like a water tower. From this eyrie ten or more real water towers could be counted in the distance. With drinks on an empty stomach, it was easy for Diaz to lose count. The view was spectacular! Though the circular motion of the restaurant made him slightly queasy.

After lunch they went for a tour of Dallas's police headquarters where they signed notarized affidavits describing the trail of murder and drugs that had led to Diaz's and Felicia's journey to Dallas. They shook hands with Bruccoli's boss, a tough-as-nails descendent of cotton pickers, and were introduced around to a clutch of other detectives. It wasn't every day the Dallas PD had a visiting Pooh Bah from Mexico.

At four Diaz, Felicia, Bruccoli and several of the detectives crowded up to the bar at The Sons of Herman Hall, a rough-hewn but friendly dive.

All these diversions conspired to ensure that Diaz and Felicia did not arrive back at D/FW International until barely an hour before the last flight to Guanajuato. Bass Smallwood was still unaccounted for. As night spread over the prairie like a magician's cape, they sat in an airport bar waiting for their flight to be called.

"Amanda knew there was heroin in those frames, didn't she?" asked Felicia.

"Probably."

"And that's why she was killed."

"Probably. But it doesn't explain why they ripped out her eyes."

"Maybe they wanted to send a message to someone. Maybe to us. Not to look too deep."

Diaz made no reply. Stonewalled, Felicia fell into a funk, glaring into the distance and sipping her diet Coke. Her lips moved in a silent monologue.

Diaz drank Kentucky sour mash bourbon for the two-hour flight. After all, he was on an expense account. Next to him Felicia snored delicately. He glanced over at her. He was determined to keep their relationship that of father/daughter, though there was no blood tie between them.

In the deserted Guanajuato airport their footsteps echoed on the terrazzo floor. The parking lot was ill lit. A sense of foreboding loomed.

Once they were out of the industrial zone near the airport, it was pitch dark except for the cone of light from the car's high beams. Felicia drove. A smear of pinpoint suns across the bowl of night, each a hundred thousand light years away, offered no solace. No one would ever cross those distances, survive the impossible coldness between the stars, thought Diaz. If no one were here, would there still be light?

Diaz nodded off.

The sudden swerving of the car tumbled him into the dashboard. He thought for an instant that he was drowning. A sharp pain ran up his arm to his shoulder, then to his brain. Fully awake, he braced his hands and feet against the erratic movement of the vehicle. They bounced off the road onto a dirt track that swept downhill like a streambed, each rut a gully. Felicia pumped the clutch wildly, jammed the gear stick into first, producing a snarling, metal-shredding scream.

The car swerved into a neck-wrenching spin, stones and dust flying in wild-assed abandon. One of the tires blew.

Despite Felicia's best efforts, the car careened out of control, finally coming to rest in a tangle of brush and an old wire fence. Diaz's nose struck the front window glass with a numbing jolt. He tasted blood.

Felicia removed the ignition key and sat still, taking in deep gulps of air.

"There was a truck on the road. It pulled out right in front of me. I had nowhere to go."

"We're alive, aren't we? You did great. But we need to get out of the car before they come down from the road."

"What do you mean?"

"It's an ambush."

Needles of fear pierced her eyes.

"Pop the trunk," he ordered. "And turn off the lights."

Without warning a burst of automatic rifle fire erupted, splintering the headlights and causing Diaz and Felicia to exit precipitously from the car into the blackness of a desert night. Above them the trunk lid rose up like the top of Dracula's coffin.

As Diaz's hand reached in to retrieve his and Felicia's weapons, a sharp, popping sound awoke the night. Diaz, gripping both Glocks, dropped to the dirt behind the car, shielding his eyes as the blinding phosphorescent light of a flare exploded in the heavens. Liberated by the ambient light, the automatic weapon fire resumed its raucous rat-a-tat-tatting, savaging the fenders and front hood of the police car. The front window shattered into a zillion shards.

The fusillade originated not from the road but from the stone ruin of a defunct *hacienda* that clung to the hillside just ahead. The firing from the ruin was erratic, wildly psychotic. Not the cool precision of a military-trained assassin. Diaz suspected it was the murderous Indian he'd glimpsed behind the wheel of the Dodge

Ram as it charged like a castrated bull down *Calle Terrapien* two days before, trying to send Diaz and Felicia to an early grave.

Pissed, Diaz discharged several shots in the direction of the ruins.

"Felicia," he said, "I'm going after the shooter. Give me some covering fire. And watch my back; others may still be coming down from the road."

Felicia took her weapon and disappeared into looming mesquite shadows on one side of the car. On the opposite side Diaz scuttled into the thorny undergrowth, the rock-hard laterite soil shredding the knees of his trousers.

Seconds later Felicia's Glock flashed from the cover of a giant clump of prickly pear. The Kalashnikov responded tenfold. Under cover of its din, Diaz scrambled forward, moving like a snake.

The automatic fire came from the rectangle of a window in the facing wall of the ruin. A second flare exploded aloft but the interior space beyond the outline of the window remained pitch black.

From five meters away, Diaz squeezed off a volley of shots into that inky pit. It was like shooting into nothingness, a hole in the universe. This only drew the assassin's attention to him. A hail of bullets shredded the thicket of *cholla* cactus and mesquite screening Diaz from view. Too young to die, he hugged the earth like a lusty whore. One shaking hand slipped inside his shirt and touched the golden image of the wind god *Ehecatl* suspended there.

The second flare reached the ground and died, but a cold light still hung over the scene. A half-moon had risen with majestic silence.

Abruptly small arms fire clattered into life behind Diaz, somewhere off to his right. From his vantage point in the dirt, Diaz could see nothing, only hear the back and forth of pistol shots between Felicia and the gangbanger creeping down from the highway. A sudden high-pitched cry of pain made Diaz's blood stand still.

Felicia was hit.

Diaz almost leaped to his feet. But common sense prevailed. The assassin, hunkered down in the stone foundation of the *hacienda*, would eviscerate Diaz before he was halfway to Felicia's position.

As Diaz again faced the hidden shooter, suddenly a monstrous shadow loomed above the ruins, mutating and effervescing into a giant glowing apparition as high as the giant steel pylons of a high voltage transmission line. In the silvery moonlight the appearance coalesced into a nightmare vision: the Aztec god *Ehecatl* risen from the bloody heart of Mexico's past. Reborn in all his primordial power! His bird head draped in feathers of unnamable colors! A vision of utter horror!

Diaz's heart pounded like some primal drumbeat. His eyes bugged out. His fingers grew as cold as icicles. The heebie-jeebies crawled under his skin like electrified ants.

Then the risen Aztec god moved! Its taloned arms reached into the black heart of the ruined building.

From the black depths of the abandoned *estancia*, the shooter screamed. Leaped through the rectangle of the window frame, from darkness into half-light as if passing through some futuristic time portal.

Diaz rose on his elbows, aimed his Glock at the killer bounding toward him and pulled the trigger. To no effect. The clip was empty.

The Indian came on in an insane rush, his eyes seared with the vision of *Ehecatl*. A knife appeared in his hand, the blade a dull mirror. As the knife descended, Diaz rolled sideways, one hand catching the attacker's ankle, pitching him into an out of control tumble.

Diaz was up and after him. Together they twisted and flailed like a pair of elemental spiders, each trying to devour the other.

Rolling in the dust, Diaz's hand touched and instinctually grasped the hard edge of an old iron fencepost lying abandoned. As the Indian drew back, retracting to propel the heel of his boot into Diaz's face, Diaz gripped the fence post in two hands and heaved it powerfully upward in an arc. At the top of the arc the blade-like edge of the ironwork sliced through the shell of the Indian's skull as if it were the soft pulp of a papaya. His brainpan breached beyond redemption, the Indian imploded and collapsed to the ground. A crushed arachnid, he twitched once or twice, then lay still.

Diaz struggled to his feet, his eyes riveted to the apparition of

Ehecatl. The image of the ancient god flickered like a defective neon sign, then blinked out of existence. Gone as instantly and inexplicably as it had first appeared.

A cosmic stillness descended. Nothing dared to move. The act of breathing was a sacrilege. Then somewhere in the distance an owl hooted three times. Or was it the call of *Ehecatl*?

Diaz broke the spell by reaching into his jacket pocket for a fresh ammunition clip. He snapped it into place.

Crouching, he pressed his fingers against the Indian's throat. *Nada.* Blood and liquefied brain matter oozed from the horrific gash torn by the iron post. The last trickle of psychotic energy seeped from the Indian's eyes. His life was kaput.

For good measure Diaz slammed his boot tip into the Indian's crotch. Motherfucker!

Then he remembered Felicia and the other attackers coming down from the road.

From that direction came the whine of a truck engine cranked to life, disturbing the night's bad dreams. The shared vision of *Ehecatl* must have sent the other assassins skittering like beetles back the way they had come, shitting their pants all the way.

Diaz found Felicia stretched on the ground to one side of the dirt track, her head braced against the trunk of a canyon oak. Her eyes registered spasms of pain.

"It's my arm."

Diaz knelt and using a pocketknife cut away the sleeve of her jacket and the blouse beneath. Blood was flowing, but not an arterial gusher. When he tied his handkerchief as a tourniquet, he felt the shattered bone beneath the skin.

"What was that…that thing in the sky?" asked Felicia.

"You mean the phantasma?"

"I guess."

"If I was a betting man, I'd say we just witnessed an intervention by the Aztec wind god *Ehecatl*. But I've never gambled in my life."

"So where does that leave us?"

"Nowhere."

The police car was ruined, undrivable, its radiator riddled with bullets, its headlights punched out and its windshield nonexistent. That made two vehicles wrecked in one week. And another departmental budget shot to hell, thought Diaz.

Behind the abandoned *estancia* Diaz found the dead Indian's ancient, rust-eaten VW Bug. The keys were in the ignition. A bottle of uppers lay on the back seat and a carefully maintained machete, its blade as razor sharp as a Samurai sword.

As Diaz helped Felicia into the front passenger seat, his hand pressed inadvertently against the yielding flesh of her breast held by its lacy packaging. The Bug's engine turned over on the first try. The tires were worn nearly treadless. Diaz popped the clutch and drove as fast as he dared toward home.

After 45 minutes in the emergency room, the lead doctor assured Diaz Felicia's wound was not life threatening. Told him to go home to bed.

Instead of sleep, long after midnight Diaz visited the whores near the bus station. A dark, thin woman he had slept with before and who knew his predilections offered up the promise of a languid blowjob and other intricacies of lust. They dickered over the price. When it was finally agreed, they walked to Diaz's apartment like old acquaintances. Her breath yielded odors of cumin, *habanero* chiles and cheap tequila.

Much later he dreamed of *Ehecatl* and woke up sweating with fear.

Chapter 29

First thing next morning Diaz stopped at *La Parroquia*, with its vast neo-gothic spires rising like giant stalagmites above the *jardin*, to offer a prayer to his grandfather. He eased soundlessly into a rear pew of the cathedral, after dipping his fingers in the font of holy water and making the obligatory sign of the cross. Women in black lace bent in prayer beneath the towering vaults. A single, camera-strung tourist wandered aimlessly, staring at the relics. Diaz knelt and intertwined his fingers as he had been taught in his youth.

Father in heaven. Protect the soul of my grandfather who is in thy company.

In the next moment, he found himself talking directly to his grandfather.

Grandfather. You taught me about ancient Mexico and her gods. But you never warned me they could come back to life. Or was last night only a hallucination? Ehecatl, or his apparition, appeared not only to me but also to my fellow officer and to my enemies. Does that make it more real? Frankly I was scared shit-less. Give me the wisdom and stoicism to accept this visitation without pissing my pants.

Then a few final words to the Deity.

Merciful God, protect thy supplicant from evil and the fear that freezes the human heart. Amen.

Feeling much better even though he was nerve frazzled and bone weary from lack of sleep and other causes, Diaz emerged into brilliant sunlight. A fruit vendor's cart was conveniently stationed at the bottom of the cathedral steps. Diaz stopped and bought a glass of fresh-squeezed guava juice.

Armando waited for Diaz at the front door of the *Judiciales* station, his face a mask of apprehension. Diaz immediately jumped to the conclusion that Felicia's condition must have deteriorated during the night.

"No, no. Nothing's happened to Felicia," said Armando. "She's fine. When I stopped at the hospital on the way in, she was sitting up in bed eating a plate of *huevos y frijoles* and reading the newspaper."

"Then what's with the stressed out look?"

"A blond *gringa* burst in here ten minutes ago demanding to see the commander-in-chief. She was talking a mile a minute, something about her boyfriend being a serial killer. I put her in your office."

"Where's everybody else?" asked Diaz.

"Ortiz isn't in yet. Quevedo was up all night staking out one of the hotels where the guest rooms have been robbed. Garcia's on a call-out. That leaves me." Armando pulled himself fully erect, hands touching his outside trouser seams, and stepped forward.

"Coffee. Black," said Diaz. "I don't know about the woman."

The proverbial blonde sat sideways in front of his desk, her gaze directed at the official framed documents on the wall behind. One beautifully smooth, three-quarters naked leg rested atop the other, equally beautiful, equally naked. This exposed flesh led to a tiny, yellow sundress that more or less covered the body of a *gringa* woman who seemed vaguely familiar to Diaz even in his hyper-nervous state.

"May I help you, *senora*?"

She turned at his voice, her eyes as skittish as a pair of feral kittens.

"I know you," she said.

This threw Diaz for a short loop. But he recovered quickly, suddenly remembering his previous encounter with the little yellow dress and its occupant at the café overlooking the *jardin*. That had been on Saturday, an eon ago.

"Inspector Hector Diaz." He bowed slightly.

"Thank God."

"And you're Jane Ryder."

She stood, faltered. Diaz leaped toward her, grasping her under the arms as she collapsed. Her armpits were moist and pungent. Armando stood in the doorway, suspended in inaction, holding two cups of espresso.

"Tequila," said Diaz.

He eased Jane back onto the chair.

"Oh, my. How silly of me. I've been wandering the streets all night."

"That can be a dangerous occupation, *senora*." Or a lucrative one, Diaz thought.

A patina of rosewater overhung the rough and ready essences of sweat and frowziness. Armando handed Diaz a shot glass of amber-colored liquor.

"Drink this."

She tossed it back like a pro. Her other hand clutched a sheaf of crumpled papers.

"I'm scared," she said.

"Of what?"

She extended her hand and Diaz took the typewritten sheets.

"I thought I loved him. But now I think he murdered that girl."

"What girl?"

"The one in the paintings at the *Galeria Rana*."

She watched Diaz as, sitting behind his desk, he skimmed through the document.

"I found them in Gregory's bag. I think it's his diary, the diary of a mass murderer. I don't know how I could have fallen for him?"

"We all make mistakes," mumbled Diaz, still focused on the pages of typescript. When he looked up at her, his eyes blazed. "Where is Gregory Gregorovich now?"

Ortiz, who had strolled into the station just as Jane was sipping her second tequila, parked the police car a block before the entrance to The Pines. In the passenger seat Diaz checked the ammunition clip of his Glock for the second time in less than twelve hours. Another official looking car pulled to the curb behind them. In it was the backup: Corporal Florio of the *Policia Preventiva* and a young patrolman whom Diaz had never seen before. He looked about fifteen.

Inside the grounds of The Pines, Ortiz and the two *Preventiva* men waited while Diaz went into the office to confirm the location of the room where Jane Ryder and Gregory Gregorovich were shacked up. The desk clerk, an ill-shaven lout in a flannel shirt with the sleeves cut off, broke out in a sweat when Diaz flashed his police ID.

No, he hadn't seen the party renting the bridal suite either coming or going today. So he couldn't say whether or not anyone was in the suite. And no, none of the rooms had telephones.

"Just stay calm," cautioned Diaz.

Back outside, Diaz led the way across the garden and up the inside stairway of the hotel wing where they hoped to find Gregory Gregorovich. They moved rapidly and in silence except for Diaz's clipped commands.

The upstairs hallway was empty. One of the florescent lights blinked on and off like a manic-depressive. Diaz found himself tiptoeing up the corridor, Glock in hand.

How silly can you get? he thought.

In the next moment, Ortiz kicked in the door of the suite. They rushed in, brandishing weapons, shouting TV cop show one-liners.

Gregory Gregorovich, stark naked, was a stick man dancing a jig, paintbrush waving in one hand. His eyes were wide with terror at this harness bull blitzkrieg. On the easel behind him, a nude Jane Drury smiled lustfully from a half finished canvas.

"Hands on your dick, *capullo*," shouted Diaz. "And don't move."

The paintbrush clattered on the tile floor.

After Gregorovich was dressed, Ortiz hustled him down the stairs, handcuffed, arms jacked hard behind his back, and along the driveway to the street. Diaz led the way through the small crowd of gawkers who gathered at the bottom of the gravel drive. Florio brought up the rear, toiling under the burden of two sports bags, an antique typewriter and the unfinished erotic painting.

The teenage police officer was left behind to keep the curious out of the bridal suite until the police were done with their forensic examination. In San Miguel this consisted of a few B&W crime scene photos and a haphazard dusting for fingerprints – activities usually performed by Felicia. In her recuperative absence, Armando would have to do.

In the interrogation room at the station, Gregorovich sat hunched over, elbows digging into the table, cheeks mashed in upturned hands, staring at the wall above Diaz's head. A water stain in the shape of an exotic dancer being flagellated with nettles manifested itself on the barren plaster wall.

"What were you planning to do to Jane Ryder when she came back to the hotel?"

Gregorovich's eyes rolled.

"Nothing. Nothing at all."

Sitting beside Diaz, Armando frantically took notes, even though a miniature recording device rested on the tabletop, its red "on" light a tiny bloodshot eye.

"Not murder her and carve out her eyes?"

"No way. I love Jane."

Diaz was slightly embarrassed by this frank declaration. He held out the typewritten sheets.

"That's not what your diary suggests."

"What are you talking about? I've never kept a diary in my life."

"We've got the typewriter you used. There's no point in pretending you didn't write this." Diaz shook the pages *senora* Ryder had discovered at Gregorovich as though they were a shaman's smudge for exorcising demons.

This baroque give and take might have continued indefinitely but for the interruption of a victory whoop echoing from the outer office. Now what? Diaz opened the interrogation room door and stuck his head through the opening.

Quevedo was on top of his desk doing a flamenco routine, his cowboy boots pounding out the rigid beat, arms in the air. Ortiz stood by, clapping his hands in encouragement. Quevedo's antics stopped abruptly when Diaz walked out into the room.

"I nailed him," said Quevedo, disingenuously. "The guy actually has a gold front tooth. And you were right, Hector, about it being an inside job. His second cousin is night auditor at each of the hotels involved. She was slipping him information about which guests were wearing expensive jewelry. In payment he was slipping her the big kahuna."

While speaking, Quevedo climbed down from his desk. Diaz put his arm around Quevedo's shoulders and walked him toward the water cooler.

"Good work, Jorge. But didn't Ortiz tell you I'm interrogating a psychopathic killer in the other room?"

Quevedo tried to look over his shoulder at Ortiz, but Diaz's iron grasp prevented him from turning his head. Besides, Ortiz had already slipped out to the washroom.

"And last night someone tried to kill me."

Quevedo felt the sudden twinge marking the onset of a tension headache. Pain throbbed in his left ear. He hadn't suffered a headache this bad since his wife caught him nailing the cleaning girl in the pantry.

"So I'd appreciate it if you'd hold down the celebrating until I get through this."

Then Diaz's cellphone rang with the bad news.

Chapter 30

Fran Kovacs, dead as a doornail, floated face down in the deep end of her pool. Sodden cotton draped over her bare buttocks like the final curtain of a Greek tragedy. The buckets of lost blood had dispersed, casting the entire pool in a pinkish hue. Diaz squatted by the edge, Garcia behind him. Ortiz approached with the skimming tool affixed to an aluminum pole. With it he pushed and prodded the body. It rocked from side to side but wouldn't turn over.

"For Christ sake, just pull her out of there," said Diaz. "Garcia, give Ortiz a hand."

They each took an arm and heaved the body up and out of the pool like helping a drunk to stand. Water cascaded. They eased the body over and lay her on her back on the concrete patio. In this process her dress scrunched up above the waist. Her eyes were missing, her throat slit from ear to ear. Ortiz whistled.

Diaz frowned, not at Ortiz but at the sudden tightening of his groin. Necrophilia was a Western disease. When, wondered Diaz, had he become infected?

"Get a blanket."

Securing the crime scene camera from its canvas satchel, Ortiz began snapping shots of the deceased. Garcia seemed to take forever to find a blanket. Diaz noted the need to control the circulation of those photos to the bottom drawer of his desk.

When Ortiz lowered the camera, he had taken enough shots to fill a medium-sized photo album.

After Fran's modesty was restored by the arrival of a blanket and her earthly remains carried out on a stretcher bound for Dr. Moza's office, Diaz slumped into a couch in the airy living room.

It was the very same spot where he had sat talking with her the first time he visited No. 83 *Calle Terrapien*. For a moment she was there again, on the other side of the coffee table, her chin thrust in the air, disclaiming any emotional attachment to Gregory Gregorovich. Twenty minutes later using a razor blade she had slashed to shreds Gregorovich's painting of tawdry Amanda. With her gory demise these details were revealed as nothing more than a red herring.

Ortiz had disappeared. He was probably in Fran's bedroom going through her underwear drawer. Garcia was out by the pool taking measurements.

Diaz closed his eyes. A trailer from his recent dream played out in the darkened auditorium of his head. A vanilla body of a woman spiraling through cerulean water. An eruption of spume as she broke the surface. Then the horror of eyeless sockets, a red smiley-face slashed across her throat.

Where had the dream come from? How had he known she was going to die? Was he turning into a fucking psychic or just going batshit?

People said his grandfather had a special gift. That he was able to reach across to the underworld. Diaz always smiled at these stories. The man was his grandfather and mentor. Diaz loved him without reservation. But talking to the dead or reading the future was bullshit.

Now after last night's appearance of *Ehecatl*, Diaz was out to sea – adrift and clueless as to what to think about the old man and his dabblings in the occult. Together they had hiked and camped across remote, mountainous backcountry, excavated virgin Aztec sites. When the old man died, his departure left an inconsolable emptiness in Diaz. Bleeding welts had appeared on Diaz's chest, hands and feet. Over the next year the stigmata had slowly faded.

Still unwilling to acknowledge a supernatural element in his grandfather's persona, Diaz consoled himself with the number of murderers he had apprehended over the last twenty years without resorting to séances, parapsychology or other hocus-pocus. In the present case his sixth sense told him he wasn't there yet, despite the overwhelming evidence of Gregorovich's psychotic dementia.

What was wrong?

His hand grazed something in the pocket of his jacket. He pulled it out. A folded sheet of typewriter paper. It was the note Gregorovich had written to Fran Kovacs. Above the signature the letters **xxx** had been typed. Each x staggered sideways – three drunk *paisanos*.

He thrust the scrap of paper back in his jacket pocket and scowled at the desolation hanging like a shroud over Fran Kovak's living room.

He had meant to call on her. The last time they met she had extended an invitation. And she too was a nicotine addict.

Now she was…*fini*. Diaz raised his hands in the air, his shoulders hunched as if he were talking to Philippe the priest over a glass of cheap brandy. Diaz had lost his religion long ago but over the years they continued to meet in one or another dingy *bodega* to lament the decline of the West. In a former life Diaz and the priest had gone to the same schools, kicked the same soccer ball across the same dusty field.

When Ortiz came down the corridor into the living room, Diaz was pouring himself a glass of water from a bottle he found in the refrigerator.

"Your name and phone number was scrawled on a notepad by the deceased's bed," said Ortiz. "Maybe there's something you want to tell me, Hector?"

"Fuck off."

"Does that mean we're done here? I've got a date tonight."

"Garcia can finish up here. We're late for an interrogation."

Ortiz's face assumed a theatrical frown of unhappiness.

"Don't try to bullshit me," said Diaz. "The only date you've got is with that pair of panties hanging out of your pocket." Ortiz shoved the black lace undergarment out of sight.

They drove in silence back to the station.

In his office Diaz stared at the diploma on his wall, remembering a freckled, sharp-nosed *gringa* in her last year of medical school at the University in Monterrey. She had dirty fingernails. How, Diaz had wondered, could a doctor have dirty nails? But she and Diaz had been erotically simpatico. She loved his thick, stubby cock; he was equally taken with the vast pink sea between her legs. At the end of the year she asked him to go with her to someplace called Providence, Rhode Island, where she was to do her residency. In the end he couldn't leave San Miguel.

All these memories. Something was stirring up the thick sediment at the bottom of his brain, crowding his head with eddies of forgotten images.

He picked up the diary pages that Jane Ryder had given him. The pages written by Gregory Gregorovich. In the middle of page two of the second entry, he found the discrepancy. It read: **i sit on the edge of the claw-footed tub, fixated by the spaces between the hexagonal floor tiles.** Neither x was cockeyed.

Diaz walked quickly into the main room of the station, looking for the stuff they'd confiscated from Gregorovich's room at The Pines. The two sports bags lay in a heap next to Garcia's desk. The archaic typewriter sat on the desktop. Diaz descended upon it. The dead weight of his finger fell on a single key, activating a metal prong. The prong ascended, struck the inserted sheet of paper. The resulting x was as inebriated as his three *paisano* buddies.

"What's up boss?"

Diaz jumped out of his skin.

"Armando. I thought you'd gone home."

"It's so crazy around here. I wasn't sure if you needed my help for something."

"Everything's under control."

"I escorted *senora* Ryder back to her hotel. And told her she couldn't leave San Miguel unless you say it's OK."

"Good."

"Boss? What were you doing just now with the typewriter?"

"I was conducting a test, Armando." Is this what they meant by on-the-job-training? wondered Diaz. There had been an article about it in the latest *Judiciales* newsletter. "To see if the x on that typewriter is the same as in Gregorovich's diary."

"Are they?"

"No."

"So if the diary wasn't written on that typewriter…"

"There must be another one like it somewhere in San Miguel."

"You're good, boss."

"Go home."

After Armando left, Diaz stood in front of the one-way glass window of the interrogation room, watching and listening to Ortiz browbeat Gregory Gregorovich. The results were as unilluminating as Diaz's more circumspect interrogation approach had been.

"I know nothing about Fran Kovacs's death," insisted Gregorovich. "Nothing. *Nada*!" He closed his eyes as Ortiz leaped to his feet and leaned over the table to shout the next question.

Diaz went through the front door, down the steps, turned left, then right, followed by a half left. Then straight uphill past the bullring. It was the cocktail hour for *gringos* and *mejicanas* alike. Diaz would have preferred to stop at several favorite bars he passed on route, but he walked diligently onward.

Fifteen minutes later, un-winded despite a pack-a-day habit, Diaz turned into the cul de sac where Brian Dillinger lived. Light shown in soft waves of red, blue and yellow through the stained-glass transom. In response to the bell an Indian woman opened the door. Her eyes were as black and tightly scrunched as apple pips.

Diaz walked past her down the hall and into the study, mottled in chiaroscuro. The room appeared empty. The wood floor creaked like an infestation of crickets. Cheap new construction, thought Diaz.

The old Ernest Hemingway style typewriter he remembered from his previous visit was still in the glass case. It bore the same trademark name as the one belonging to Gregorovich. **ROYAL**. The cabinet door was locked. Diaz shook the handle, rattling the glass.

"Considering a smash and grab, *cabron*? There's nothing in there that's worth more than a meal for two at a halfway decent restaurant."

Dillinger, reflected in the glass of the no-longer-shaking cabinet door, used one hand to push the double doors of the library closed behind him and turned the key. A chrome-plated .38 revolver rested easily in the other. Slowly Diaz turned, his hands held away from his body, palms forward.

Dillinger laughed.

"Well, if it isn't Inspector Diaz. What a surprise. Is this a raid? Or did you just come by for another chat?"

Dillinger stepped close and pressed the barrel of the pistol against Diaz's temple. Then proceeded to run his hand under Diaz's arms, around his waist and up one leg and down the other – ankle to cock and balls to ankle again. Diaz was unarmed.

During the frisk Diaz could have broken Dillinger's arm, commandeered the bling-bling .38 and cold-cocked Dillinger three times over. But he wanted Dillinger's confession.

"You look all keyed up, Hector. Overwrought. May I call you Hector?" Without waiting for an answer, Dillinger continued: "People your age get heart attacks when they get too excited."

"I'm here to take you into custody."

"For what?"

"The murder of Amanda Smallwood, Fran Kovacs and others to be determined."

"What could possibly connect me to those deaths?"

"For one, the fact that Kovacs's murder is insider information, known only to the killer and the police. And two, I believe Gregorovich's fake diary was created on the typewriter in your cabinet. By you or someone known to you. Maybe the woman who was here the other evening."

"You're too clever for your own fucking good, Hector. But I'm afraid I'm not ready to perform my *despedida* in the bullring just because you're a smart ass. I'm sure my partner in crime will come up with a creative solution."

Dillinger nodded toward a shadow-drenched corner of the room. Lieutenant Morales rose from a dark leather armchair. Diaz recognized him from the black etching of his silhouette, even before he stepped into the light. It occurred to Diaz that the two of them had been waiting for his arrival. As though someone had called and given them a heads up. Armando?

The Lieutenant rocked back and forth in what appeared to be a state of high anxiety. This made Diaz more nervous. Morales disdained the usual pleasantries.

"I'll be straight with you, Diaz. We had a nice little thing going with Bass and his gallery. Black tar. Mexican brown. A couple of

kilos every month. But *senorita* Smallwood wanted a bigger cut.
Like all women, she had a greedy streak. Brian agreed to take care
of the problem. But, as you know, he got carried away with the
details. Someone needed to be found to take the heat. The Russian
pornographer was the perfect sweetheart, since he was already on
the run from a rape charge in L.A. It would have worked, too, if
you had found Gregorovich and that Canadian *puta* sooner. But
Brian got antsy and decided on his own you needed to find another
mutilated corpse as an incentive to hunt down Gregorovich."

Diaz staggered under the weight of this rush of words. His
cojones shriveled with a sense of impending doom. His own. He
got a grip and said:

"But why the eyes?"

"Collector's items," Dillinger said, holding up a specimen
jar in which two pairs of off-white orbs, suspended in a vaguely
green fluid, languidly floated around each other like disembodied
ping-pong balls.

Diaz fought down the urge to spew his lunch.

"Brian's an odd duck," Morales said.

A fucking mad dog, thought Diaz.

"After that my orders were to close down the entire operation,"
said Morales.

"Meaning Bass Smallwood was measured for a shallow grave."

"Something like that."

"Why are you telling me all this?"

"I thought you should know everything leading up to Brian
Dillinger's unexpected death."

Dillinger was fixing a drink at the mini-bar, his back turned
toward the room. His white T-shirt imprinted across the back
with some heavy metal band memorabilia. The first bullet from
Morales's standard-issue .45 obliterated the memorabilia, slamming Dillinger into the cabinet. Glass splintered and rained down
in the brief silence before the next gunshot. And the third. Each
making Dillinger's body jerk like a dyspeptic hip-hop dancer.

"There's your killer, Diaz. Ready to be hung up, photographed
and measured like a prize marlin."

Diaz felt suddenly liberated, light as a helium-filled balloon.

"So you're not going to kill me," he said. "I get to walk out of here whistling the national anthem with that scumbag's ear in my pocket as a keepsake."

"However you want to play it, Hector. The owners of the import-export business I work for don't want to stir up a firestorm caused by your death. After what happened last night out on the *campo* when the Special Forces or whoever they were came to your rescue, my principals understand you have powerful friends in the ruling cabala. They want the bad publicity to end. You get the glory for killing the real psycho-killer. I get my long deserved promotion."

The Lieutenant stepped toward Diaz. "No, Hector, I'm not going to shoot you," he said. He drew back his .45 to strike Diaz across the face. "But I will take some payback for the other day."

At the last moment Diaz dove sideways just under the striking trajectory of the muzzle of the .45. The spirit of *Ehecatl*, resident in the amulet suspended around Diaz's neck, rose up like a shimmering metallic bat in the opposite direction, drawing Morales's attention. Or was it the light glinting on the broken glass of the cabinet.

Diaz hit the floor, rolled and bounded to his feet next to Dillinger's desk where the Nazi dagger sat next to a stack of unopened mail. Without a thought, Diaz grasped the hilt of the dagger and drove the double-edged blade sideways through Morales's gut with every ounce of strength he possessed. The blade eviscerated Morales like the horn of a bull through the underbelly of a *picadores*' horse.

A look of imbecilic surprise effused the Lieutenant's face, as he staggered past Diaz to the edge of the desk where he leaned heavily on the desktop, intestines oozing between the lips of the dagger's cut. Morales' eyes rolled up and he withered to the floor. Diaz watched alertly, but there was no reason to strike Morales again. He was dead meat.

There's your promotion, Diaz thought, looking down at Morales's scabrous features, his paratrooper fatigues soaked in blood. In seconds the face transformed itself into a Toltec death mask.

Diaz wiped his fingerprints from the handle of the dagger and dropped it next to Dillinger. He sniffed the end of the barrel of the gaudy .38 then stashed it in his pocket. Chrome plated, handle inlaid with bone and not fired in recent memory. Dillinger, the tough guy. The killer of women.

"Pussy," muttered Diaz.

Considering the positions of the dead pair, Diaz knew nobody would believe they died together in a fight. But the facts would show that Dillinger murdered and disfigured two *gringa* women. And no one gave a shit about Morales. No catchy *narcocorrido* would celebrate his pissant demise.

But had justice been served? Not yet, thought Diaz.

A relic in one of the display cabinets caught his eye. He hefted the 600-year-old obsidian blade. The edges of the volcanic glass were still razor sharp.

Twisting the sacrificial blade in a circular motion, Diaz removed Dillinger's eyeballs as easily as liberating two fat oysters from their shells. He held the gore-spattered baby blues in his cotton handkerchief while cleaning the blade and its handle on the edge of Dillinger's T-shirt.

When Diaz opened the library doors, the house felt as silent as a tongueless man. Stepping into the hallway, Diaz locked the French doors and polished the door handles with the corner of his suit jacket. The Indian woman was nowhere to be found but he discovered a powder room under the stairs, where he deposited Dillinger's eyes in the shitter and flushed. He made sure the front door locked when he pulled it closed. Outside in the street he tossed his wadded-up handkerchief down a storm drain.

A night fog licked at the gutters with a cold tongue. A few blocks away yellow light beckoning through the open door of a *bodega* promised hospitality. The shot of mezcal burned. When the barman looked up from polishing a glass, Diaz nodded for him to pour another.

Flipping through his wallet, Diaz came upon the business card of the young woman he had met at the *Galeria Rana*. A vague recollection of her pretty face hung in the air before him. He dialed the number. It rang and rang but nobody bothered to answer.

Diaz wondered what kind of mood Martina would be in if he dropped by out of the blue. He hadn't called her all week. With a shrug he downed the second shot of mezcal, threw some coins on the bar and, stepping from light into bone-chilling darkness, headed in her direction.

Acknowledgements:

Chapter 3, in slightly different form, appeared in Melissa Mann's awfully big adventure: *Beat the Dust*.

Muchas gracias to everyone who helped along the way, including, but not limited to, Jay Parini, Ben Fountain, Michael Ray, Hannah Tinti, Dani Shapiro, Michael Marin, John Burnham Schwartz, Valerie Martin, Susan Tomaselli, Anthony Neil Smith, Rachel Kendall, Tony Black, Todd Robinson, Allan Guthrie, Lou Boxer, Keith Rawson, Cameron Ashley, Jimmy Callaway, Laura Roberts, Jed Ayres, Scott Montgomery, the Writer's Garret, Brian Lindenmuth, Sandra Ruttan, and last but never least, Jon Bassoff.

CPSIA information can be obtained at www.ICGtesting.com
Printed in the USA
LVOW041133030612

284435LV00007B/6/P